Alyssa Arrives

Alyssa Arrives

SAGE MALLORY

THE *Alyssa* SERIES

Also by Sage Mallory

Alyssa Awakens

Alyssa Arrives

Author's note: This story occurs after the events of *Alyssa Awakens*. While this story can stand alone, you will understand the backstory and the interpersonal interaction better if you have read that book first. Either way, enjoy!

1

FRIDAY, MARCH 5, HOME

"Oh god, yes! Keep going just like that!" Alyssa wailed at Robert as he pounded his cock into her while holding her ankles out wide. "I'm coming again! Come on, Babe, come in me one more time!"

"You like this, Baby?" Robert asked. "You love my fucking, don't you? You love this cock hitting your spots just right." Sweat dripped from his chin onto her chest, then rolled to puddle in the hollow between her collarbones.

Alyssa's pussy tightened around his thrusting cock. Every move tugged her lips, the stretch electrifying her body. From the heat spreading across her breasts and up her neck, she knew Robert smiled because she was turning red, like she always did before a big orgasm. *Let him see that it's real.* She held her breath and flexed her abs, pushing her pussy as far onto Robert's cock as she could as her orgasm broke free, flexing every muscle from head to toe. Physical pleasure overrode her capacity for speech, leaving only a loud throaty noise to escape her lips.

He released her ankle, bringing his finger and thumb together to squeeze and pull her nipple, distending her breast and extending her pleasure with the pain as he fired spurt after spurt of cum inside her. Alyssa's eyes fluttered and rolled back before her body fell slack.

Alyssa awoke to Robert snuggling her from above, bearing his weight on his knees and elbows. "Mm. Three times. That's what I needed tonight, Babe. You give it to me so good."

"It's all you," Robert said with a kiss. "I just do what your dirty mouth tells me to."

"Even when my dirty mouth is full of your cock?"

"Then I just watch your eyes and your breathing to know what you want."

"Then I'll keep telling you. Everything you do makes me come."

"I'll keep listening. I love making you come."

"Then hear this. Roll beside me. Hold me. Let me kiss your talented mouth again."

They lay entwined for a while. It was late. The last two hours had rumpled the bed, but they didn't want to sleep. She slid her fingers from his chest, down his belly, and back again. Robert stroked her side and down her outer thigh with his free hand.

"I didn't think you would have me back after what I did," Alyssa said as she squeezed Robert's chest to her.

"Me either. I'm glad we worked it out."

Alyssa gasped playfully. "Worked it out? What about me watching you fuck Jessica seven ways to Sunday as punishment is working it out?" She smiled up at her husband, putting her fingers across his lips before he could respond. "I'd do it again in a heartbeat to stay married to you. I love you, Babe, more than I can say. I'm glad we worked it out."

Robert squeezed her. "I was referring to this past week, really. We have talked more and made love more than we have in a long time. I guess figuring out an open marriage kept us talking and horny."

"I guess it did." Alyssa smiled at him, then raised her head. "Are you sure you want to go through with this? Yes, it's my idea, but I'm still nervous. What about you?"

"Yeah, me too. But you want this, this freedom to branch out, to explore. I get the same freedom, and we established ground rules that protect ourselves. It is, at least, fair. I'm nervous, but I'm willing to try. One-month free trial, right? Then we evaluate?"

"God, Robert, you sound like an infomercial. Yes, one month, so we can avoid cold feet after the first try, but we reevaluate on April 1. Don't forget the emergency ripcord if things get ugly. Everything stops forever with the word *confessional.*"

"There is that. I hope we can trust ourselves enough to give this a fair try. Telling each other everything and reclaiming each other right afterward should help. Are you sure you don't want to call for clearance beforehand?"

"It's one of the things I learned from people in Houston. Getting permission breaks the mood, and worse, it diminishes our trust in each other." Alyssa patted Robert's chest. "I have to trust you to pick good partners, and you have to trust me to do the same."

"I will." Robert patted Alyssa's ass. "We start tomorrow?"

"Might as well. We have an agreement. We have separate plans during the day. We can open hunting season, right?" She poked Robert's side. "You've had your eye on that waitress at the country club, anyway. Now's your chance."

"Not fair. I could just as easily say you have the hots for that guy in your book club."

"Ooh yes. And a couple of the women too."

"Orgy at the book club tomorrow," Robert said, laughing with his wife. "Seriously, we will be discreet, right? I mean super discreet. We live here. Bad behavior could hurt me at the bank, you at the restaurant, or worse, embarrass the kids."

"That's right. Super discreet. My first priority is to protect the family, and you most of all. We will do this well, and we will enjoy it together."

"We will, Baby. Love you."

"Love you, too, Robert." She turned off the bedside light and snuggled against her husband to sleep.

2

SATURDAY, MARCH 6, THE GOLF COURSE

ROBERT CHATTED WITH Chris and Sam by the golf carts, waiting on Bryce to complete their regular Saturday foursome.

"He's late and doesn't have time to warm up," Chris said with a laugh. "I'm so glad he's your partner today, Robert."

"Yes. And we are playing for a hundred today." Sam grinned.

"There is his car. He's pulling in now." Robert shook his head. "At least I didn't have to forfeit."

The black Porsche pulled into a space, but the petite blonde stepping out of the driver's door was Summer, Bryce's wife. She opened the trunk and bent inside, stretching the blue shorts tight across her fitness-instructor ass. All three men watched her lift her golf bag. She walked to the threesome and put her bag on the back of Robert's cart. "Bryce sends his apologies. He got called out of town last night. He asked me to play in his place because this is your big money week. Sorry I'm late."

"No problem, Summer," Sam said. "We are glad you came. We have a couple of minutes. Did you want to hit a few balls?"

"No. I'll just play. I played yesterday after my class. I probably hit harder than you guys anyway." She grinned.

"Well, if that is the way you feel, maybe you should play from the blue tees with us, since you are Robert's partner," Chris prodded.

"Nope. You guys were just laughing that Bryce was late on hundred-dollar week. The last laugh is mine because Summer is a better golfer than her husband, and she plays the reds." Robert extended his hand to Summer for a high five.

"Let's go," Summer said as she slapped his hand.

By the sixth hole, Robert and Summer had won four of the five from Sam and Chris. Robert had done fine, but Summer was on fire. Her shots had all landed in the middle of the fairway, even when she had to use a fade or slice. The good-natured ribbing among the three men had continued, but Summer silently focused. After the men had hit their tee shots, they went to the red tees for Summer to hit. She hit to the left, well into the woods. "Shit. Robert, think we can find that? You guys go ahead. We will come play Robert's ball after we find mine."

They drove into the woods where Summer's ball appeared to have gone. They drove slowly among the trees, looking. "Robert, how long have you known Bryce?"

"Hmm. I'm not sure. We moved here in 2010 and met you that winter, so ten years?"

"That's what I thought. Does he confide in you? Tell you his secrets?"

"That's hard to answer. I don't know what he keeps from me, but I'd say we have some serious conversations. He told me when you had that breast cancer scare a few years ago. Do you mean that kind of secret?"

"Has he ever told you about his affairs?"

Robert stopped the cart. He gaped at Summer.

"I figured." She removed her sunglasses and looked at Robert with puffy pink eyes.

"Summer, I'm so sorry. I didn't know."

"I understand. It's probably best. You would have been in an awkward position." She hung her head. "He didn't get called away on business. He told me he did, but he left his phone lying around and he got a text saying, 'Can't wait to fuck you all weekend.' I didn't open it, but a blonde with big boobs picked him up this morning. He said she was his intern."

"Oh my. Summer, you must be hurting." He put his arms around her as she began to cry.

She sniffed a few times, then leaned back. "It happened before. After Joanie was born, I caught him with the babysitter. He blamed me for not dropping the baby weight fast enough to look sexy. I bought that shit, so I fired the babysitter, forgave him, and opened the fitness center. That helped, but as I think about it, he goes on short-notice weekend trips several times a year."

"Summer, what are you going to do?"

"I'm not sure. I came to play in his place so I could see how obvious he's been. I'm relieved you didn't know."

"No, he didn't broadcast cheating on you. Of course, he probably knew we wouldn't approve. I haven't heard any gossip about it, at least."

"That is something, I guess. I don't know how to react. I can't fire the big-boobed bimbo this time, and teaching the fitness classes keeps my boobs small. He hasn't touched me in months, anyway. I don't know why I worry."

"Come on, Summer, go easier on yourself. You are a beautiful woman, a sexy woman. If Bryce is having an affair, your beauty is not the reason."

"So I'm a bitch, then?"

"Oh. Shit, that came out wrong. No, Summer, you aren't a bitch. What I should have said is that if Bryce is cheating on you, then the reason is Bryce. No man would want to stray from you."

"I'm sorry I snapped. This hurts, and I'm looking for ways I caused it."

"You didn't cause it. I'm sure of that."

"I'm searching for reasons so I know what to do next. I can't figure it out." She looked up at him. "Robert, if Alyssa cheated on you, what would you do?"

Robert coughed and pointed to their right. "Oh, look. There is your ball."

"The fucking ball is exactly where I fucking aimed it," Summer huffed. "So, please, answer my question."

"Well, um, Summer, I, uh…."

"Oh shit. She cheated on you. I'm sorry. I didn't know. I was asking hypothetically. I didn't want to upset you." She put her head in her hands. "You don't have to tell me what happened. Forget I asked."

Robert put his arm around her shoulders. "We've been in these woods a while. Why don't we get your ball and go win the hole. We can talk more as we go along, but we don't want Sam and Chris to get suspicious. Think we can do that?"

❧

Robert and Summer lost the sixth hole, but by the turn, they had won seven of nine. The three men joked back and forth in the clubhouse and had a drink, while Summer drank quietly before heading for the back nine. The pair had not spoken about their spouses' cheating since the woods. The eleventh hole had Summer deep in the woods again after her tee shot.

"I'm about sixty yards over there on the right, but take your time getting there. I'd like to talk some more, if you don't mind." She took off her sunglasses and wiped her eyes.

"Sure." Robert took a deep breath. "We left off when you asked me what I would do if Alyssa cheated."

"Robert, you don't have to talk about it."

"No, it's okay. It didn't go the way I ever imagined it. When we were first married, we joked that if one of us cheated, the cheater would get thrown out naked and penniless. It sounds like a good solution: quick, decisive, and painful. Real life only provides the painful portion, and it spreads it evenly between both people. When Alyssa told me, I left, not her. Back home the next day, I wanted to punish her, hurt her the way she hurt me, but if there was a way, I wanted us to stay married. I made her atone for what she did, then we talked. We talked a lot, both about what got us to that point, and what we wanted out of our marriage going forward. We are just now moving forward."

"That sounds awful. Why stay together?"

"Simply put? We love each other. That holds true no matter who else may be involved. Until that isn't true, we save our love for each other."

"What do you mean, 'no matter who else may be involved'?"

Robert drove the cart closer to Summer's ball. "We have been speaking in confidence so far. Can you keep what we are discussing completely to yourself? Even years from now?"

"I can."

"Please make sure. We do not want this to ever become known."

"I understand. You have my word."

"We have decided to not be monogamous."

Summer gaped a moment, then took a breath. "You have sex with other people?"

"Conceptually. Today is day one of our trial period. That's the idea though. Like I said, we don't want that to get out. It could hurt us around town."

She looked at the ground as if searching for her ball. Without raising her eyes, she mumbled, "So if I asked, you could sleep with me?"

"Summer, I'm not sure that's a good idea. You're upset—"

She looked at him, eyes blazing. "Damn right I'm upset. Do you know why I drove his precious Porsche this morning? To leave it in a parking lot with the keys in it. He loves that car more than he does me, probably for the pussy it gets him. I think sleeping with one of his friends might be a better way to get even."

"I know how you feel. Really I do."

"I bet you would have done me on your couch in front of Alyssa when you found out. Why not do me now? We could do it in Bryce's car and leave cum on the seats."

Robert gave a thin smile. "You're right. In that moment, I wanted revenge, and doing you on the couch would have been vengeful. I'm glad I didn't have that option."

The fire receded from her face. She looked at her shoes. "So you don't want to sleep with me either, even though you can. What is wrong with me?"

"Summer, we've been friends for years. Under normal circumstances, I bet sex with you is a life-changing experience. And in a Porsche? Even better." He grinned and saw her mouth turn up at the corners. "Because we have been friends for so long, I know you. You're a wreck inside, switching from mad as hell to wallowing in self-pity with no stops in between, and rightfully so. I care too much for you to jump at the chance to sleep with you. Please, let your emotions settle a bit, and let me be a friend to you."

Robert put his arms around her shoulders as she sobbed. She

turned to him and nuzzled her face into the base of his neck while her body hitched with each jagged breath. He was rubbing her back as Chris and Sam drove toward them.

"Are you guys ready to play?" Chris yelled at them before he recognized Summer was upset. "Oh, sorry. Is she all right?"

"She just got some bad news. We are going to call it a day. You guys finish. I'll get her home safely. I'll pay you for the forfeit next week."

"No, we will pay you," Sam insisted. "You two were going to win, anyway. Summer, is there anything we can do? Can we call Bryce for you, or do you want Debbie to come by?"

Summer turned to Sam. "Thank you, no," she said, her voice catching. "I'll be fine. I just need to go home."

"Are you sure?" Chris asked. Summer nodded. "If you need anything, let Carol or me know, and we will be there."

Robert pulled in front of Summer's house and opened the passenger door for her. He walked to the front door with his arm around her waist, supporting her. "Do you have your key?"

She dug in her purse. "Here. Damn, I wanted to leave those in the car."

"Funny, but probably not your house keys too. The registration shows your address, and with a key, the thief would make off with more than just a hundred-thousand-dollar car."

"Noted for later." She squeezed his waist while he opened the door. They walked into the den. Summer let go of Robert and walked to the small bar along one wall. "You want one?" she asked as she poured herself some Eagle Rare over ice.

"Sure. I'll have one with you, as long as you promise that after I leave, you won't spend the rest of the day finishing the bottle."

"No promises, Robert."

"Please do your thinking while you are sober. It ends better."

"There are no good ends right now."

"I know that too. Remember you have friends around who can help you find the good ends."

"No. Not for me. Everyone is Bryce's friend. If I throw him out, I throw away everything I value along with him."

"Not everything. You would be surprised how many people are your friends."

She downed her drink and poured another. "No, I know what is what. Bryce is the life of the party, everyone's friend. People will have to choose between us, because it is too hard to remain friends with both halves of a divorced couple. I'll be left out. I either get to live with the cheating bastard, or I start life over with only twenty-two fitness centers and no friends for support."

Robert sipped his drink. "I don't think so."

Summer ran out of the room. Robert stood by the bar, sipping his drink. He didn't want to be there, but he didn't want to leave Summer. She seemed too fragile to be by herself all weekend. He finished his drink and sat on the sofa. Just as he came to rest, he heard, "Robert, could you come help me, please?"

Robert shook his head and stood, heading down the hallway into the back of the house. "Where are you, Summer?"

"I'm in the guest room. Third door on the right."

Robert walked in and stopped. Summer lay against the headboard of the bed, her open legs facing the door, wearing nothing but a tiny lace bra and even smaller lace panties. "Help me, Robert. Please help me feel desirable again. Please show me that a good man still wants me."

"Summer, please think through this."

"I thought about what you said, Robert. I'm not offering myself to you to get even with Bryce. I don't want to do this in his car, or his office, or our bed. That would make it about him. I chose the guest room because this is about what I need from you, the same way I would feel it in a hotel, or a field, or any other anonymous place. I need to feel wanted. Please…please, want me. Make me feel something good."

Robert sat on the bed beside Summer. He leaned to kiss her, placing his hand on her sculpted stomach. She put both hands on his cheeks to return his kiss. She opened her mouth and thrust her tongue against his lips. Robert opened his mouth and extended his tongue to meet hers. His hand traveled in widening circles around her belly, brushing the top of her panties and the undersides of her breasts. His mouth found her earlobe and then the spot on her neck beneath it.

Summer's back arched, then she grunted when he stood to remove his clothes. "Very nice. Go slower. I love it when a man strips for me." Just as she said that, Robert stumbled onto the bed when his shoe got tangled in his pants. They laughed while he removed the rest of his clothes before standing again, presenting his body and hard cock to her. "Oh yes. Beautiful cock." Summer licked her lips.

Robert returned to nibbling her neck and rubbing her firm abs. He liked the way his fingers rippled over her defined muscles and tight skin. When she reached down to stroke his cock, he pulled her hand away. "Not yet. Let me show you how much you are wanted." He closed both her hands onto the headboard behind her, then brushed his fingertips down the insides of her arms and armpits to the sides of her breasts, drawing goose bumps from her skin and a quick hiss from between her lips.

He traced the edges of the lace until he found the clasp between her mounds. He flicked it open but left the see-through cups in place as his mouth found her collarbones and his hand teased her side. He kissed lower onto her chest and moved his hand to her hip, then the outside of her thigh. Robert used his tongue to slide first one cup and then the other off her breasts to the side, dragging them slowly as he licked across her nipples. He sucked a nipple into his mouth and flicked it with his tongue, enjoying her gasp as it hardened between his lips. He moved across her chest to the other nipple, making it harden as well.

Robert brought both hands to cup the outsides of her small breasts, caressing them and hefting them against the slightest sag. He kissed between them, then circled the right one with small wet kisses, working closer to her areola and nipple. When his mouth arrived there, he blew across it and watched the nipple rise and the pink circle crinkle. He worked back over the kisses he had placed and repeated the tortuous process on her left breast. Summer's hips writhed against the bed as she struggled to keep her hands on the headboard. "Fuck, that feels good. You are going to make me come just from that."

Robert kissed the underside of each breast, then worked down her toned abs, kissing and nibbling between the defined muscles. He lingered at her navel, licking into it as he moved his hands down her outer thighs to her knees, then returned up the insides, stopping just short of her pussy before reversing course. He kissed lower, and when his hands came up Summer's legs, he slid his fingers inside the waistband of her panties. "Raise your hips," he said between kisses, working farther down her body. She did, and he pulled the panties below her knees. Summer wiggled her legs to work them to her feet and off. He kissed down just to the top of her shaved mound, rose and brought her foot to his mouth to suck her toes.

"Oh, you tease," Summer groaned.

"You like having your toes sucked?"

"This is my first time. It's good, but I was ready for you to lick my pussy. God, I'm so turned on."

"Sit back and enjoy." He sucked her toes one at a time, then kissed up her arch and the inside of her ankle and calf. She whimpered when he sucked the back of her knee before nibbling up her hamstring. Her hips moved toward his mouth as he planted a kiss right where the back of her leg met her cheek, and he licked up and around to the inside of her thigh to the little hollow between the tendons.

"Yesss, lick me," she whispered, so Robert pulled back, moved his knees between her legs, and sucked the toes on her left foot, repeating the journey he took on her right leg. This time, when he slid inside her thigh, he moved straight to the base of her pussy. He stuck his tongue between her dripping and open inner lips and licked all the way to the top. When he reached her clit, he flicked it twice. Her thighs clamped together, and she growled as her orgasm burst from her. Her hands grabbed his hair and pushed his face into her pussy. He stopped flicking her clit but kept his mouth attached to her. When she released his head, he started again at the bottom and licked to the top. He tongued around the inside of her opening. He pulled her lips one at a time with his mouth. As her breathing grew ragged again and her legs began to quiver, he slid a finger inside her, pushing on the upper surface of her vagina. He sucked her clit one time, then raised his head to watch her face.

Her eyes flicked from the ceiling to his face when he released her clit, then back again to the ceiling. Her hands held her breasts, and she pinched her nipples between her fingers. He watched her mouth as his finger searched inside her. She gasped when he hit the spongy spot he had been hunting. He returned his finger to it, rubbing across it as he flicked her clit concurrently with his tongue. She began grunting in time with his finger strokes, increasing her volume. "Oh fuck." She prolonged the words until her belly hollowed inward and the sound faded. Then her abs jumped up with a gasp as she clamped down on him again.

Robert kissed his way up her body after her legs relaxed, taking his time to let her sensitive pussy recover. He reached her mouth. He kissed her tenderly for a moment. When her kisses became more urgent, he grasped his cock and lined it up at her opening.

"Give it to me. I want it so bad," Summer whispered in his ear.

Robert slid about halfway in on that first thrust before her tightness stopped him. She was dripping wet from her previous orgasms, and she felt hot around his cock. He pulled back until he was almost completely outside her, and pushed back in, going a little farther. He continued to work his way in over the next several strokes, finally touching the end of her tunnel with his cock.

Summer looked at his face and grabbed his sides with both hands. "You feel so good. Fuck me. Please fuck me."

Robert pulled back to tease her opening and rammed his entire cock into her. He kept pounding away with long, hard strokes and shifted his eyes between her tits bouncing and her face flushing as another orgasm built. He felt her legs tremble against his hips, so he slowed his strokes and leaned back.

"God, no! Don't you tease me now! Fuck me. Let me come."

Robert leaned back some more and lifted her thighs outward and back, just enough to tilt her hips. He thrust forward slowly, watching her face. In and out he went, Summer begging for release, until her breath caught as he found with his cock what he'd found with his finger earlier. Knowing where to stroke, he picked up his pace and maintained his aim, rubbing her sensitive G-spot with his cock on every movement. Summer's tits kept bouncing and flushed pink, the blush spreading up her neck and down her belly. Her legs pushed against his hands, trying to wrap around him and pull him deeper. Her stomach fluttered, causing her cries to break and restart, and her legs squeezed against his hands harder. Robert kept fucking her, his own release building. Robert felt her hard cervix rub against the head of his cock as it moved with her orgasm. The sensation pushed him to finish, and he splashed cum deep inside her, spurt after spurt filling her as he continued to pump and deliver the last few drops.

⁂

Robert stayed above her, weight on his knees and elbows, as her body went limp. Her legs fell lewdly open, and her arms dropped from his back to the mattress. Her eyes closed. "Mm. That was good." Summer purred. Robert moved to get off her. "No. Stay there. I want to feel you a while longer."

Robert stayed in place and traced a finger along Summer's hairline, ears, and neck as she lazed beneath him. His cock softened. It slid out of Summer, releasing a glob of their combined cum down her ass and onto the bed. "So much," she whispered. Robert rolled off her and lay on his side, propping his head on one hand and grazing her stomach with the other. After a few minutes, he reached to the foot of the bed and pulled the sheet and blanket over them, then returned his hand to her body.

Summer opened her eyes and turned to face him. "That was magnificent. Thank you."

"It was my pleasure."

"Why did you change your mind?"

"You mean about sleeping with you?"

"Yes."

"I was worried what you would do if I didn't."

Summer recoiled. "So that was a pity fuck?"

"No. That didn't come out right. I didn't give you a pity fuck. I had sex with you because you are dear to me, and you were hurting. You doubted your own worth, and you were spiraling downward, based on what you said in the den. You needed to feel loved, to feel desirable. I wanted to remind you that you are."

"So this was a rescue fuck?"

"Not that either." He raised the covers and looked at her body. "Look at yourself. You're beautiful and sexy. Yes, you needed me to have sex with you to feel that way again. But I wanted to have sex with you because you are so alluring. When I saw you lying here in your lingerie, I was all in."

She smiled. "Jesus, you certainly were all in. I'm glad you stayed. If you had left, I might have done something stupid. And I would have missed out on the best sex I have ever had." She rolled to her side and rested her hand on his chest. "I can't believe Alyssa cheated when she could get what you just gave me at home. What happened?"

"To be fair, I hadn't made love with her the way I just did with you for a long time. We both got a little complacent and rushed in the bedroom. Schedules get hectic, kids are at home, you know how it can be. We just didn't prioritize time for good sex, so we had serviceable sex. I don't think that is the only reason she cheated, but exactly why she cheated when she cheated might be better coming from her."

"You think she would talk with me about it?"

"I don't know. Maybe. If you let her know what is happening with you."

"So why are you two nonmonogamous? If I had you beside me, I'd never get out of bed, much less look for someone else."

"Maybe it's because, even if you have great sex all the time, you just want something different. Even if it isn't as good, it can remind you how good what you have really is. Right now, I'm going along because Alyssa wants to try it. She is pretty energized about it."

"So even with me lying naked and full of your cum, you are just going along?"

"I didn't say I wasn't enjoying you. I struggle with knowing she wants sex with other people. Well, the men at least. It is gut-wrenching to think of another dick inside her. I get the same freedom, but that doesn't preclude jealousy."

"So maybe I shouldn't talk with her. I don't want to make her feel jealous or threatened."

"You won't. I will tell her everything that happened. It's part of our agreement. Then we will reconnect." Robert thought about Alyssa reclaiming him.

"You mean she will make love to you after you're with someone else?"

Robert refocused on Summer. "Yes, and I will make love with her after she has someone else. We want to reaffirm that we love each other more than anything else." He moved his hand beneath her chin. "What are you going to do this weekend? You aren't going to do anything dangerous or stupid, are you?"

She sighed. "I have some thinking to do. If you hadn't been here, I probably would have gone to a bar looking for a revenge lay, which would have been stupid and dangerous. Thank you for worrying about me."

"I told you, we are friends. Of course I worried about you. You won't go looking for a bottle tonight, will you? That could lead to something stupid."

Her eyes sparkled. "I'll make you a deal. You fuck me to another huge orgasm, and I won't need a bottle or a stranger to get through the weekend."

"That's a deal," Robert chuckled as he rolled on top of her.

3

SATURDAY MARCH 6, THE LIBRARY

No orgy at the book club today. The children gathering for story time at the library provided a low rumble outside the club's meeting room. Alyssa laughed to herself as she looked out the glass wall into the main lobby of the building.

"Hey, Alyssa. You look like you are having a good day."

Alyssa looked up at the youngest and best-looking member of their club, Cole Griffin. His skin and body had that late-twenties perfection that made every woman in the club jostle to sit beside him in their meetings, and his clear blue eyes and perfect smile had that confident hunger that made sitting next to him arousing. "Hey, Cole. Just remembering something my husband said last night."

"If just the memory can make you smile, you should share the happiness with the rest of us." He smiled at her and touched the empty chair beside her. "Anyone sitting here?"

I love his perfect teeth. "No, nobody is sitting there, and no, I don't think I'll share what my husband said." *He wouldn't be interested in me. He has a hot young girlfriend. Robert's right though. I might if I had the chance.* Alyssa's nipples started to tingle. *It is hunting season.*

Cole laughed. "Fair enough. I wouldn't share things my girlfriend said either."

"Do you two have big plans tonight?"

His smile faded. "No. We broke up."

"I'm sorry. I shouldn't have mentioned it."

"Don't worry about it. She got a job in Seattle. I didn't want to move, so we just said goodbye."

"Just the same, I'm sorry that happened."

"Thanks. Now I just keep busy and hunt for the next one."

"So you are back in the book club. And this month's book is a romance. That's a little tough."

He smiled broadly. "I'll probably read it for pointers."

"I bet you don't need any pointers. A tall, good-looking guy like yourself will probably have ladies all around when you hit the market." She gasped. "I didn't mean that like it sounded. I just mean that women like tall, handsome men." She shook her head. "That didn't come out right either. I just mean I hope you will be fine, and I will stop talking now, before I swallow my other foot."

Cole laughed again. "Thanks. It's good to know you find me so attractive. I'll let you off the hook. We did just talk about your husband's sense of humor."

Alyssa blushed and put her hand to her forehead. "Sometimes my mouth gets ahead of my brain, and things just tumble out of it." The leader of the book club called the meeting to order. *Saved by the bell. Did I want to be?*

Alyssa jumped at the knock on her car window. She looked over at Cole's smiling face and rolled it down.

"Alyssa, I'm sorry to ask, but my car won't start. Could you possibly give me a ride to my apartment? It isn't too far."

"Um, sure. Did you need to call a tow truck or something?"

"I called the roadside assistance. They are backed up and won't be here until after five."

"It's noon. I think I would change roadside companies. Hop in."

Cole smiled and got in. "It's about three miles straight down this road. Thanks for helping me out. I couldn't have waited in the library all afternoon."

"Big plans this afternoon?"

"I am grilling steaks to celebrate before I go out tonight. Hey, if you are hungry, would you like to join me for lunch?"

That didn't take long. Why not? "You know, I don't have lunch plans. I'd love a good steak. Thanks. I will join you." *He might be packing something big, like Paul in Houston. No. Discretion, Alyssa. Be careful.* Alyssa's nipples hardened.

"Excellent. They won't take long to cook."

"What are you celebrating?"

"Tonight is the first time I'm going out since my girlfriend left. I thought I should celebrate."

"Smart idea. We already know I don't think you will be without a girlfriend long, don't we? I'm still embarrassed by the way that came out."

"Don't be. I'm flattered that a beautiful woman like you would find me attractive. You boosted my confidence for tonight." He pointed ahead. "Here, on the left."

They walked into his apartment, and he scurried to pick up a few stray items. Alyssa looked at the few photos on the living room shelves. *No pictures of any ex-girlfriend here.*

"I had planned on baking a potato, but that takes too long. Are you good with just steak and salad?"

"That sounds good to me." She joined him in the kitchen. "Is there anything I can do to help?"

"That would be fantastic. Could you start on the salad? The lettuce, carrots, and cucumber are in the bottom drawer of the fridge."

Alyssa crossed to the fridge and bent straight-legged to reach the crisper. *Bet he's taking a good look. These jeans always make my ass look good.* She looked back at him before standing. *Gotcha.* Her nipples, tingling before, hardened. "And where is a bowl?"

"Right up there, top shelf." He pointed at a cabinet in front of her.

She reached up, knowing her short sweater would reveal a glimpse of her flat tummy and her breasts would get a nice lift in his view of her profile. She couldn't reach but stayed extended long enough for him to get a good look. "I can't reach it. Can you help?"

He stepped behind her and reached up, pressing his body against hers from his hips through his chest, keeping her against the countertop. Alyssa held her breath when she felt his cock against her ass. *He's getting hard, and it's big.* He set the bowl down in front of her and drew his hand along her arm as he stepped back to the steaks. Alyssa's pussy became more sensitive to the seam of her jeans rubbing back and forth as she moved to the island beside him. "Mind if I work here? It's easier to talk than when I'm facing the cabinets."

"Sure." He put his hand on her arm. "Glad to have you close by."

Alyssa tore the lettuce, then picked up the cucumber. *Let's see how this goes.* She smiled up at him. "This is big. Do you usually put all of it in?"

"Mm, I usually use bigger, but you can put in as much as you want and see how you like it. Most of my guests start with part of it but end up putting all of it in," he said, smirking back.

Alyssa felt her pussy lubricate. "Okay. I'll see how much fits. Maybe I'll learn something new."

"Maybe so. I'll put the steaks on." When he came back in, he picked up a bottle from the counter. "Would you like some wine?"

"It's a little early in the day, but since this is a celebration, why not? I'll have a glass."

He poured the glasses, and they walked outside to the grill while the steaks cooked. They chatted on the small patio, standing close so their soft touches seemed inadvertent. He put the steaks on a plate, rested one hand on Alyssa's lower back, and guided her inside. "We need to let these rest for a minute, then we can eat. More wine?" He gestured the open bottle toward her glass.

"Just a little. I have to drive after we eat."

He topped off her glass. "We wouldn't want you to be out of control."

"No, we wouldn't." She raised her glass. "Here's to you getting over your girlfriend."

He leered at her. "Sounds good to me." They took a swig. "You go to the table. I'll bring the food in a minute."

Alyssa sat with her back to the kitchen. Cole's hand appeared from her right, holding a plate with steak and salad on it. He set it on the table, then ran his hand along her back, from the bare shoulder in the cut-out sweater on her right, across the back of her neck, and across her bare left shoulder. The hair on the back of her neck stood, her nipples hardened, and her pussy moistened. She shifted in her seat to no avail. *Yep. I'm going to fuck him. I'll just have to keep him from telling anyone.*

He returned from the kitchen with his plate and sat. They ate and chatted. She laughed at his jokes and touched his arm beside her. He complimented her and reminded her that she thought he was attractive. They finished the bottle of wine. Their feet bumped together. Finally, Alyssa leaned back in her chair. "That was good. You know what to do with a big piece of meat." She bit her lower lip while making eye contact. *Might as well be forward about it.*

He laughed, then his smile turned serious. "I'm glad you like it. I do have a bit of practice with big meat."

Alyssa leaned forward. "I bet you do. You know, I'm a little tipsy after the wine. Do you mind if I wait a little before leaving?"

"I thought you might wait here a bit. You would be more comfortable on the couch." He stood and offered her a hand. When she stood, he cupped her ass to guide her to the couch.

Here we go. She turned to face him. "Mmm. I like a gentleman who helps himself to my seat."

"I knew you would." He leaned to kiss her. She responded, wrapping both hands around his neck and pulling his head toward her. Their mouths opened, and their tongues wrestled. His hand remained on her ass, and his second one moved to squeeze her breast. She dropped one hand to his ass and moved the other to his cock, hard and bulging in the leg of his pants. *Oh yeah. He is big.*

"That's it, baby. You want that big cock? You'll love when I split you open with it."

Corny, but he's young. "Yeah, I want that big cock. Show me what you can do with it. And don't call me baby." She pulled the hem of his polo out of his pants and over his head, then tossed it to the floor. She rubbed her hands down his chest and down his firm abs before returning to grip his ass and cock through his pants. "Very nice. I love your body."

Cole slid his fingers inside her sweater to cup her tits, then pulled the top off over her head, dropping it. Without pausing, he reached the clasp of her bra and pulled it roughly off her and dropped it atop the sweater.

"Mm. Love your tits." He cupped them again, one large hand wrapping completely under each breast, squeezing and pulling it high until he licked the nipple.

The pulling and squeezing hurt and stretched, sending hot ropes through her body to her clit, making it tingle. "Love you loving my tits."

He flicked her nipple again with his tongue. Alyssa arched her back, seeking more contact.

Cole unfastened and lowered her jeans to her knees. He pushed her back so she plopped onto the couch, then raised her feet to remove her shoes before pulling the jeans off with her socks. He leered at Alyssa between her knees when he gripped her panties at her hips. "Lift your hips."

Alyssa did, and thought the cool air should steam when it touched the heat between her legs.

He unbuckled his pants and dropped them to the floor. He stepped out of his shoes and the trousers and pointed his cock at her. "This is what you want, isn't it? You want my big cock, so much bigger than anything you have had before. You want this?"

It is big. Not as big as Paul was, but big. "Yes. I want your big cock."

"It's bigger than your husband's dick, isn't it? That's why you want it."

Alyssa stiffened. "It is big, and I want it. Leave my husband out of it."

He smiled. "I understand. You don't want to say, you just want to feel. I can do that."

Cole climbed on top of Alyssa, turning her lengthwise on the couch and placing one leg along the top of the headrest, then pushing the other foot to the floor. He sucked her nipples briefly as he aligned the head of his wide, long cock to her opening, then he moved his body higher to prepare to fuck. He rubbed the head twice over her slit to tease the inner lips apart enough to push the tip between them, then thrust forward with his hips.

"Uunh," groaned Alyssa as the head caught her lips and dragged them painfully as he pushed farther before pulling back.

"Yeah, you like that." He grinned as he started back in, again pulling her relatively dry lips painfully.

She put both hands on his hips. "Go slow. Give me time to adjust." She moved one hand to flick her clit and increase her arousal.

"Oh, you will adjust in a minute." He pulled back and pushed in slower this time. "I'm not even halfway in, but you will take it all soon enough."

He was right. Her pussy hurt from being stretched, but it got juicy and accommodated his size in just a minute or two. When she slipped her hand from his hip to his side, he pounded into her, driving the head of his cock into her back wall with all he could muster and mashing her fingers onto her clit. His large balls slapped against her asshole. She came, dripping juices down her ass, and Cole never broke rhythm. He pulled back. "I don't want to come yet." He stood and pulled her hand to raise her off the couch. "Come over here." He bent her over the arm of the couch, pressing her face into the seat, and put his cock inside her again. He drove all the way in, making Alyssa moan into the cushion.

He resumed banging away at her, filling her full, then leaving her empty with the long, hard strokes. Her vagina stretched farther with the deeper penetration this position allowed, making Alyssa sore yet driving another orgasm upward. She reached under herself to flick her clit and help things along. Her orgasm hit, and her legs quivered and gave out, letting her hips rest on the arm of the couch while she spasmed. Her hip bones hurt from being rammed into the hard frame beneath the thin cushioning. Alyssa stiffened her legs to raise her hips off the arm.

No! Not right now! Alyssa felt her pussy suddenly empty, and Cole grunted. She felt his hot spunk land in her hair and down her back twice before he rammed his cock deep into her, filling her with the rest of his load. "Oh yeah, sexy. You loved this big cock, didn't you?"

"It was good, Cole. You really gave it to me." She rose from the arm of the chair. "Bathroom back here?" She walked toward the hallway.

"Yeah. When you come back, maybe we go again."

Alyssa walked to the bathroom and sat on the toilet, letting the cum drain out of her. After a minute, she stood and looked at herself in the mirror. *Shit. He pulled out. That strong first shot would have been so powerful hitting inside me, and it got in my hair. A double negative.* She wet the end of a hand towel and wiped what she could out of her hair, then cleaned her back as best she could. She used a hairbrush to make herself look presentable.

"Next time, come inside me," she said as she returned to the living room. "I love that feeling, and I don't have to clean my hair."

"Oh no." He shook his head and grinned. "I always come a huge shot on my women's bodies first. I like to see if it can reach their heads, but face or tits is good too. Then I put the rest inside to mark them as mine."

"And you never thought what…your women…might want?"

"They want to feel my fantastic dick. You liked it, I can tell. I mean, shit, your legs gave out. And you did just say 'next time.'"

"I liked it, and I came. I'm telling you what I like." She reached for her clothes and began to get dressed.

"I thought we would go again. After all, let's not pretend you came in here for lunch. I'm getting hard already, see?" He wagged his dick in his hand.

"I have to go. I have other things to do today, and I've stayed too long already."

"Not even a quick one?"

"I have to go." *I need to get home.*

"That's all good. I'll see you again soon, right? You'll want some more. I know you liked this big cock."

"We'll see." She grinned, slipping her sweater over her head, then sitting to put on her shoes. "Let's make sure you understand though. I'm married, and this needs to stay between us. Not a word to anybody. Not your friends, not your work colleagues, and certainly not anybody at the book club. If we want to do this again, we have to keep it our secret."

"No problem. I get it. You don't want your husband to find out."

"I don't want anybody to find out." She stood and ran her fingers across his bare chest. "Not if we want to do this again. Can you keep our secret?"

He grabbed her breast. "I'll keep your secret. You just be ready to come back for more."

4

SATURDAY, MARCH 6, HOME

Alyssa let the hot water flow over her body. She had brushed her teeth, douched, and washed her hair twice so that all traces of Cole would be gone. The soreness in her pussy remained, and bruises were beginning to form on her hips from the arm of the couch. *I went outside my marriage for that? I thought it would be better. It's going to hurt when Robert reclaims me, but I want him to make me feel good. I'm so horny for him right now.* She closed her eyes and dipped her head into the warm spray yet again. *Maybe I won't even tell Robert. It's only our first day, and I don't want to seem too eager.*

A cool draft roused her. She opened her eyes and grinned as Robert's hands grasped her waist.

"I heard the shower running and thought I would join you. Can I wash you?"

"I'm already clean. Why don't I wash you?" She leaned to kiss him and wrapped her arms around him.

"Sounds wonderful, Baby." He smiled and wet his hair.

Her hands worked the shampoo into his hair longer than was needed before she spun him with his back to the showerhead. "Lean back." She pressed her breasts into his chest as she reached up to rinse the shampoo away. She rubbed her hard nipples across his chest before stepping back and getting her hand full of body-wash to clean him. She washed down from his shoulders and chest to his flat belly, then grabbed his hard cock. "Let's get this especially clean." She knelt to rub suds down his legs and took his clean cock in her mouth. Her head bobbed as she sucked him and licked the underside of his cock.

"That's good, Baby. I didn't know I was getting a spit shine."

She pulled off his cock and stood. "You got the VIP wash. What do you say we take this to the bedroom?"

"I like it. Let me rinse off." He spun in the water, then turned it off. They dried each other before stepping out of the enclosure, then kissed their way into the bedroom and fell onto the bed. He pulled her against him. "Baby, our agreement is to talk after. I need to tell you something, and I think you need to tell me something, too, don't you?"

Alyssa winced, then let out a big breath. *I knew I'd have to tell him.* "How did you know?"

Robert's head reddened for a moment. "You usually don't need a shower after book club."

"True." She looked at the far wall and sighed. "So, day one of our agreement, and we both stepped out. Wow. We were in a hurry."

"Maybe not. I didn't leave the house this morning with anything on my mind but golf. We got some bad news, and it just kind of happened. What about you?"

"I wasn't looking for sex, but I was thinking about our agreement when I got to the book club. When the good-looking young man flirted with me, I flirted back." She gazed at him and licked her lips. "Let's talk, then I really need you to reclaim me. I've been horny for you all afternoon."

"Horny for me, or just horny?"

"Horny for you. I fucked a big dick, but what I want is your perfect cock." She stroked his cock and kissed his chest. "Sounds like you have the better story. Would you like to go first?"

Robert smiled at his wife and rubbed her hip. "If it gets me closer to you reclaiming me, I'll start. I've been horny for you this afternoon too."

"Did you hit on the waitress?"

"I didn't hit on the waitress. Summer showed up in Bryce's place today. He and I were paired today, so by chance she ended up with me. On the course, she told me that Bryce is having an affair."

"Damn. How did she know?"

"He surprised her with a business trip last night. She saw a text from the intern who picked him up this morning. It wasn't about business."

"Poor girl. I'll call her later."

"Naturally, she was upset. She asked me what I would do if you cheated on me. She saw through my stammering, and I told her about our arrangement."

"Shit. Will she keep it to herself?"

"We've been friends for ten years. She won't say anything to hurt us."

"I hope you're right."

"She ended up sobbing on the course, and I drove her home. She started drinking, and I was afraid that she would do something rash. She asked me to sleep with her for revenge, and I refused because she was so emotional."

"So you don't have anything to tell me."

"No, I do. I refused her when she first asked. She went into the back, but I hung around to try to settle her down. A few minutes later, she called for assistance in the guest room, where she was in her underwear on the bed, pleading for me to prove to her that she is still attractive. So I did."

"Oh, so you had sex with the beautiful blonde aerobics instructor only because you felt sorry for her?" Alyssa smiled.

"No, I did it to show my friend that she is indeed a beautiful blonde aerobics instructor and worthy of any man's attention. But it wasn't a hardship."

"Did you enjoy it?"

"Yes. The sex was good, but the best part was when she told me she wouldn't do anything dangerous this weekend."

"Dangerous?"

"Like drink herself into a coma or go looking for a random guy to sleep with. She was pretty desperate for validation."

"Ah. Dangerous. Did you have to promise a return visit this weekend?"

"No, but you may need to help her work through everything."

"I'll call tomorrow. Tell me, is her body as hot as it looks?"

Robert leaned back to appraise his wife's face. "Even better. You bad girl, do you want a shot at her?"

"I might, but I'm really gauging your interest."

"I still want your body the most, Baby."

"Mm. I'm hornier now than when we started talking." She fondled his chest.

"So what is your story?"

"Like I said, when the young guy in the book club flirted with me, I flirted back. He broke up with his girlfriend, and I told him he's too good-looking to be single long."

"Sounds like you were looking for something today."

"Maybe. I didn't intend to, but when the opportunity arose,

I took it. Anyway, I played that off like an accident, and nothing else happened until I was leaving. He knocked on the window and said his car wouldn't start and asked for a ride to his apartment."

Robert chuckled. "You bought that?"

Alyssa chuckled also. "No. I let him think I bought it. I accepted his offer for lunch. I got a good steak out of it."

"Glad you were able to get something for your trouble."

"We drank a bottle of wine and flirted hard during lunch, I acted tipsy, and we fucked on his couch."

"You don't sound excited. Did you not enjoy it?"

"His dick was big, and I came, but he didn't have any finesse. He just pounded away, like the size was all I needed. To top it off, he pulled out and came in my hair before shooting the last drabs inside me. You know how I like that first hard shot inside."

"Maybe you should teach him how to use it."

"What?"

"You should teach him how to use his big dick. He's young, sleeping with young women who don't know how to tell him what they like from a big dick either. You could make him a star."

"You won't be jealous of me going back for his lessons?"

"I probably will be, especially if you teach him what you like. I don't want him to know you that well. I'm still coming to grips with this. It's only our first day. Of course, I did suggest it."

"Babe, I'd never want him over you. I understand what you're saying though. I don't want you finding a better lover than me either." She kissed him and stroked his already hard cock. "Now that we have talked it all through, I need you to make me yours again. It feels like you like what you heard."

"I like what comes now. Lean back on the pillows and open your legs for me."

She lay back. Robert lifted her right hand to his mouth and kissed each fingertip and the palm before nibbling down her arm to her elbow and the inside of her bicep. Shivers went from that soft spot inside her bicep down her side to her abs, making her quiver.

Robert extended her hand over her head to hang off the corner of the mattress before kissing down through her armpit and the side swell of her breast and her side. When he reached her hip bone, he kissed a line across to the other hip bone. Alyssa chased his mouth with her hips, wanting him to kiss lower.

Robert moved on his knees across her and reversed his nibbling kisses up her left side, finishing with each fingertip. When he placed her left hand beside her right, Alyssa squirmed her hips on the mattress in search of the touch her pussy needed but Robert withheld.

He kissed her forehead, then her eyebrows before gently kissing her closed eyes. By the time he sucked on her neck just below her ear, Alyssa's nipples were hard and her pussy wet, and that spot, so sensitive on normal occasions, connected with her vaginal walls, making them clench and grip, seeking something hard to resist them. She rubbed her thighs together in a vain attempt to find some relief for the need that kept building, but she only intensified it.

Robert kissed down the inside of her neck muscle to the hollow between her collarbones before cupping each breast and capturing her hard nipples between his fingers. *He's going to make me come from this alone.* "God, you're making me come. Keep going, Babe."

Robert released her tits to rub her belly with his fingertips while he nibbled and kissed her breasts around the areolae. He kissed across the valley between them, shifting his focus from one to the other, inching closer to her nipples. When he sucked the first one hard, her pussy let a small rush of fluid run down her ass. She groaned with the small release.

Robert kissed down her stomach, nibbling in the sensitive hollow between the abs and obliques, all the way to her mound. He blew across her puffy outer lips before kissing down the inside of her left thigh. Alyssa tensed her body, her desire driving her mad. She arched her back and chased his mouth with her hips, craving his touch on her sparking pussy.

He raised her calf and kissed the back of her knee and down to her toes, sucking on each one. The rough surface of his tongue between her toes tickled, and Alyssa let the break from pure sensual stimulation relax her muscles. "Fuck, Robert, you haven't done that in so long," she purred. "Do it again." He put her foot down, then picked up the other one to suck those toes and nibble his way to her knee. Alyssa spread her legs wide, inviting him to finally lick her wet, open pussy lips. Alyssa's leg quivered when he ran the back of his finger from her arch to her crotch, then pulled it back to her knee, where he resumed nibbling, licking, and kissing up her thigh.

He nipped her skin with his teeth before he reached her outer lips. Shocks went through her pussy to her nipples with each bite. "Do it! God, eat me!"

Robert blew across her clit, making her stiffen. He dove his mouth to her slit and stuck his tongue between her lips. He pushed the lips apart, pressing first one side, then the other before licking her entire opening from bottom to top, stopping just shy of her clit. Alyssa rocked her hips downward, trying to force contact between her clit and his tongue, but he grabbed her hip bones and held her in place. Her muscles rippled beneath his fingers, but he held her in place, preventing her from humping against his mouth. He repeated the long lick, starting again at the bottom of her opening and stopping before reaching her clit, fighting to hold her hips down. He repeated the trip a third time, this time slipping a finger inside her and licking her clit when he reached it.

Her thighs clamped down on his head, and her back arched as she climaxed. He continued to lick her lips as her thighs fell to the sides, opening her and shifting her opening upward. He added a second finger to the first and stroked her front wall, stimulating the spot he knew she liked. After a few minutes, her knees had risen and her thighs quivered. Robert raised his head and withdrew his fingers.

"Oh, I'm close. Make me come again. Please."

Robert tapped her clit with his finger, then positioned the tip of his cock at her opening. He thrust inside, getting about half his cock inside before pulling back and plunging in a second time, letting his balls rest on her ass and the tip of his cock push against the top of her vagina.

"Unnnh, god," Alyssa moaned while grabbing his sides and holding him inside her. She relaxed her grip, and Robert slid his hips up her body so his cock was pointed into the back of her vagina, and he began pumping up and down, pushing her into the mattress. Alyssa groaned with the stimulation. *I can feel it against my ass. God, my pussy's sore, but I want it. I want Robert to take me.*

With one long stroke, Robert pushed against the back of her vagina one last time, then moved his hips backward, tracing a line inside her from the back, across the top, and to the front without pulling back. Once he hit her cervix, he pulled back and resumed thrusting, pressing his head against it on every stroke. He lifted her right leg and sucked her toes as he fucked her. He used his left hand to press her abdomen down, intensifying the impact his cock had inside her, and flicked her clit with his thumb. Alyssa's entire chest felt like it would spontaneously combust, and she threw her head back with a wail, her pussy squeezing Robert as she came hard. Fluid ran down, and she felt the sheets get wet beneath her cheeks. Robert thrust deep into her and cried out as his cum shot from his cock against her cervix. He held himself inside, grinding the underside of his cock against the firm knot, driving both their orgasms higher. He hugged her leg to his chest, steadying them both as he finished emptying inside her.

Robert kissed her instep tenderly before laying her leg down and lying down beside his wife. "I love you, Baby."

Alyssa rolled her head toward his. "I love you too. Thank you for reclaiming me. My god, did you reclaim me. You are a master when we have time for foreplay." She kissed him, holding his cheeks in both hands and feeling the warmth of his body as she pressed against him. She broke the kiss and laid her head on his chest, draping one arm and one leg across him.

"You are mine again, Baby. I'm so glad. You said I reclaimed you. Didn't you just reclaim me too?"

"No way. I'm letting you rest a minute, then I intend to reclaim you for myself. Two outside fucks deserve two lovemakings, don't you think? Besides, I'm so horny for you, you aren't getting out of bed yet."

"That sounds good to me."

She kissed him and stroked her hand along his chest and belly in lengthening moves. When she reached his cock, she wrapped her hand around it. "This is starting to harden, but let's see if I can speed things up." She rose to her knees and inched down his body, dragging her hair along his torso as she moved her mouth to his cock. She took the head into her mouth, savoring the taste of their combined juices. She sucked more of his length into her mouth, licking what she could and swallowing the juice, feeling him swell against her lips. *I love when he swells in my mouth.* She pushed her mouth lower, replacing her hand as the head reached her throat. She relaxed and swallowed as she pushed her face all the way against his stomach.

Robert groaned and reached down to pull her hair to the side so he could see where her lips met his body. "Oh god. You have it all." He watched as her head pulled back, revealing his still-hardening dick, shiny with her saliva. She pushed down again, taking him into her throat and staying there. *Yeah, he's hardening and stretching my throat. Definitely doing this again.* Alyssa dropped one hand to her pussy and stroked her clit. Alyssa kept his cock in her throat, not breathing as he reached what felt like his full hardness. Her face reddened, and her eyes ran, but she fought the urge to pull off for a breath. She undulated her tongue against his shaft until she finally pulled off, gasping for breath.

"Jesus, that's good, Baby. I've never felt anything like hardening in your throat. But are you okay?"

She looked at him, tears running down her cheeks, panting and fingering herself. "Never better." She wiped her eyes and straddled him. "Now I reclaim you." She lined up his cock at her opening and plunged down, the cum and looseness from their first coupling allowing her to take all of him at once. She arched her back, and her eyes rolled back when his head reached the end of her tunnel. Robert caressed her breasts. Alyssa rolled her hips, grinding her clit and pushing the underside of his cock against the bottom of her dripping slit. She moved his hands to her hips. "This is me reclaiming you. Don't make me feel good, let me make you feel good. Just hang on."

She leaned back to vertical and started fucking his cock in earnest, making sure to press the tip of his cock into all the places she loved and hitting it with her hard cervix. She squeezed her vaginal muscles to grip him tighter.

Alyssa watched him watch her body as she rode him, his eyes only leaving her bouncing tits when he watched her cunt swallow his cock. She looked down to see what he saw. Sweat flew from her body to land on his chest and the sheets. His cock appeared and disappeared inside her, whipping the cum it pulled out into a froth that coated her lips and his shaft.

She felt his cock thicken and the head flare out inside her. Knowing he was about to come, she flopped forward to rub her nipples against his chest and grind her clit against his pubic bone. *Come inside me and set me off.* She slammed her hips back and forth, relishing each thrust into her sore pussy, nearing orgasm. Robert dug his fingers into her hips, holding her in place when his cock hit bottom, and erupted inside her. The strong spurt against her womb set off her own orgasm, making her pussy muscles flutter along his spasming cock.

Alyssa sagged onto Robert's chest. Both their stomachs pushed against the other as they panted to catch their breath. Their bodies were hot and slick with sweat, but neither wanted to break away from the closeness they felt. He wrapped his arms around her back and stroked from shoulders to ass. "I love you, Baby. I am yours always."

She raised her head, focusing her eyes on his. "Did I do well? Do you feel how much I love you?"

"You were great. I always feel how much you love me, not just when we are making love."

She pressed her arms against his sides and squeezed. "I don't want to move from right here."

"Me either, but Clay will be home soon, and we will need to feed him. Want to cook together after a shower?"

"Sounds good." Alyssa winced as she climbed off Robert and waddled to the bathroom.

"What's wrong, Baby?" Robert asked, following her.

"My pussy is really sore from today. I told you Cole had no finesse. He just pounded away."

"Baby, if you were that sore, we could have waited."

"Robert Davis, let me make one thing clear. If I get sore, or injured, or die because I use our open arrangement, then however much it hurts, you will reclaim me. There is nothing, no pain, no inconvenience, no event that will keep me from reinforcing our marriage and my love for you. Whatever the pain, I will make sure I lie down beside you as your wife as soon as we are together again. You are more important to me than any soreness or inconvenience. Never offer to delay reconfirming our love after one of us plays. Do you understand me?"

"I understand, Baby. I see how important it is. Just remember I love you, and hurting you is never something I want to do."

Alyssa grinned. "Not even if I asked you to, maybe, spank me?"

Robert grinned back at her. "Only if you earned it, Baby."

"I'll try to earn it. I want to try it once, at least." She shuffled to the shower.

5

SUNDAY, MARCH 7, SUMMER'S HOUSE

ALYSSA WONDERED WHAT to say while she waited for Summer to answer her door. *I'll see how she is. That will tell me how much detail she needs.*

A tired-looking Summer invited Alyssa inside. "Thank you for coming to check on me. I hope you don't mind; I just threw on some clothes."

"Oh, Summer, don't worry about primping." Alyssa gave Summer a hug, and Summer held on to Alyssa. "I was worried about you after what Robert told me."

Summer squeezed Alyssa one last time, then let go. "I was worried when I saw your name on my phone. He told you everything?"

"He did. I'm proud that he resisted you, and I'm proud that he gave in too. Sounds like you needed it. I'm a little jealous, but that is part of our arrangement. Like I said on the phone, you are my friend, and you are hurting, and I want to help you, even if that just means lending an ear."

"I have coffee on. Would you like some? I drank a bottle of wine last night, and I need the caffeine."

"Oh, did I call too early?" Alyssa took the coffee and followed Summer to the living room couch. "I thought we could talk before Bryce came home."

"Not too early. I was still sleeping, but you waited late enough. I would like to talk with you about this." Summer wrung her hands in her lap. "I don't understand why he needs someone else. I have done everything I can to be a good wife for him. I got in shape after Joanie. I never refused him in the bedroom, when he was still asking. Why does he need the bimbo with the big boobs?"

"You told Robert this had happened before. What did he say back then?"

"He blamed me. He said I was too fat after Joanie was born, and I turned him off. So he fucked the babysitter. I've been in great shape since, but he hasn't touched me in months." She started to say something else, then stopped. Alyssa waited. "Can I ask you something? Robert gave me the best sex of my life yesterday, by a long shot. If I could get that treatment occasionally and half as good as that all the time, I'd never leave the house. I don't want to seem rude, but you have that at home every day. Why would you need to cheat? And why do you want other people now?"

Alyssa pondered Summer's expression. Her eyes were open and a little bloodshot. Her mouth was open but not slack, like she was awaiting enlightenment. *She looks like she can handle hearing the whole truth. I hope I can handle telling it.* "I thought about that a lot. When I first cheated, I was stranded in Houston, horny, drunk, and Robert and I had been going through the motions in the bedroom for months, maybe longer. I met a couple with an open marriage. They told me how it worked while I had mind-blowing sex with both of them."

"Both? The wife too?"

"Oh yeah. She was great, and her husband was the best pure fuck I've ever had."

"Whoa."

"Oh yes. Amazing." Alyssa took a long blink. "I went out of control that week, but I learned a lot about myself, what I want, and who I care about. I care about Robert more than anything in the world, and I am thrilled to be married to him." Alyssa looked into Summer's eyes and held her hand. "I learned that I want variety in my sex life though. I like the feel of different partners. I love the thrill of having someone for the first time. I really love the taboo of fucking someone other than my husband." She sighed. "But if Robert wants to stop when our experiment is over, I'll give it all up to be with him."

Summer released the breath she had been holding. "One man can't satisfy you?"

"Not exactly. Look at it like this. Robert can satisfy me. He can gloriously satisfy a woman, as you found out. But I want that additional thrill that comes from the unknown, the forbidden. He is willing to let me have that, so long as he gets the same opportunity, and we come home to each other afterward. If anyone gets in the way of our marriage, then we stop."

Tears spilled from Summer's eyes. "I don't think Bryce wants that. I think he just wants to keep me at home while he plays."

Alyssa hugged her friend. "I'm sorry if that's true. You deserve so much more. And he is missing out."

"Missing out on what?"

"You, Summer. You are a great friend, a loving mother, a beautiful and devoted wife, and if I may say so, a very sexy woman. If Bryce is willing to overlook all that for a bimbo, then he's a fool."

"You think I'm worth having?"

"Yes, I do. And I bet Bryce thinks so too."

"No, he wants his bimbo, and I'm just the domestic help."

"Do you want to find out if that's true?"

Summer looked across the living room at a framed picture from their wedding day. "I'm afraid."

"Afraid of what?"

"I'm afraid he doesn't love me anymore. I'm afraid he does love me but can't keep his dick out of other women. I'm afraid I end up alone no matter what the truth is."

"I understand. There's no way to know the end unless you are willing to find out. Then you can figure out the ending." Alyssa kissed Summer's cheek, lingering much longer than a friendly peck. "I don't see how you could end up alone, no matter what."

Summer gasped at Alyssa's kiss. "Are you saying you want me?"

"I do want you, but I'm saying more than that. I'm saying that you are a dynamic, beautiful woman. Even if your marriage is over and you throw Bryce out, you will only be alone as long as you choose to be. There will be men, and some women, knocking themselves out to be with you."

"I don't think I'm interested in women."

"Not everyone is. Are you interested in the truth of your marriage?"

"Yes. I need to know if there is anything left."

"I have a thought. Do you want to fuck Robert again?"

"God, that would be good, but how will that tell me what Bryce thinks?"

"Have us over for dinner next weekend. You and I dress sexy. You sneak off and have a quickie with Robert. And get caught."

"Jesus, Alyssa, are you out of your mind? That won't save my marriage."

"I said caught. I meant seen. Maybe you go beside your hot tub. I could see you from the bathroom window and call Bryce in. His reaction will tell you how he feels."

"What if he feels like killing us?"

"Then we tell him the truth. You found out about his affair and wanted to know if he still cared. If he does, then you guys talk it out with a counselor."

"How will we know if he doesn't care?"

Alyssa sighed. "If he doesn't care, he'll probably try to fuck me for revenge."

"Don't fuck my husband. Not until I decide what to do. Don't help him leave me."

"I won't. I could never do that to you. If he asks, I'll say no, but we'll know he's done."

"Does Robert know about this?"

"How could he? I just thought it out sitting here. I'll talk with him. He won't like it because Bryce is a friend too, but he'll help. So do you want to find out?"

Summer looked at her wedding photo again. "Jesus. I guess so. I need to know, but I don't want to know. Can you think of any other way?"

"Another way he can't lie about? No. We can keep thinking. If we come up with another way, we will just have a pleasant dinner next weekend."

"I'll set up dinner."

"I'll talk with Robert."

6

SUNDAY, MARCH 7, HOME

Alyssa stepped back when Robert threw his hands in the air and let them drop to his legs with a slap that filled the kitchen.

"What do you mean you want me to get caught with Summer?" Robert asked.

"We want to see if he gets jealous because he still loves her or tries to fuck me because he doesn't."

"So you fuck Bryce too? Jesus, Alyssa, this is our friends' marriage we are meddling in. What are you thinking?"

"No, I won't fuck Bryce. I won't hurt Summer that way, and I won't hurt you that way either. Don't say it wouldn't hurt you—Bryce is one of your friends, and that would certainly not keep our agreement about discretion."

"You're right. Alyssa. I absolutely don't want you to have sex with him. But I also don't want to have sex with his wife."

"You mean you don't want to have sex with the hardest body we know? You liked it yesterday."

"I did like it, and she is hot, but they are both our friends, and we need to help them with their marriage, not create some kind of trap to end it."

"That's just it, Robert. Summer thinks it already ended. She wants to know for sure."

"Then she should talk with him. It's how married couples communicate."

"It's also how married couples deceive each other. If he's already lied about his affairs, how does she find the truth?"

Robert stroked his chin. "Fair question. I don't know, but surely there's a better way than this."

"I wish there were, Babe." Alyssa stepped to Robert and held him against her. "I don't want to watch you fuck Summer. This open arrangement may work for us, but I don't think I'm ready to watch again." *Watching you fuck Jessica as retribution for what I did in Houston was hard enough.* "And I don't want to sleep with any of our friends, especially Bryce if he's been having affairs." She squeezed him and pressed her face into his chest. "She doesn't know how to move forward. Summer needs our help, and I don't see a better way to get an honest answer from him."

"Maybe a private detective or a lawyer?"

"She knows he's cheating. She needs to know if he still has any feelings for her. Robert, I'm afraid of what she might do if this doesn't work."

"You think she'd hurt herself?"

"Maybe. Or hurt Bryce. Or maybe just put up with it and become more depressed. I don't know, but she seems unstable to me."

"She's unstable, their marriage is unstable, Bryce is caught red-handed, and you want to throw us having sex into that mix. What could possibly go wrong?"

"I know it's a long shot, but she's counting on it to work." She looked up at him. "Will you please help us?"

"How could I say no to those eyes? I'll help, but how about only a little kissing and feeling?"

"You may not need to actually fuck, but he needs to see that she would. You will need to get some clothes off, and she'd probably better have your cock out."

"Alyssa, there is no way this ends well. You know that, right?"

"Babe, with you involved, it always ends well. It will work."

❧

Alyssa was cutting chicken when Clay walked into the kitchen. "Mom, how long until we eat?"

"Probably an hour. Sooner if you help."

"Okay." Clay started working on the salad. "Mom, can we talk a bit?"

"Sure, honey. What's on your mind?"

"I know you moved back into the bedroom, and you've been kind of loud. I guess you and Dad settled your argument?"

Alyssa blushed. "You weren't supposed to hear. We have been more active lately. I'm sorry if we embarrassed you."

"I'm not embarrassed," Clay said with flushed cheeks. "I'm eighteen. I know how I got here. And I've heard those sounds from your room for years. It's kind of good to hear that you two are still, well, interested, even though you're old."

"We're not that old, thank you very much. And yes, we are still 'interested,' as you put it. And yes, we are working out our disagreement. We get better every day. Were you worried we wouldn't? You stayed pretty quiet after we talked about me sleeping in the guest room."

"I was scared. You two had argued before, but you'd never slept apart. Jeremy's parents slept apart before they got divorced. Are you getting divorced?"

"No, sweetie. We aren't getting divorced. We needed to work through some things."

"What kind of things, Mom?"

"Husband and wife things, sweetie. You'll understand when you're older."

"I talked with Susan, Mom."

"Oh." *Shit. He and his sister don't have any secrets. She probably told him everything I told her.* "She told you about my trip?"

"She told me that you had sex with a lot of people, including women. She said you almost got raped, and that you didn't tell Dad until you got home. She said you lost your mind there."

"All that is true, Clay. I was a shitty wife on that trip. It almost cost me everything I care about—Dad, you, Susan. I did lose my mind in a way."

"You didn't even think about us, did you? You didn't think about how you could destroy our family?"

"I did think about it. I cried about it. But I couldn't resist what I was learning about myself and what I was experiencing. It was a hard time, but I came out a stronger person."

"You had some life-changing week, and made it harder for us when you got back."

"That week after I got back was the hardest week of my life. I didn't know if we would stay a family. Dad was furious with me, and I thought we would get divorced. Susan was just as upset, and you didn't want to be around either. And it was all my fault. I hurt all of you."

"Hard for you? God, Mom, don't you get it? We learned that

you were slutting around Houston. The person who takes care of the family. The person who helps us make the right decision. The person we look up to. And you just threw it away for, for, for what? Some dick?"

Alyssa slumped back against the countertop. "I'm sorry, sweetie. I didn't know you knew, or we would have talked sooner. Your dad and I have always talked with you two like adults, but we didn't talk with you like that this time. Yes, I had sex with several people in Houston, and I have no excuses for that, or even a decent explanation." She stood back up. "Like I said earlier, I ended that time a stronger person, and I learned what I want in my marriage. It turns out our marriage may be better after this episode. We are trying very hard. I hope you understand I still intend to take care of our family and I still want to guide you in your decisions. I hope you can still look up to me as your mom and as a person."

"So you guys are going to have sex with other people?"

Jesus, she really did tell him everything. I'm going to have to talk with her about choosing what to share. "That is really between your Dad and me, but yes, we are trying to expand our marriage."

"God. Now I can't even have my friends over. They already think you're a MILF. I can't imagine how bad it would be if you slept with one of them."

"Oh, Clay. Don't worry about that. I would never hurt you that way. And none of your friends should ever know how our marriage works." *They think I'm a MILF?* Her nipples hardened.

"Promise me, Mom. Not even when we all go to college. You know how guys talk." He looked at her a moment. "So are, like, you and Dad going to bring people over? Will you use the guest room?"

"No, sweetie. We have decided that the most important thing is to be discreet. We aren't going to let this hurt the family. We don't want to embarrass you, Susan, or us. This house is just for me and Dad. Nobody else. He and I agreed on that."

"What if this doesn't work out?"

"Then we return to a traditional marriage. I will give up exploring to stay married, and your dad will too. Our family comes first."

"What does this mean for me?"

"It means you go to school every day, and you come home, and we have dinner together, just like always. It means we have family time together, and we attend your events and all the other things we do together, just like we always have. It means Dad and I sleep in the same bed, and make loud love, and love each other, and love you and Susan, just like we always have. Nothing should change for you. You should not see any differences."

"Mom, please be careful. We all lose if you two screw this up."

"We will, sweetie."

"Susan said she slapped you when you told her."

"That she did. Twice. Do you feel you need to as well?"

"No, but you deserved it."

"I did. I probably still do. Can you forgive me instead?"

He looked at the countertop.

She stepped toward her son. "Are we okay, Clay?"

He stepped to her and wrapped his arms around her shoulders, resting his chin on her head. He squeezed her tight as she pressed the side of her face into his chest and wrapped her arms around his waist. She could feel his ragged breath as he worked to say, "Yeah, we're okay."

She held him until he let go. She looked up and smiled, then hugged him once more. When he let go, she resumed cutting the chicken. "Clay, I deserved the things you said to me, and the way you said them, so you aren't in trouble. But"—she pointed the knife at him across the island—"remember I'm still your mom, and you need to show the proper respect from here on out. Understand?"

"Yes, ma'am."

"Good, now finish making that salad."

⚬

Alyssa waited in the den for a few minutes after Robert headed to bed. *I want to show him I want him, just because of who he is.* She turned off the TV and entered their walk-in closet to change. Robert was already changing. She took off her shirt slowly, watching his eyes, lifting the hem to her chin, then whipping it off, letting him stare at her full tits and hard nipples. She turned around and slid her shorts and panties to the ground, bending at the waist and sticking her ass and pussy out at his hardening cock, looking back at him over her shoulder. *Gotcha. You wouldn't turn this down.*

She stood and reached into the drawer, pulling out the gauzy nightgown she had placed there for this purpose. She raised it over her head, never breaking eye contact with Robert, whose cock was reaching full mast. She let the nightie drop down her arms and over her body, barely reaching her upper thighs.

Robert looked her up and down. "Mm. Nice show. What is the occasion?"

"Robert, you are a wonderful man, and I love you more than all the world." She stepped toward him and grasped his cock. "And I don't need a special occasion to want to have a night of great lovin' with my husband. I want to make love to you, Robert, just because I want to."

"That sounds wonderful, Baby." He reached around to grip both ass cheeks and pulled her against him. He kissed her as he lifted her off her feet. She wobbled a moment, then wrapped her legs around his waist. "Do you want to start here?"

"That wasn't my plan, but when you lifted me up, I swooned. Put that hard cock in me now, Babe." She reached behind her, finding his cock and lining it up with her wet slit. She rubbed the head to tease open her lips. "Lower me and fill me up."

Robert lowered her, sliding in a couple of inches before her lips grabbed at his skin. He flexed his cock, lifted her, and lowered her again, this time getting deeper. He flexed his cock again, stretching against the walls and making her wetter. He raised her and lowered her, this time all the way down.

"Oh fuck, Robert. That feels so good like this." She started to grind her hips, still supported only by his hands and cock. He lifted and lowered her for a minute or two, then backed her against the doorframe. She grabbed the side of the frame behind her head, supporting some of her weight, as Robert began pounding into her. Her pussy clenched as her abs thrust her hips toward his. "Oh, you're hitting all the right spots. Don't stop."

He nibbled her neck up to her earlobe, sucking it into his mouth and tracing the folds with his tongue. Her body shot the pleasure from her neck to her pussy and back again, creating a storm in her belly. His fingers dug into her cheeks as he held her, and the hard doorframe punished her tailbone and spine. *God, that hurt is so good.* "Pound me, Babe. Give me that cock. Make me come. I'm so close."

He sucked hard on her neck and drove his cock faster. She undulated her hips to grind her clit on his pelvic bone. She clinched her ass cheeks as she came. "Oh fuck. Oh fuck. God, god, god." She moved her hands from the doorframe to his neck. "Carry me to the bed, Babe. I'll make you glad you did."

He kept her impaled on his cock and waddled the five steps

to the bed. He set her ass on the edge. "Lie back, Baby. Let me fill you right."

Alyssa lay back. Robert put her ankles on his shoulders and leaned forward, bending her almost in half. He pushed all the way into her. She moaned with the breath he drove out of her. He pulled all the way out, then lined up to go all the way in. He repeated the exit-entry stroke until Alyssa was grunting with each thrust. He stood straight up and fucked unevenly. The position pressed his cockhead into her G-spot, but the randomness of the moves kept her guessing where and when the electric sensations would originate. They all accumulated in her belly, on top of her vagina.

"I'm coming, Baby," he said, and he buried his cock in her, then rotated his hips so his head circled across the sensitive flesh surrounding her cervix. He fired into her again and again. She felt how his rotating cock coated her walls with hot cum between his cock and her pussy.

Robert stayed inside her for a moment, then pulled out and lowered his face to her gaping pussy. "Baby, I'll eat mine, but never bring me someone else's. Deal?"

"Never, Babe."

He dove in, licking her lips up to her clit. He barely grazed the slim ends of her inner labia, circling and circling. He inserted a finger to rub the front wall of her vagina, and Alyssa's head jerked up from the pillow when he pressed her G-spot. He kept his finger on that rough tissue while his tongue shifted to her clit, flicking it in time with his curling finger.

Alyssa pressed her clit against his mouth. Robert accelerated. She clamped her legs against his head as she wailed through her climax. Her hips bucked twice in rapid succession, then waited for another spasm. After another pause and spasm, her legs fell open, her head fell back, and her hands slid beside her hips.

Robert spun Alyssa to lie in the bed, then climbed in to spoon her from behind. "I love you, Baby. What a lovely way to tuck me in."

"Mm, I love you too, Babe, and I think you tucked me in. You wore me out." She placed her hand atop his on her breast.

"What brought that on, Baby?"

Alyssa squeezed his hand. "Like I said, I love you. You are amazing. You are a great lover, and I wanted to show you all that tonight. No reason beyond that. I'll give you the full seduction another time."

"The full seduction?"

"I was going to give you the full seduction: caressing, blow job, long, lingering lovemaking until we fell asleep. I couldn't resist going straight to fucking when you picked me up. God, I almost came. That was so hot."

Robert laughed. "I'll expect the full seduction another time. Tonight was hot, I'll admit."

"We aren't done. I feel like a sexual piranha. I want more and more."

"Sexual piranha? That's a new one." Robert stroked her breast with his palm. "You could entice me to go again."

"Maybe not against the doorframe. My ass will be sore all week."

Robert chuckled and moved his hand to rub her hip. Robert's cell rang on the nightstand. "It's a little late for a call." He rolled to answer it. "It's Tanya Cook. I wonder what she wants."

"Answer, and she'll tell you." Alyssa sat up.

"Hey, Tanya. Is everything all right?"

Tanya was never one for quiet conversation. Alyssa chuckled as she lay beside him, hearing every word. "Robert, why do you assume something is wrong when I call? It can't just be, 'Tanya, it's good to hear from you?'"

"Okay. Tanya, it's good to hear from you…so late on a school night. Is everything all right?"

Tanya cackled into the phone. "That's fair. Yes, something is wrong, and I called late thinking Alyssa would be there. Am I right?"

"Yes."

"Put me on speaker."

Robert hit the button. "Alyssa can hear you."

"Hey, Alyssa. I need your help. Your husband has responded no to the high school reunion again this year. Can you help me change his mind?"

Robert shook his head at Alyssa.

She smiled at him. "I don't know, Tanya. He's never wanted to go before. What's the big deal this year?"

"This year, I'm chairing the committee, and at least twenty people have asked if he's coming. A lot of old friends want to see him. If nothing else, it would be good to catch up with you two."

Robert spoke up. "Do I get a say in this?"

"Nope. You have given the incorrect answer, so I'm appealing your decision to the boss." She laughed. "But really, people have asked about you. Will you think about it?"

"Tanya…"

"Alyssa, will you remind him how much fun your last reunion was?"

"I've never gone to mine either, Tanya."

"Oh, goodness, then you both need to come so you can decide if you ever want to come to any. You might end up having a good time by accident."

"We'll see," Robert offered.

"Alyssa, would you do me a favor? Bat those beautiful brown eyes at him and ask him to go, just this once. You know he can't refuse that."

Alyssa laughed and gave her best bedroom eyes to Robert. She lowered her voice to a husky whisper. "Will you go, Baby? Just this once, for me?"

"Ah! Mercy! You both know me too well. I'll go, I'll go. Just don't sic the eyes and the voice on me again!"

"Great! You just made a lot of people happy! Now, Alyssa, make good on what your eyes just promised. Have a great night, you two!" The line went dead.

"I don't want to go."

"I know. That kind of mingling has never been your thing, even though you're good at it. But we can go see Tanya and some of your other friends. In fact, let's get a room there, and when you're ready, we can slip away, and I'll make you happy you went."

"Will you bring that nightie?"

"Maybe something better."

"Okay. We'll go, and we will stay the night."

She reached for his cock. "Get ready, Babe. Tanya told me I had to make good on what my eyes promised." She did.

7

FRIDAY, MARCH 12, SUMMER'S HOUSE

Robert shook his head as his wife emerged from their closet. "You aren't being fair, Alyssa. That outfit would make any man want you, even one who doesn't cheat on his wife."

Alyssa twirled, showing two thin chains crossing her bare back, holding a gold halter top low across her tits and ending two inches above a black miniskirt. The only other thing she wore was a pair of strappy heels.

"Bryce is screwing a blonde bimbo with big boobs. I have to provide a reasonable alternative when he sees you with his wife. If it makes you feel better, Summer will be wearing a sexy outfit too."

"Your boobs are fantastic, Baby. He'll notice." Robert sighed. "This is their marriage we are meddling in. Are you certain she wants to go through with this insanity? Are you sure you want to?"

"I talked with Summer two hours ago. She's nervous, but she needs to know. She said this week has been unbearable."

"God help us, we'll help her, but remember you are not to fuck Bryce."

"I remember. I'm not interested."

"I know, but don't let your libido kick in when you see Summer and me. You know you get horny when you dress sexy. You'll be keyed up, and then you'll watch us together. I worry about you. You are, after all, a sexual piranha."

"Yes, I'll get horny in this outfit, then you will make me wet with Summer, but it is all for you tonight, Babe. I promise."

⁂

Robert observed him when Bryce opened the door with a smile. "Robert, Alyssa, come in." He shook Robert's hand and hugged Alyssa, like always. What was new was that Bryce's lower hand trailed across her bare back as she pulled away. "Wow, Alyssa, you look great. New outfit?"

Robert noticed Alyssa shiver slightly as she smiled at the compliment. "Yes. Summer and I wanted to dress up tonight. Did you like her outfit?"

"Hm, she looks like always. Not as hot and sexy as you."

"That's my wife you're talking about, Bryce."

"Of course. My apologies if I overstepped. I was only trying to be complimentary."

"I thought I heard the doorbell." Summer entered the foyer with glasses of wine for Robert and Alyssa. She hugged Alyssa, then Robert. "Thank you," she whispered in his ear.

"You look great, Summer," Robert said, releasing the hug. She wore a green version of Alyssa's halter top and a pair of billowing short-shorts with slits up the sides to the waistband. Her bare feet were tipped with green toenails.

"See? Alyssa carries the look better."

"Bryce, you never did know when to stay quiet," Robert said with a frown. "Is it time we started the grill?"

"It is hot already. Let's put on the steaks." Bryce and Robert took the steaks to the grill while the women went to the kitchen.

"Robert, I'm sorry if I said too much about how Alyssa looks. She does look good tonight though. You are a lucky man."

"Bryce, have you noticed your wife? She looks every bit as good."

"Maybe, but she nags me about spending more time together. We spend lots of time together, and I need some time for me."

"Maybe she's trying to tell you something. Have you talked with her about it?"

"Nah. It's the same shit she always says. I've heard it before. She will get over it."

Robert shook his head. "You still in for golf tomorrow?"

"I think so. There is this project at work that might call me away though. It is hot and heavy right now."

"If you can't play, just send Summer in your place. She did great last week until she got some bad news."

"Yeah, she told me. I didn't realize she was close to a great aunt, but she was pretty upset that she died. Thanks for letting her play for me and for bringing her home."

"Thanks for going through with this, Alyssa. Do you really think it will work?"

"I do," Alyssa said. "Just take Robert out by the hot tub and make out. That's where you don't have security cameras, right? Make sure you get undressed some. I'll see you from the guest bathroom window right there and call Bryce in. His response will tell you what to do."

"I need that certainty. He's been distant all week, like he

always is, and he had to work late a couple of nights. He hasn't worked late that many nights during one week in a long time. I think we are done, but I want to know for sure."

"We're here to help you."

⁓

The steaks came off the grill. While they rested, Alyssa opened a second bottle of wine and prepared the plates. Bryce brushed his crotch against her ass as he carried the bread to the table. *He's taking a lot of liberties, and he's hard.*

During dinner, conversation started normally, but Bryce's eyes stayed on Alyssa's chest. Before they had finished their salads, he removed his shoe and nudged Alyssa's foot across from him. *That's no accident. His shoe is off, and now he's rubbing my foot.*

Alyssa noticed that Summer became quiet before dessert and that Robert used Bryce's name more frequently to draw his attention away from her chest. *He's not even trying to be subtle, even at the table with Summer and Robert. It is flattering though.*

Robert frowned at her and stood up. "Why don't we clear these plates and help you guys clean up?"

What did I do? Alyssa stood and saw her reflection in the wall mirror when she turned to take her plate to the kitchen. The peaks of her hard nipples were poking out the gold halter. *He thinks Bryce's attention is turning me on. I'll show him who turns me on during the ride home.*

The four gathered some dishes to take to the sink. One load delivered, Summer looked at Robert. "Robert, will you help me close up the grill? Bryce and Alyssa can get the dishes in the dishwasher." Alyssa made eye contact with Robert and gave an almost imperceptible nod. *Here we go.*

"Sure. Lead the way."

৶

Robert watched Summer's naked back as she walked to the patio. Despite his misgivings about meddling in his friends' marriage, his cock puffed up just enough to feel heavy as he walked.

They covered the grill. With nervous eyes, Summer pulled him beside the hot tub. "I'm sure he's in there trying to fuck Alyssa anyway, but are you ready to go through with this? They will watch us through that window." She pointed to the small window about fifteen feet to their right.

Robert nodded. "If you're sure you want to, let's start."

Summer put her arms around Robert's neck and kissed him. She pushed her tongue into his mouth. Soon they were not faking the passion, and Robert ran his hand under her halter to cup her breast. Her nipple was already hard when he flicked it with his thumb. "Oh yes. I've wanted this all night," she murmured into his mouth. Robert moved his other hand to her ass, sliding it through the slit on the side of her shorts and onto her bare cheek. Summer dropped her hands to open his pants.

"Summer, can we simply get caught without having sex?" Robert asked, remembering this was a test, not a real affair.

"Robert, I need you in me. If he gets mad, then I save my marriage. If he doesn't, then I get to feel your wonderful cock while my marriage crumbles. Please me. Please?" She dropped his pants to his ankles and bent to take him into her mouth.

Robert looked skyward as Summer sucked his cock to the back of her throat. When he looked down, he took in her toned back, bare save the two chains holding her halter in place. He ran his hands across her shoulders while she sucked his cock to full hardness, then slid his hands under her top to grip her breasts. He pulled her upright, gliding his hands down her naked sides and back between the slits in the sides of her shorts. He cupped her bare cheeks with both hands while he kissed her, then turned her around and pushed her back gently, nudging her to bend over against the hot tub.

Summer gasped as Robert pulled the loose shorts to the side and placed his cock at her opening, which was glistening and spread with her arousal. He rubbed his head along her slit twice, then pushed forward. "Oh fuck, yes. Give it to me." His hips met her ass before he pulled back and slowly filled her again. He plunged into her again, moving his hands underneath the sagging halter to grip her breasts, using them to pull her onto his cock faster with every stroke. Summer moaned and pressed her hands against the hot tub, thrusting against him like she was trying to get more of his cock inside her.

Robert looked at the window his wife was to use to spy on them. It was dark. He slid the hand closest to the window from Summer's breast to her hair and pulled her head back. "Oh yes. Use me. I'm so close," Summer moaned.

"Yes. Me too." He pushed into her and ground his cock against the end of her vagina, pulling her hair and breast to hold her in place. Her ass cheeks clenched, and she spasmed around his cock, pushing him over the edge. He filled her cunt with cum, grinding his cock inside her while they orgasmed. She rose, he moved his hand from her hair to her belly, and he supported her as her legs wobbled without pulling his cock from inside her.

When her legs strengthened, she let him slide out and stepped forward. A glob of their cum rolled down her thigh and out the loose leg of her shorts, stopping just above her knee. "Well, even if he didn't see us, he will know what we did. Are you ready to go back inside?"

"I guess we should. Let's go see what happened."

Alyssa bent to load dishes into the dishwasher, and Bryce patted her ass and lingered on her cheek with a gentle caress. "Thanks for doing that. You look great doing it."

Alyssa stood. "Bryce, stop it. You're drunk. I'm not your wife. I'm Robert's, and he wouldn't appreciate the way your hands and other parts have roamed over me tonight."

Bryce stepped back. "Sorry. I'm just showing a beautiful woman my appreciation for being beautiful. If you ever want me to appreciate you more, let me know."

"Finish the dishes. I need to powder my nose." Alyssa walked to the guest bathroom to look out the window. She turned on the light to orient herself, then turned it off again. She stepped to the window and opened the blinds. She looked out to see Summer bending to take Robert's cock in her mouth. Alyssa reached under her halter to pinch her nipples. *I've been horny all night, and those two look good.* She slid one hand from her breast to the hem of her skirt, lifting it to rub her pussy when Robert bent Summer over to fuck her from behind. *God, Robert. Yes. Give it to her.* She looked at Summer's tits swinging underneath the loose halter that hung below them. *I'm going to let him fuck me in this halter so I can look like that.* She straightened, remembering why she was there. *Time to get Bryce.*

She moved to the door and whispered loudly to the kitchen, "Bryce! I need you in the bathroom." He appeared only seconds later. "You need to see this. Keep the light off." She walked in front of him and stood at the window. He stood behind her, and his head came over her shoulder.

"Well. Look at the slut. One picture of this, and the divorce is easy. You want a copy?"

Shit. I didn't think about him using this. I have to stop him. "Wait. If you take a picture, the flash will give us away. You know, we could get even a different way." She reached back with her hand to feel his pockets for his phone, brushing across his hard cock as her hand slid from one side to the other. She felt his hands palm her sides and slide forward under the loose halter, caressing her belly before cupping her breasts. Alyssa moaned as she watched Robert pull Summer's hair.

"What's that? In the kitchen you were high and mighty, and now you want a revenge fuck? That's a quick change."

"It is a quick change, but it's right. We get even, and nobody needs to know." She held his hands on her breasts. *Can't let him think about a picture again. Can I get by with a blow job? He'll take a picture over my head. Shit!*

"Then that works. I'm gonna love holding your big tits while I fuck you." Bryce moved a hand to the back of her leg, then trailed it up, pulling her skirt over her ass. "No panties. I think you had something in mind already."

I did. Fucking Robert as soon as we got home. "Do you like that bare ass?"

"Oh yeah." She felt his hand move and heard his zipper being pulled down, followed by the tip of his cock rubbing around her pussy.

There will be hell to pay with Robert and Summer, but if I don't keep him distracted, a picture will ruin everything. I hope they will understand. She reached down to spread her lips for him. "Go quick. They sound like they are about to finish."

"We won't worry about them. If they catch us, we'll just say we caught them first. It might be good for everyone."

He pushed his head into her, then pulled back and drove in deeper. *Thank god I'm wet from watching.* She pushed back against him, hitting his hips with her ass. *Thoroughly average, but I'm so turned on already.* Bryce held both tits in his hands, squeezing and using them to pull her against him on every stroke. "Don't come in me, understand?"

"You sure? All right."

Alyssa's climax stole upon her quickly as she watched Robert pull out of Summer. She saw the cum roll down Summer's leg, and Alyssa moaned with Bryce's thrusts. *Fuck, that's sexy, and I love the way Bryce pulls my tits.* She neared her orgasm as she felt Bryce pull out and pump his load over her naked back, skirt, and ass, groaning. The warm fluid triggered her climax. She stifled a scream on her forearm and flopped against the windowsill.

⁓

Robert and Summer walked into the kitchen and heard the sounds of sex from down the hall. They looked at each other with long faces, then hurried to the guest bathroom, arriving just as Bryce and Alyssa came. Summer turned on the light.

Bryce had both hands under Alyssa's halter, his bare ass hanging out above the pants bunched at his knees. Alyssa's skirt was around her waist, her back was covered in cum, and her head rested on her forearm across the windowsill.

"Bryce! You asshole!" Summer yelled and slapped the back of his head. Robert caught her and pulled her back while Bryce laughed.

With the lights on, Bryce's smiling face reflected in the window, and he made eye contact with Robert. "Hey, Robert. Why don't you take Summer, and I'll keep Alyssa tonight. I can't get enough of these tits. I'll bring her to you worn out and happy in the morning. What do you say?"

Robert looked at Alyssa, who hadn't raised her face from her arm. "Alyssa?"

Alyssa groaned. "Babe, you two should go home. We can talk later."

Robert restrained Summer and walked toward the kitchen.

"Come on, Summer. We don't want to be around this." She tensed, then sagged into him, sobbing. He walked her to his car and went home.

8

FRIDAY, MARCH 12, HOME

Robert turned on the lights as they entered their great room. The car ride home had been quiet, except for Summer's ragged breathing as she silently wept. He led her into the seating area, then turned toward the kitchen.

Summer spun toward him. "Why did she do that? She wasn't supposed to fuck Bryce. She promised," she said through her tears.

"I don't know. She promised me too. I guess our little plan didn't work out so well."

"No. Well, yes. At least I know." She shuddered another breath. "He threw me away like garbage." She put her face in her hands and wept.

Robert put his arm around her shoulders. "At least you know."

"What do I do now?"

"For tonight, you stay here."

"Robert, I don't feel like having sex, even though Bryce traded me."

"No, Summer, I don't either. He was out of line with what he said. You can stay in the guest room, or you can sleep, just sleep, with me if Alyssa doesn't come home. In case you want a shoulder to cry on."

"I'll figure out where to sleep later. For now, since I'm staying, I need another drink."

Robert nodded and made them each a bourbon and water. They sat, saying little. Robert was pouring another round when the front door opened. Robert glared at his wife's back as she locked the door behind her. He clenched and unclenched his fists, then counted to ten to gather himself.

"Alyssa, what the hell did you do?" Robert asked his wife as she entered the room. "There was one promise you made to the two of us about this cockamamy scheme of yours. Your word gets less and less reliable every time you give it."

"Guys, I'm sorry that happened, but—"

"But what, Alyssa?" Summer growled. "But you wanted to fuck my husband, and this was your way to do it? But you wanted to hurt your family and mine? But what?"

Alyssa lowered her head. "But we didn't count on Bryce wanting to take pictures. He didn't want revenge, he wanted evidence for a divorce. He'd been after me all night, so I let him fuck me rather than take pictures. I'm sorry. It was all I could think of. It wasn't what we agreed, but I thought you would understand. Can you forgive me?"

"Shit, Alyssa. You need to think a bit more before hatching any plans." Robert shook his head. "So why are you here? Weren't you staying the night?" Robert crossed his arms.

"After you left, I sent him to the couch while I cleaned up and ordered an Uber. When I went to the front door, he tried to stop me by threatening to throw Summer out. I reminded him of his cum on my skirt, and what I could say if he tried to hurt her."

"Alyssa, what are you doing?" Robert asked.

"I would never actually say anything. Now it's up to you, Summer. What will you do?"

"What if he accuses me of having sex with Robert?"

"Of the three of us, who will corroborate that story for him?" Alyssa asked. "After all, we had dinner, Bryce got a little drunk and out of line, and we brought you here while he slept it off."

"I can't believe that didn't go worse," Robert said to his wife. "Don't go messing in other people's marriages again. And stop breaking your promises. Agreed?"

"I won't. So, Summer, what do you want to do?"

"For now, I want to sleep. I'm too drained to think."

Alyssa walked Summer to the guest room. "Summer, I really am sorry I let Bryce fuck me. I didn't want to hurt you, but I thought pictures might hurt worse."

"I understand. It hurt to see it though. And the way he laughed…that was awful."

"Do you need anything? T-shirt, panties, nightgown? A hug?"

Summer hugged Alyssa. "Thank you for being a friend. I'll be fine. I'm going to sleep. We can talk more in the morning."

"How is she?" Robert asked Alyssa when she came into the bedroom.

"Tired. I bet she's in there crying her eyes out. I would be if I had been tossed aside like that."

Robert gritted his teeth. "Kind of like you tossed me aside?"

Alyssa's mouth dropped open. She stammered a bit, finally blurting, "I didn't have any choice."

"Jesus." Robert turned his back to her and counted to ten before facing her again. He pointed his finger at her, then pulled it down and took a deep breath to calm himself. "Baby, this can't happen again. You were stuck with bad options, but we need to trust each other to abide by our boundaries. You promised me you wouldn't fuck Bryce, and I walk in and see his cum on your back. That hurt me. Can we keep our marriage out of everyone else's?"

"It won't happen again, Babe, unless…"

Robert threw his hands in the air and let them fall. He couldn't believe she was trying to justify her behavior. "Goddamn, Alyssa. Unless what?"

"Unless you want to fuck Summer again while I watch. God, that was so hot. I fingered myself and almost forgot to bring Bryce in. That halter showed her pretty tits, and when your cum rolled out of her, I orgasmed."

He held his chin in his fingers while he stared at his wife. She was living up to their agreement, even though she had used it poorly tonight. She wanted only to help her friend, and to get turned on by her husband. How could he be too upset with that? He watched her hopeful look fade as he pondered her activity tonight. She wanted to connect with him, and much more delay responding would hurt her. He sighed, shook his head, and took her in his arms with a smile. "Now's not the time to fuck Summer, don't you agree?"

She beamed up at him. "Agreed. But it was so hot. I'm horny now thinking about it." She squeezed his ass. "You know, we need to reclaim each other. Can I show you something in the bathroom?"

Robert followed her into the bathroom. She stood in front of the tub, looking to her right at the mirror on the wall. "Do you like the way this halter hangs loose on my tits, Babe?"

"I do, Baby." Robert nestled behind her and let his hands drift up from her belly to cup her tits under the thin top.

"Oh, that's good. Pinch my nipples. I've wanted to feel your hands here all night."

Robert pinched her nipples while he licked and nibbled the side of her neck just below her earlobe. "You were showing your body tonight. Did it make you horny?"

"Yes."

"Who did you want to show your body to?"

"You, Babe."

Robert pulled her nipples and bit her neck, making Alyssa hum. "Only me?"

"You and Summer. I wanted to join you. I wanted both of you to fuck me."

"Not Bryce?"

"No. He's not a good man. I never wanted him."

Robert pinched her nipples again. "Are you sure?"

"Yes, Babe. Oh yes. I wanted you to see me."

"Why don't you show me, then?"

Alyssa leaned forward, making the top sag well below her pendulous breasts. "Look in the mirror, Babe. Look at my tits hanging there, my hard nipples, hanging out for anyone to see behind this little top. That's what I saw when you fucked Summer, and it's what I want you to see when you fuck me."

Robert stared at his wife's tits hanging below her and the halter top hanging below them. "Oh wow. That is hot." He ran his fingers up the backs of her legs. "But that isn't the only thing you were showing tonight, was it? I didn't see any panties, did I?"

"No, Babe. I wanted to let you inside me if I got the chance."

Robert pulled up her skirt and teased her lips with his finger before dropping the hem back down. He reached for the zipper, then stopped. "That has Bryce's cum on it. Take it off before coming to me."

Alyssa smiled and said, "Yes, Babe. Never another man's leavings when I come to you. I know the rules." She unzipped the skirt and let it fall to the floor in a ring, then stepped her feet to the side. She reached down to pick it up as she bent forward against the tub.

"Leave it there. Remember why it is on the floor and not on your waist." He stepped behind her and rubbed her ass cheeks down to her pussy, then back again. He gave her a swat on one cheek then the other, leaving a pink handprint on each. "That's for breaking your promises. You have been a bad girl tonight."

"Uhn. I won't do it again, Babe. Now, please, reclaim me. Make me yours again."

Robert knelt behind his wife, then leaned forward to kiss her wet lips. Alyssa gasped. He kissed across her ass cheeks and back to her hamstrings, then back to her pussy. He spread her lips with his tongue and dipped lower to flick her clit before raising his tongue up toward her anus. She was already wet, and as he kept licking her, a drool of her juice and his saliva ran down her legs.

"Please, Babe. I'm so ready. Give me your cock."

Robert chuckled and flicked her clit with his tongue again. "Do you want it now?"

"Yes."

"Do you need it?"

"Yes. Please fuck me."

Robert kept licking her as her hips squirmed. Her breathing quickened, and she moaned softly between gasps.

"What do you want, Baby?"

"I want you to fuck me. Reclaim me. Please."

Robert rose and lined his cockhead up at her open, wet entrance. He looked at her reflection in the mirror, watching her breasts wobble with every uneven breath, then looking at her face between long strands of hair. He reached forward, pulling the hair back into a ponytail so he could see her face. He shoved forward, making Alyssa shiver and groan.

Alyssa uttered noise but not words. Her throat strained, and her mouth became an *O* shape. Her eyes opened wide, and her face flushed red. Robert stayed inside her until she breathed again, then he dropped her hair, held her hips, and began pounding her with his cock. He watched her tits swing unrestrained inside the dangling halter. He felt her pussy clench around his cock, and he held her up by her hips as she came. He reached beneath her top and grabbed both breasts, then pulled to have her stand.

"Lie back on the tub surround, Baby."

She lay back on the tub surround, and he lifted her ankles to his shoulders. He pulled the sides of the loose halter between her tits, leaving them hanging uncovered to the side. He gripped them and inched into her while flexing his muscles to make his cock as wide as possible inside her. He leaned forward, bending her and tilting her hips to reach as deep as he could, only stopping when he tapped the end. He ground his hips, rubbing the head of his dick around her cervix, making her groan again. He pulled back and began giving her long, full strokes. He pulled on her breasts, stretching them toward him. He felt his orgasm building, so he gave her nipples a pinch, then leaned back, pressing the head of his cock against her front wall, the way he knew she loved. He thrust into her and up, working her G-spot with every stroke. He watched her face flush again and fired into her, pressing deep and splashing cum inside her.

Alyssa's pussy clamped onto his cock when he filled her. Her legs flexed, pushing against him and raising her hips. She squinted her eyes closed and growled deep in her chest. Her body remained tense for almost a minute while Robert stayed buried inside her and held her legs up to keep her from falling into the tub.

When her legs relaxed, Robert lowered her feet to the floor

and leaned forward to kiss her chest. "I love you, Baby. I have reclaimed you, and you are mine."

Alyssa stroked the back of his head. "I love you, too, Babe. I am yours again. Always."

Robert offered both hands to help Alyssa stand. He lifted the halter over her head. "Let me take you to bed, Baby."

She hugged him. "Love to, Babe." They walked hand in hand to the bed. Robert pulled back the covers, picked Alyssa up, laid her in the bed, then covered her. He kissed her forehead and slid into bed beside her. Alyssa rolled to lay her head on his chest, draping her arm across his body and a leg over his. "This is what I wanted all night, Babe. I just wanted to be loved by you and held."

Robert kissed her head and caressed her back with one hand and her side with the other. "Me, too, Baby."

Robert was reaching for the bedside lamp when Alyssa's phone dinged with a new text. "Who's texting this late?"

"Let's see." Alyssa opened the text. "Jesus. It's Cole from book club. Look what that dumbass sent." She handed Robert the phone.

"Is that his dick? On a dinner plate? Interesting way to ask you to lunch. He is quite confident. It covers most of the plate, so perhaps he should be." Robert laughed. "Kids today."

"Robert, I told him to be discreet. This isn't discreet. And he called me Baby twice. I told him never to call me that."

"So are you going to meet him and give him his first lesson on how to use that giant dick?"

"I shouldn't after this stunt."

"I'm still uneasy about all this, but it's up to you, Baby."

"It is a big dick. I don't want to hurt you, Babe. I know I crossed a line tonight, and I don't really want to step out tomorrow too. And I don't want him to think I'm at his beck and call. No lesson for him tomorrow."

"Your call. If you want to go, go. We're trying this, so we have to experiment and stretch some. I'll be all right. But if you want to teach him how to be patient instead, do that."

"I'm not going. I will text him back, and if he is ever this indiscreet again, or if he calls me Baby again, he will never learn how to use that cock."

Robert laughed again. "You're training him in a lot more than how to use that dick, Baby. You'll whip him into shape."

Alyssa sent the text and set down her phone. "There. He won't misunderstand that message. And I told him not to text back because it is late. He'd better not." She kissed Robert. "Let me sleep in your arms now, Babe.

Robert reached for the lamp again, only to be stopped by a soft knock at the door. "Come in, Clay."

The door opened, but Summer, rather than their son, entered. She still wore the halter and shorts, her hair was mussed, and her eyes were puffy and red. "Guys, I think I need to go. I just can't get to sleep on my own, and I don't want to bother you. I'll go home and stay there."

Alyssa sat up, holding the covers in front of her chest. "Summer, do you want to go because you want to go back to Bryce, or do you want to go because you don't want to be alone?"

She stared at Alyssa, who waited. "I don't want to go back with him. I just can't be alone tonight, but I don't want to call my sister this late."

Alyssa got out of bed and hugged Summer. "You aren't alone, sweetie. You're with us. This is a big king-size bed. Sleep here and you will feel better in the morning."

"You two are naked. I'm interrupting."

Robert sat up. "Summer, you aren't interrupting. If it will

make you feel better, we will put on some pajamas. Alyssa, get Summer something to wear. I bet she would like some PJs rather than her clothes."

"I really don't want to intrude. I'll just go."

Alyssa squeezed her tighter. "Nonsense. You're sleeping with us, and that's that. Come with me. We both need nighties, and Robert needs shorts."

"Actually—" She looked at the floor before continuing. "—if you two are more comfortable naked, I sleep that way too. We are just sleeping, right?"

"Just sleeping is what I promised you, Summer." Robert looked at Alyssa. "I offered just before you came home, Baby. We're adults here, and we can just snuggle and sleep, even if we are naked. Are you ready to go to sleep?"

Summer just pulled her halter top and shorts off and laid them in a chair beside her. Alyssa guided her to the bed and held the covers for her to slip beside Robert before following her in. Summer laid her head on his chest and hugged him with one arm while she silently wept. He stroked her hair and cheek, and Alyssa stroked her back and arm. They both kissed her head as she drifted off to sleep. Robert turned off the light.

9

SATURDAY, MARCH 13, HOME

Alyssa woke with a small hand rubbing her nipple. After a flash of confusion, she remembered Summer had slept between her and Robert. She pulled Summer's hand to her mouth and kissed the fingertips, then rolled to face her. The light coming through the blinds backlit the unbrushed blonde hair, a glow framing her face. "Good morning. You look like you feel better. Do you?"

"I do. Getting some sleep worked wonders. Thank you for letting me stay."

"You're welcome. We were glad to help, if we helped." Alyssa put Summer's hand back on her breast. "You can stroke me again if you like. It felt great."

"I didn't realize I liked doing it, but I do," Summer said, almost under her breath, as she traced her fingers along the curves of Alyssa's tits. "You have beautiful breasts."

"Thank you. So do you." Alyssa moved her hands to Summer's breasts to mirror Summer's movements.

Summer looked from Alyssa's tits to her face. She raised her head off the pillow and moved forward to kiss her. Alyssa closed her eyes and let Summer kiss her a moment before moving her own lips and slipping her tongue to tease Summer's lips. Summer opened her mouth, and they kissed in earnest. Summer pulled back. "I've never been with a woman. I've never been turned on by a woman."

"Me neither before a few weeks ago. It's nothing to be ashamed of." Alyssa kept caressing Summer's breasts. "Do I turn you on?"

Summer looked into Alyssa's eyes and whispered, "Yes."

"Do you want me to kiss you?"

"Yes."

Alyssa kissed Summer softly. "Do you want me to caress you?"

"Yes."

Alyssa ran her hand along Summer's side, down her hip, and down her thigh, then back up to her shoulder, while stroking Summer's nipple with her other hand. "Do you want me to make you come?"

"Yes."

Alyssa kissed Summer's mouth, then moved to her neck, nibbling and licking from her earlobe to her collarbone. Her hand continued to caress Summer's side as she moved to suck Summer's nipples into her mouth and pull them away from her body.

Alyssa slid down the bed as her mouth kissed down Summer's hard abs, her ass dragging the covers off them as she moved. She nibbled in the gaps between the defined muscles, making Summer jerk when she hit a sensitive spot. Alyssa nudged Summer's body onto her back so she could move between the blonde's legs and tease her thighs. Summer raised her knees and opened her legs.

Alyssa caressed Summer's hamstring down to the soft flesh beside Summer's pussy, then back up until her calf prevented going farther. Alyssa used her other hand to support her weight as she nibbled on the hollow between the tendons where Summer's thigh met her body. Summer's hips chased Alyssa's tongue, showing her impatience with Alyssa's teasing, but Alyssa shifted and kissed above her mound, teasing her further.

Alyssa blew across Summer's clit and wet slit, drawing a giggle from Summer. "That tickles. Do it again." Alyssa did, and Summer fluttered her stomach. Alyssa blew across her one more time, and Summer clamped her thighs around Alyssa's head. Summer relaxed her grip, and Alyssa relented, digging her tongue into Summer's opening and swirling it around before licking up to flick her clit. "You taste like Robert," she laughed before going back for a second lick.

Summer gasped and tensed her legs. "Robert, you scared me."

Alyssa looked up to see Robert on his side with Summer's breast in his hand. "Shhh. I've been watching. Let me help you come."

Summer guided Robert's hand to her other breast, then pulled his head to the nipple nearest him. "Oh yes. Make me come."

Alyssa resumed licking and put a finger into Summer to rub her G-spot. When Summer bucked, Alyssa intensified her rubbing there. She flicked Summer's clit with her tongue, rubbed her G-spot, and felt Summer's vagina tighten on her finger. Summer's thighs quivered, and Alyssa looked up to see her pale white tit blushing pink between Robert's fingers. Alyssa added a second finger and rubbed the outside of her anus with her other hand, and Summer convulsed in pleasure. Her knees drew up and rolled her hips toward the ceiling as she tucked into a ball around Robert's head. Alyssa's mouth jammed against her clit, and she switched to sucking it, making Summer scream.

Summer collapsed back onto the bed, and Alyssa slid up beside her. She and Robert caressed her body until Summer opened her eyes a minute later. "That was wonderful."

Alyssa kissed her forehead. "I'm glad you liked it."

"You eat pussy better than anyone I've ever had. Thank you. And thank you for letting me sleep here. You didn't have to do that."

Alyssa put two fingers across Summer's lips. "We're your friends, and we wanted to help you with this. You were most welcome." She ran her finger along Summer's slit. "You're delicious, by the way."

Summer jerked her hips when Alyssa reached her still-sensitive clit. "Can I return the favor?"

"You want to taste me?"

"Yes, but I've never been with a woman before. Can you help me?"

"Just do to me what you like done to you. I'll tell you what works."

Summer looked at Robert. "May I pleasure your wife?"

"If she said yes, so did I. Make her come."

Summer kissed Alyssa, then moved down her neck and chest to her breasts. She licked and kissed down the center, then across the lower curve of the left one before kissing back all the way to the far right. She nibbled around Alyssa's areolae, jumping from one to the other while the nipples hardened. She sucked one nipple as far into her mouth as she could while pinching and rolling the other one, then switched and repeated the process.

Summer kissed down Alyssa's flat belly, pausing at her navel long enough to lick the bead of sweat along its edge, then down farther to her mound. Summer moved her head to the inside of Alyssa's knee and began a slow ascent of nibbles up her thigh. She reached Alyssa's glistening lips and blew across them, just as

Alyssa had done to her. Alyssa moaned. "Oh, that didn't tickle. That's good." Summer blew one more time, then dropped to Alyssa's other knee to kiss up her soft thigh again. Like he had done with Summer, Robert took one of Alyssa's breasts in his hand and the other in his mouth, elevating her pleasure.

Summer bit Alyssa's skin right beside her engorged pussy lip with her teeth. Alyssa twitched with the shock. Alyssa's pussy clenched at Summer's tongue when she shoved it in, then shuddered when she flattened it to lick up to her clit. Alyssa regretted teasing Summer when Summer stopped short of touching her own clit and licked back down to the soft skin above her anus, then licked back up.

"Please…"

Summer slipped a finger into Alyssa and curled downward to press on the back wall as she flicked her clit with her tongue. The fingering and flicking continued until Alyssa moaned with every breath. Summer then rotated her finger to the front wall, finding Alyssa's G-spot and rubbing it. Alyssa clamped her legs on Summer's head and held her breath while her orgasm exploded within her. After a moment, she let her legs splay out on the bed and exhaled. Alyssa's head lolled a minute before she recovered her strength and made eye contact with Summer, who was smiling down at her.

"Did I get it right?"

"Mm-hmm. You can do that again anytime." She held out her arms, and Summer crawled into them. Alyssa stroked her back and turned to kiss Robert beside her. She reached with one hand to grasp his cock. "I think you liked watching that."

"I did. You two are beautiful together."

"It's your turn. Summer, see if you like watching this." She pressed Summer's shoulder and rolled her off.

Alyssa moved to Robert. She nudged him onto his back and

straddled his hips. She grasped his hard cock and lined it up at her pussy. "God I want this right now," she said, looking at him and rubbing his head on her wet lips. "Will you let me have it, Babe?"

"It's always been yours, Baby. Take what you want."

She plunged down, taking the entire length into her. She exhaled in a shudder and put both hands on his chest to steady herself. She rose and plunged down again with the same response. She ground her hips to stimulate the area around her cervix with his cockhead before shifting to a hard riding stroke. Her tits bounced and her hair flew around her face as she thrust her hips onto him over and over. "I'm going to come. Are you close?"

Robert put his hands on her hips to steady her as she sped up. "Getting there, Baby, but not yet."

"You are so good." She slammed down onto him a few more times, then fell to rub her tits on his chest as she came. After a moment, she resumed riding him with the same energy as before. She looked down at Summer, who had moved closer and was watching. "Tease his nipples and kiss him. He loves that."

Summer hesitated a moment, then rolled to flick Robert's nipple as she latched onto his lips. Alyssa was bouncing his body, and Summer backed away with a jerk, holding her hand to her lips. *I bounced their teeth together, I bet.* Summer watched Alyssa ride Robert and timed stroking his nipple with her thrusts. After a few more strokes, Robert held Alyssa's hips against his, and he came deep inside her.

Alyssa stayed where she was until she felt the last of his cum dribble into her, then she lay forward to kiss her husband. "Thank you, Babe. I love you."

"Love you, too, Baby."

She moved her hips, then froze. "You came so much, Robert. I feel flooded."

"Well, that was quite a show before you climbed on."

Her mouth twisted into a devilish grin. "I have an idea, if you two don't mind me leaving for a while. I think Cole needs his first lesson about his place when he chases another man's wife."

"What are you thinking, Baby?"

"He needs to learn about who gets to come inside me and what he has to do when he gets the chance."

Robert shook his head. "What about teaching him patience?"

"Teaching him his place in the pecking order will be better, and your huge load will teach that better than anything."

Robert chuckled. "If that is what you want, go. I'll entertain our guest."

"Thank you. This will be quick, I promise." She turned to Summer while keeping Robert's cock, and his cum, inside her. "I'm sorry to eat and run. Are you going to stay a while?"

"I think so, if you don't mind. I need to go home today, but I want to talk with my attorney first. Being with you two has helped me decide about Bryce. If he can't love me for me, he's out."

"You can stay as long as you need, but you'll be in the guest room most of the time." Alyssa pointed to her nightstand. "Would you hand me my phone, please?"

Summer handed Alyssa her phone and took the opportunity to suck on the nipple that hung close to her face. Alyssa typed the text without moving. "This is delicious. A cock inside me and lips on my boob."

"While you text your young lover?" Robert asked, half-smiling. "You are pushing our limits, Baby."

Alyssa rose, still astride Robert, so she could see the red skin on his head fade back to white. *I'm making him upset. He thinks I'm going after a better lay.* She needed to reveal her thoughts. "I know. Your huge load gives me the chance to set a limit, Babe. I haven't sent this text yet. If it bothers you, I'll stay." *Please let me go. This could be fun.*

Robert sighed. "No, you can go. Teach this boy some manners, then come back to me."

"I will." She leaned down to place her forehead on his. "I will always come back to you. You know that, right?"

"I do. We are still early in this though. I need to remind you where you belong." He patted her hip. "Just so his big dick doesn't make you forget."

He needs to know he won't be replaced. Alyssa looked into his eyes. She slid her hand between them and placed it on his chest. "I belong right here." She used her other hand to pull his hand to her chest. "And you belong right here. Here is where you stay. Always."

"All right. Send your text. Then hurry back."

She kissed him long and slow. "I will." She turned to Summer. "Will you take care of him while I am gone?"

"Of course. We will make some breakfast."

"If you want to, he likes it when I cook naked or in lingerie. Clay is at practice this morning, so you will have the house to yourselves. Feel free to dig through my clothes for whatever you might want to wear…or remove."

Alyssa got off Robert and sped to her closet, where she put on some cotton panties, a calf-length brown T-shirt dress, and sandals. She felt Robert's cum squish between her legs. *This will be fun.* "I'm going," she said to Robert and Summer. "Be back soon. Love you, Babe."

"Love you, Baby."

10

SATURDAY, MARCH 13, COLE'S APARTMENT

Alyssa kept her thighs pressed together while she waited for Cole to answer the door.

"Come in, Alyssa," Cole said as he opened it. "After last night's message, I was surprised to hear from you." He bent to kiss her.

She put a finger to his lips and pushed into his apartment. She smiled at the freshly sprayed citrus smell and the beer cans in the garbage. She moved through the kitchen into the living area, stopping in front of the couch she remembered from her last visit. "I had a change in plans this morning, but I don't have long. I thought I could show you what I like."

"You like this big cock, baby."

"Don't call me baby again, or I'll leave and never come back. Are we clear?"

"It's just a nickname. What's the big deal?"

"Only my husband calls me baby. You don't get to."

"Then why are you here with me and not with him?"

"That's my business. You may not have been with a married lady before, but it is different from the young, single women you are used to. Understand that you are the guy on the side, and you get what she wants to give you. I'll give you some of me, but he gets all of me. Understand?"

"Sure. Whatever works to get you naked. I won't call you baby anymore. You still want to fuck?"

"I'll make you a deal. You have a big cock, and it's good to fuck, but you don't use it as well as you can. Let me show you more. You do what I say, and you can be more than just a big dick. You can be an addiction. Would you like that?"

"You're already addicted to fucking me. What do you mean I don't use it well?"

"A big dick is pleasing, filling. A big dick with some finesse is amazing and addictive. You rely on that fullness to please your partner, and you do please her. I'll show you how to be so much better, if you will listen."

"We are still going to fuck, right?"

"Oh yes, we'll fuck. I want that big dick, I just want it better."

"So show me."

"A big dick is hard to take in. Starting with some strong foreplay helps her relax and get wet." She put her arms around his neck. "Give me a soft, slow kiss, then kiss my neck the same way."

He lowered his mouth to hers. His kiss started soft, then he clamped his hand behind her head and pressed his tongue into her mouth. He eventually moved to her neck and sucked hard. She felt a pinch under his lips. *Christ, that will be a hickey.* "Easy there. You are trying to warm me up, not take me in a nightclub bathroom. Kiss gently." He slowed his actions. "Good. Now caress my ass."

He grabbed her ass and squeezed hard, lifting her to her toes.

"Caress. You already know how to have a fast fuck. Slow down. Take your time and make me wet." He continued to nibble her neck, and let his hands rub across her ass, then brought one up her side to caress her breast. "Very good. Kiss down my chest." He kissed down her chest to the neckline of the dress, then around it up to her collarbone. *There you go.* "Now raise my dress until you can grab the hem."

He bent, reached to the hem, and pulled it to her ass. "Nope. Drop it. Now put your hands on my ass and use your fingers to raise the dress a little at a time." One hand at a time, he pulled his fingers up, dragging the soft material up to bunch in his hand before reaching his fingers out again. After more than a minute, the hem of the dress reached his fist. "Now pull it up and off, still slowly."

He pulled it up her back in one swift motion. The front caught under her tits. "Come on. Take it back down. Pull it up slowly. Make me anticipate being naked. Let me feel the cool air on my skin a little at a time." This time, he moved slower, though he still caught the front of her dress under her tits in just a couple of seconds. He slid his hands to her sides to free the dress, then took it up over her arms, leaving her in only her panties. "Better. Now kiss my breasts. Keep building my arousal."

He sucked her nipple hard, biting down with his teeth.

"Cole! This is about building anticipation. Caress me with your mouth. Make me tingle. Relax. This builds your desire as well."

"Oh yeah. I want you now."

"Keep taking your time and you'll have me. Kiss my breasts." He licked and kissed her breasts, moving between them quickly and focusing on her nipples. He pinched the other one, making her gasp from the pain. She slapped his hand away. "Kiss. Make me feel relaxed and wanted."

He looked at her with a frown and bit her nipple with his teeth. She winced. "It's also about what I want."

"Yes. You want me to come back for more. You want every woman to come back for more, right? Sometimes patience pays off." She pulled his face from her breast. "Let's move on. Take off your clothes, then take me to the couch and take off my panties."

He stripped off his clothes and her panties in three quick movements, then pulled Alyssa to the couch.

"Lie on your back."

He lay on the couch and held his big erect cock in his hand, pointing it upward. "Now you get this. Get over here."

She walked beside his head. "I'm not wet enough yet. It's time you ate me. I'm going to climb on your face, and I will slide back to your cock when you have made me wet and ready." She swung one leg over his head, resting her knee above his head. She brought the other leg onto the cushion as well, then lowered her pussy onto his mouth. He licked her slit a couple of times. Her lips parted, and some of the cum Robert had put there earlier fell onto his tongue. He kept licking and got another glob. He pushed her ass up off his chin.

"Are you wet enough yet? I'm about to drown." He looked at her open pussy as more cum dripped out. "Whoa! You are full of cum. I'm not eating cum!" With a scowl, he pushed her ass farther up, and she leaned to the back of the couch as he squirmed out from under her. He gave her ass a final shove as he cleared it, almost flipping her over the arm of the couch onto the floor. *He's pissed.* Alyssa caught her balance and suppressed a giggle. *Time for some insight, if he'll take it.*

"Cole, if you want to fuck married women, sometimes you have to fuck them after their husbands do. Cum isn't so bad. How many women have swallowed your cum? Do you think they thought it was dessert? They didn't. They did it because it pleased you. If you will eat out a woman with cum in her, you can have more married women than you can imagine."

He waved his arms like a football referee signaling an incomplete pass and shook his head. "I'm not gay. I don't want to eat cum." His eyes narrowed, and his jaw muscles flexed.

Alyssa waited for his tension to abate, trying hard not to smile at his irritation. *He doesn't want to do anything that might be construed as gay. Next lesson.* "Eating a cum-filled pussy doesn't make you gay, it makes you a dedicated lover. You're getting her ready for your big dick, remember?" She bit her lower lip and made her eyelids heavy, making a show of how she wanted this lesson to end. "You're getting me ready for your big dick."

"I think you are ready now."

"Not yet. You need to eat me some more and loosen me with your fingers." She nodded to the couch. "Ready?"

He grimaced, then got back under her. She let her pussy linger above his lips before dropping down to let him tongue her opening. She squeezed more cum out, then began grinding her pussy on his face. "All right. Tongue my clit and put two fingers in me." She tilted her hips to grind her clit on his mouth. He shoved two fingers inside and fucked her with them, drawing more cum out to land on his chin. "Easy. Get me ready for your dick. Let me enjoy it." *The boy has no touch. I give up. Might as well get the big reward.* She ground on him another moment, then started sliding her wet pussy down his body. By the time she had her nipples on his mouth, she reached back and lined up his head with her opening. She kept sliding back until he was inside her, then she rested while her pussy adjusted to his girth. Cole slammed his hips upward, jamming half his length into her. Alyssa yelped.

"God, that's too much. Slow down. Find the right spots." *Oh fuck, I'm splitting open. It's so good, but he needs to learn.* Alyssa pushed her hips onto his to slow his thrusts.

He pulled back and slammed upward again. "No more slow-ing down. I'm in, and I'm big enough to hit all the spots, right and wrong. Hang on while I fuck you." He grabbed her hips and held her as he rammed his cock up into her over and over. He hit the end of her tunnel after he got all the way in, and he punished her cervix with his head.

Alyssa put her hands on his chest. "You are hitting me too hard. Slow down."

Cole smiled, rammed his cock into her, and held it there before pulling back and ramming home even harder. "That's how you need it."

"Aahhhh," Alyssa groaned while he hammered away. *God, it hurts, but I'm coming.* Alyssa pulled both her nipples as he stretched her over and over. Her juices flowed out and over his balls onto the couch as she closed her eyes and moaned. "Come inside me," she whimpered as her pussy convulsed. Her sensitive clit screamed at her as he continued to fuck her hard, his girth pulling her lips tight and rubbing it against his shaft.

He swelled after only a couple of minutes, then he pulled out and shot his cum skyward to land on Alyssa's back.

"No! I said come inside me. I love that feeling." She let her head droop onto his chest while she caught her breath.

"Not going to happen, baby." He grinned as he rubbed his cum from her back to her ass, smearing it across her tight pucker. "I always mark my women. Regardless of what they want."

Alyssa waited a moment longer and raised her head to scowl at him. "I'm leaving," she said as she climbed off to put on her panties.

"I know. You'll be back. Just like all the others. It was good to stretch your pussy again."

She paused with her dress over her head. "No. I get better than this all the time. I tried to help you, but you won't learn, so

I'm gone." She dropped the dress over her body, tugging it into place when the back stuck to the cum on her ass. She picked up her purse and opened the door before he spoke again.

"Wait, Alyssa, I was only playing."

"That just proves you aren't ready for me. Bye, Cole." She sped home.

11

SATURDAY, MARCH 13, HOME

Robert looked from the kitchen table when Alyssa walked in from the garage. "That was quick. Did you shorten the lesson?" He and Summer were wearing bathrobes, and the breakfast dishes sat in front of them on the table.

"I ended it. He isn't interested in pleasing me, and you give me better at home every day. I won't see him again."

"Don't get me wrong, Baby; I'm not upset at that turn of events, but won't you miss his big dick? The excitement?"

Alyssa scooped some of the cold eggs out of the pan and sat at the table to eat. "No. It is big, but it's a one-trick pony. I'd rather have your cock any day. And he's not exciting. You make me feel so much better. Someone else can teach him."

"Um, just how big is it?" Summer held her hands about six inches apart.

"Bigger than that." Alyssa held her hands up, then pulled out her phone. "Here. He sent me this picture last night." She opened the text strand with Cole and pulled up the picture.

Summer gasped. "Shit, that's a dinner plate. He's got to be what, nine, ten inches long?"

"Probably that long, and thick. It is delightfully filling, but then he just beats you to death with it and expects you to like it because it is big. If you're thinking of a rebound man, I can introduce you, but I wouldn't advise it."

"Another man is not in the cards right now. But that is one impressive dick." She smiled and licked her lips. "I talked with my attorney. There is some work to do before I can file, but his detective got some photos this week. I thought we would end up divorced, so we hired a detective to get some evidence while this week played out."

Robert sat up straight. "He wasn't outside your house last night, was he?"

"No. We had what we needed by Thursday at lunch. It seems he nails the bimbo almost every day."

"You had me worried there for a minute."

Alyssa put her hand on Summer's shoulder. "Where will you go?"

Summer reached up to cover Alyssa's hand. "My sister lives about twenty miles away. Joanie was there last night, so it will be easy for her and me to stay there. It's closer than driving across town." She stood up. "I already showered. Would you mind if I borrowed some clothes? Something that doesn't say 'party girl'? I don't think showing up at home this morning wearing the same clothes I wore last night would make things go smoothly."

Alyssa stood. "Sure. Come on, we'll find you something." She looked at Robert. "Are you going to play golf?"

"Bryce texted earlier to beg off, so we are canceling today.

He may be there when we arrive, Summer. The clothes may not make any difference."

"I'll take an Uber so you two aren't there. It will be fine. I bet he goes to see Bimbo as soon as I arrive."

❧

Alyssa finished putting the breakfast dishes away while Robert walked Summer to the door. *Those two have always been close. They get each other's quirks. I'm glad he was there for her last night.*

Robert returned to the great room. He stopped walking and stared at her a moment, the hint of a smile at the corners of his mouth. "I think you need to shower."

"I do indeed. Want to join me?"

Robert shook his head. "I'll wait. You wash that boy's cum off your back and throw the dress in the laundry, then come to the bed. You can request that I reclaim you."

Fuck, that made me wet. "Be ready, Babe. I need you bad."

Alyssa washed quickly but took some time gently rubbing her tender pussy and letting the warm water run over it. *Jesus, Cole did a number on me. This is going to hurt.* After a few minutes, she got out, dried off, took three Advil, and went to the bed, where Robert waited under the covers. "I'm clean, Babe." She smiled and winked at him. "May I request that you reclaim me?"

Robert took his time making a show of looking at his nude wife from head to toe. "I want you back. I also saw you in the shower. You're sore, aren't you?"

Alyssa hung her head. "Yes."

"We can wait, Babe. I want to reclaim you, but I refuse to hurt you."

Alyssa snapped her head up to look at her husband. "No! I told you I will bear any pain for you to reclaim me."

"I know. But I won't hurt you. We can wait."

"Thank you, Babe." She held her face in her hands a few seconds, ashamed that her trip to see Cole impacted her time with Robert. She took a deep breath before straightening. "He really hurt me today. That's why I'm never going to see him again." *I know!* She smiled and clasped her hands in front of her chest. "Would you accept a substitute?"

"A substitute? For you? How does that work?"

"Not a substitute for me. A substitute for my pussy. Would you reclaim me by fucking my ass?"

"That's not quite our deal."

"I know, but you don't want to hurt my sore pussy, and I don't want to wait, so what about that as a compromise?"

Robert chuckled. "If that is what you want, who am I to refuse?"

"I'll be back in a few minutes," Alyssa said with a grin as she headed to the bathroom and closed the door.

She returned in about fifteen minutes with a couple of hand towels and a bottle of lubricant. "I've done some research. I'm prepped for you, Babe." She leaned over her husband and kissed him. "How do you want me?"

Robert raised his eyebrows. "How do you recommend, madam expert?"

"I want to see you while you reclaim me, Babe. I'll lie on my back and you fuck my ass." She laid one of the towels on the bed, then lay back on it and dripped some lubricant onto her fingers before sticking one into her ass, swirling it a bit before adding a second. Tingles shot up her spine and returned to clench her pussy and ass open and closed. *Oh, that's good, and it's not even his cock.* She handed him the bottle. "Bring your cock to my mouth, Babe. Let me get you hard while I open up."

Robert knee-walked beside her head and let his cock flop

into her open mouth. She sucked the tip inside and bobbed her head, humming around his shaft while she continued to spread her asshole with her fingers. She held eye contact with him while he worked his cock slowly in and out of her mouth. His cock hardened quickly. *I love it when he hardens in my mouth.* She took him into her throat for a few strokes before pulling off and gasping. "God, lube up and get inside me. I'm ready. Just go slow. Your cock feels huge right now."

"You made it that way," Robert laughed as he backed up to her hips. He poured a palmful of lubricant and slathered it on his cock. Some dripped off the tip onto her inflamed pussy before rolling into her crack. Alyssa smeared her fingers one more time in her ass, then pulled them back. He lined up his head at her open pucker and pushed. Alyssa felt pressure in her bowels as his head caught, her ass not yet ready to accept his full size.

"Keep it there and press harder," Alyssa said as she moved her hands to her tits.

Robert pushed a little harder, and the tip of his cock slipped inside. Her skin stung as it stretched around him, the pinches riding the same path as the anticipatory tingles had a moment ago, clenching and relaxing her pelvic muscles. She gasped and saw his eyes bug and then narrow as he felt his head enter her. Alyssa pulled her nipples. "Push farther before you stop."

Robert pushed until about half his cock was inside her ass.

Alyssa released the breath she had been holding. "Hold there. Let me get used to you." She closed her eyes and took a few slow breaths. Her belly bloated a bit, and she concentrated on relaxing.

Robert held still and caressed her outer pussy lips while she adjusted. "I'll get this later, Baby." He ran a finger around her swollen clit. Soft sparks flew from her clit, joining with and multiplying the ones from her ass. They settled deep and warm in her belly, making her quiver in that same spot where her biggest orgasms always started.

Alyssa grunted and twitched her hips. "Oh yes, you will. I still owe you my pussy. My ass is just a down payment. God, you feel good. All right. Give me some more."

Robert pulled back and slowly reinserted, pushing a bit more with each stroke. After five or six, his balls rested on her. He waited for her to adjust to his full length. Alyssa pushed a sweaty strand of hair away from her face. "Yes. Now fuck me, just go slow."

Robert pulled back and began a slow, rhythmic fuck. His movement was so slow that her breasts barely jiggled as he moved. He rubbed them with his fingertips as he stroked, circling the entire breast, then working his way in toward her nipples. Even preoccupied with a big cock in her ass, Alyssa held her breath, wanting what she knew would come next.

When he reached her nipples, he pinched them between his fingers and accelerated his strokes when she groaned and closed her eyes. Her nipples electrified her chest, pleasure arcing between them until it built and flowed through her body, deep in her belly.

With a soft hum, Robert moved a hand to her breastbone and patted her, silently urging her to be still. *He doesn't want to come yet.* She stopped moving and looked at his sweating face, his eyes closed, his lips pursed as he controlled his breathing. She lay still, resisting the urge to squeeze his cock with her ass, delaying the gratification of feeling its full hardness for letting him last longer inside her. The thought made her pussy throb. She felt some juice roll down her perineum. *He makes me hornier even when he is completely still inside me. I have it so good.*

Robert began thrusting again and moved a finger to strum Alyssa's clit, releasing her anticipation with the first flick across it. Alyssa flexed her body, forcing air from her lungs with a sound more animal than human.

Oh fuck. My ass is so full, and my clit is on fire. I didn't know how good his big cock would feel back there. Alyssa gazed at Robert as her breathing recovered, though it was shallow and rapid. She stretched her legs to the side, straightening them in almost a full split. She then pulled her legs back farther with her hands, straining her hamstrings and her hip joints, opening her body. "Nothing between you and my ass, Babe, not even my own legs. Nobody gets me this open, ever, just you. I'll only stretch like this for you, Babe. Fuck me hard. Fill me deep." Alyssa's abs cramped when she pushed her hips forward to meet his thrusts.

Robert tapped one hand on Alyssa's clit and pulled her nipple with the other one. Her hands fought to hold her legs open as she wailed. He shoved his cock deep into her, and his cum boiled deep inside her bowels. Her orgasm exploded. Robert stroked slowly while Alyssa's orgasm abated, then stopped when her legs fell limp on the bed. He lowered his face to hers for a slow kiss. "I love you, Baby. You are mine again."

"I love you, Babe, and I am indeed yours. That was wonderful." She wrapped her arms around his neck. "Stay in me until you go soft. I love that feeling."

"So you want more anal?"

"Not with anything bigger than you. I feel so full, and so good. I meant what I said. I only trust you enough to be so open and vulnerable. You know just how to make me come. But I want to tighten as you soften, not all at once." Robert lay above Alyssa for a while, kissing her and caressing her face, neck, and chest. His cock finally softened enough to slip out of her ass. She smiled at him. "Let's get clean. Now will you shower with me?"

"Absolutely."

✦

Robert turned when he heard a knock on the bedroom door. "Come in, Clay," he called out as the door opened. "What's going on?"

"Mom, Dad, I know we are going to the Leas' lake house tomorrow, but Sawyer and I want to go rowing and maybe get some lunch. Can I skip, please?"

Robert's eyebrows raised. "Wait, Sawyer, the gorgeous six-foot blonde on your crew team?"

"Robert! That girl is younger than your daughter," Alyssa called from the closet. "You need to be looking at me, not young girls."

"Baby, she is impossible to ignore. I noticed her. Everyone notices her. I'm not hitting on her. That"—he winked at his son—"is apparently what Clay is doing."

Clay rolled his eyes. "We just want to practice and get a bite to eat. The first regatta is coming up next week, and we haven't rowed together much. I'm not hitting on her. In fact, it was her idea."

Alyssa laughed. "Of course, you can get some practice in, sweetie. I'll let Carol know in case her boys want to do something else as well."

Clay smiled. "Thanks. Tell them I look forward to next time." He turned and left the room.

"He and Sawyer have been spending a lot of time after practice lately," Alyssa said. "I think he likes her."

"You think he plans to bring her back here tomorrow after they row?"

"I'll be disappointed if he doesn't." Alyssa stepped out of the closet and wrapped her arms around her husband. "So long as they don't want us to entertain them when we get home. I think we'll have other plans then."

Robert leaned back and looked at Alyssa. "What do you have in mind?"

Alyssa sighed. "For years, I've told Carol how good you are in bed. With Clay not coming up, she'll have her boys stay home. She'll try to fuck you tomorrow. If you do, I'll need to reclaim you when we get home. So we will not be able to entertain the teenagers."

"Whoa, Baby. That's a lot to address. You think Carol will try something? Why? She hasn't before. And thanks for bragging on me, but maybe you could have kept that part our secret?"

"I let it slip that we are trying being open when we were at lunch last week."

"You let it slip? Alyssa, we agreed to be discreet about our arrangement. How does 'we have decided to try an open marriage' just slip into the conversation?"

Alyssa hung her head, then straightened but cast her best puppy dog eyes. "I didn't mean to. She was complaining about how some guy she had met had shown no finesse. I must have mumbled Cole's name, and she heard. She jumped right on it and wouldn't let it go. The only way I could stop her from raising her voice and making a big scene in the restaurant was to tell her about it. I'm sorry. It was an accident."

"You were honest. You didn't think to lie?"

"You know I'm not as quick with comebacks as you are. I told her to keep the secret."

Robert shook his head. "What's done is done. Then what happened?"

"She tried to be subtle, but I could almost see her jumping up and down in her mind, thinking about sex with you." She made eye contact with her husband and blew a long breath through pursed lips. "I know you like her body, so if you want to, go for it."

Robert gripped Alyssa's shoulders with both hands. "Hold on there. These are our friends. We have known about her cheating a long time, but we don't need to participate. She has a great body, but after what just happened with Bryce and Summer, why do we want to make the weekend a smorgasbord of marital meddling?"

He held up his hand to stay her response. "And when were you going to tell me this?"

"She says Chris has known about her cheating for years. He actually encourages it. She says it turns him on. It wouldn't have been an issue if Clay were coming. With the kids not there, she'll try something, and she will probably want me to entertain Chris while she does."

"Entertain? What does that mean?"

"She didn't say. She says he likes to hear about what the other men do to her while he masturbates. I may get to practice talking dirty, or I may just keep him company while he thinks about it."

Robert wondered what Alyssa had been keeping from him. Had Carol tried to get Alyssa to cheat on him? If Carol liked it so much, and she talked with Alyssa about the men she fucked, had that made Alyssa more comfortable doing what she did in Houston? A knot hardened in his stomach, and he sat on the bed. "How long have you known this stuff? We never talked about this before."

Alyssa smirked. "She has told me about her lovers for years, but this is the first time she ever mentioned Chris's feelings. I'm not sure I believe her, but I'll give her the benefit of the doubt."

Robert held up his hand to stop her while he swallowed his anger. Alyssa's smirk told him she accepted Carol's casual attitude toward marriage, maybe for a long time. He kept his hand up while he took two more deep breaths. "Is that why you were so quick to fuck those people in Houston last month?"

Alyssa's face fell. Her smirk twisted into a gasping *O*, and her hands flew to her cheeks. "No. No, no, no, no. I never thought about Carol when I was in Houston. That was all me, and the circumstances."

Robert pondered that response. As far as he knew, she had never been unfaithful to him prior to that week. If Carol had bragged about it for the years they had been friends, it would likely have happened earlier. He took a different approach. "And you never tried to talk her out of cheating for all those years? You found it acceptable?"

Alyssa flew to her husband, wrapping her arms around him. "No, Babe. I never found it acceptable. I tried to talk her out of it for the first few years, but she ignored my advice, so I provided a friendly ear. I never dreamed of joining her, if that's what you're thinking. I didn't do anything like that, never thought about it, until last month."

Now it wasn't even cheating when she fucked someone else. He stroked his chin as he pondered the changes that realization wrought in his life. His breathing slowed, and the knot in his stomach released. He wrapped Alyssa in his arms and kissed the top of her head. "I did consider that, but you convinced me I was wrong. Thank you." If what Carol had told Alyssa was true, then their friends had had a similar relationship for years. "Do you believe Chris likes her sleeping around?"

"Maybe. She never kept it much of a secret. Not from me, at least."

"Come to think of it, she does like to flaunt her assets when the men are around. Those low-cut shirts and bikini tops advertise her boobs." He chuckled.

Alyssa laughed and poked his ribs. "So are you going to fuck her and come all over those great tits of hers or not?"

Robert shook his head. "She does have magnificent tits, but I am uneasy getting involved in this. I play golf with three guys, and I could sleep with two of their wives in one weekend. That sounds bad to me."

"It's your call, Babe. It will be within our arrangement as long as you come home to me. Why don't you see how it goes?"

"We'll see. We always have a good time at the lake. I don't want to ruin that by messing up a friendship."

12

SUNDAY, MARCH 14, THE LAKE

"HE REALLY IS the perfect fit?"

Alyssa rolled her eyes at Carol's question while they sat in the bow of the anchored pontoon boat, the radio keeping their conversation from their husbands. "He is for me. You may feel differently. You know, Carol, he's my husband, not a gigolo. I don't like talking about him like he is a piece of meat."

"I'm sorry to be so crude, but you know how I am. You have always bragged about how good he is in bed, and now I find out that you have an open marriage. It makes me want to try him out."

"Obviously. Your clothes are so tight and revealing, it is clear you're baiting him."

"Chris calls this my 'fuck me' outfit. I wear it without any underwear when I am hunting guys. I can flash with the short hem and deep neckline or just let the soft fabric reveal what is underneath."

105

"If you say so. Open marriage or not, I don't relish the thought of pimping out my husband."

"You don't like sharing Robert? Chris loves when I tell him about my lovers." Carol winked. "And I love doing it."

Alyssa sighed. "I'm coming to grips with sharing him. It was my idea, and I want to be open, so we're working on it. If he wants you, he knows I'm okay with it. I'm still jealous. He is mine, remember." She looked at the two men sitting in the stern. "So why does Chris like it? He doesn't go outside? Just you?"

Carol smiled. "Yeah, just me. I love him, but he has never satisfied me in bed. I started cheating before we were married. I didn't know it then, but he knew before the wedding. He followed me a few times and even had pictures. The thing is it turned him on. About five years in, I caught him jacking off to some of the pictures he took of me and another guy. We talked it out. I still 'cheat,' but with his permission. Sometimes, I let him catch me with the other guy. The rest of the time, I tell him what the guy did to me. Chris fucking loves it. He comes so hard, and I get bigger dick. It's a good arrangement."

A booming clap of thunder interrupted the conversation. "Time to go to the house," Carol said as she walked to the covered part of the boat. She and Alyssa were barely seated before Chris had the pontoon making its best time toward their lake house. Despite the Bimini top, the four of them were soaked by the cold downpour during the twenty-minute ride. They scampered, dripping and shivering, into the lake house's basement.

"You two shower down here. Chris and I will use ours." Carol directed Alyssa and Robert to the bathroom in the corner of the basement. "Why don't we meet in the den to play cards when we are dry? Chris can start a fire so we can warm up. It's the weather we get in March, right?"

"Um, Carol? We didn't bring any clothes. Do you have anything we can borrow?"

"Oh, right, Alyssa. We aren't the same size, and neither are the guys, but let me see what I can find. I'll be back in a minute." Carol smiled at her friend. "Go ahead and warm up in the shower. I'll give the clothes to Robert."

"Okay. Thanks." Alyssa watched Carol and Chris ascend the stairs and turned to Robert. "Will you fuck her? She's going to offer."

Robert shook his head. "No, Baby. The prospect clearly bothers you. We are open, not hurtful."

"Please don't take that into account." Alyssa shifted her weight from one foot to the other, wringing her hands. "If you want to, go ahead. I won't be upset."

"Baby, you look like a prisoner waiting to be tortured. I won't put you through that."

"I'm just cold." Alyssa dropped her hands to her sides, then took his in hers. "And… I'm excited too. I want you to rock her world. Fuck her ragged. Show her that I have better at home than she gets anywhere, no matter how much she cheats." She looked in his eyes. "I think I want to see that."

"What? You want me to rock the world of the biggest philanderer we know? Thanks for the vote of confidence, but that's a tall order."

"Oh, you can do it. Just get her warmed up the way you do, then put that cock beside her cervix over and over. Nobody can resist that."

"You want to watch? When you watched me with Jessica, you didn't like it."

"That was different. That was in our bed, and you were punishing me for what I did in Houston. This is intended to make Carol come screaming over and over. That makes me wet, Babe."

"That's the rain, Baby. Let's warm up in the shower. We'll see what happens." They walked to the bathroom door and turned when Carol called to them from the stairs.

"Here you go. I found a pair of sweatpants and a T-shirt for you, Robert, and some shorts and a T-shirt for you, Alyssa. They should fit, but if they don't, you can borrow our bathrobes. The dryer is right there." She pointed to a door opposite them. "Run your clothes so you can wear them home. See you upstairs."

Alyssa and Robert stripped off their clothes while the shower warmed up. Alyssa pressed herself into Robert, and her hand found his cock. "This is how you rock her world, Babe. Give it to her the way you give it to me, and she'll be left limp and panting."

They entered the shower together and huddled under the warm water. "All right, I'll fuck Carol if I get the chance. With us playing cards, I don't see that happening."

"Carol is pretty devious, and Chris is in on it. Don't be surprised when it happens."

They dried off and dressed in the clothes Carol had provided.

"Jesus, Robert. Those sweats are so tight I can tell you shave," Alyssa laughed.

"That's fair because your cut-off shirt shows your nipples when you lean forward and the bottoms of your boobs when you stand straight. I like it." Robert put his hand at the leg of her shorts and slid up to her bare pussy. "And I bet she has a smaller pair of shorts you could have worn. These look like they are for easy access."

"Careful, big boy. I can see your cock getting harder. You'll split those sweats."

"I think that's the plan. You ready to play whatever game she has planned?"

Alyssa smiled. "Yes, Babe. Just make sure you win."

⁓

Alyssa stopped when she entered the living room from the basement. Chris sat in a T-shirt and sweatpants almost as tight as Robert's, but his cock wasn't outlined. Carol wore a loose outfit of shorts and a T-shirt like Alyssa's. She was flashing her pussy toward the basement door by raising her foot into the chair and showing the bottoms of her large breasts by reclining over the low back of her chair. Four bottles of beer and a pack of playing cards sat on a low table. "Have you been waiting long?"

"No." Carol leered at the pair. "And yes."

"Y'all come on and sit down," Chris added. "The fire is warm, and the beer is cold. Let's play some spades."

They played a couple of hands of spades. Carol kept her foot in the chair and her pussy pointing at Robert through the open leg hole the entire time. Alyssa chuckled to herself, watching Robert watch Carol rub her breasts from underneath while she considered her plays, returning his eyes to her open crotch as she laid her card. Robert's dick made a huge, curved bulge down the leg of his sweatpants. Alyssa felt a twinge of jealousy in her gut every time Carol stared at it.

God, that's hot. I want him to wear sweats like that all the time. Alyssa sat more demurely than Carol, but her boobs were on display when she bent forward. She winked at Robert when she caught him looking down her shirt while she dealt. *I'm so turned on. When will she do something?* She looked into Chris's lap, where his smaller cock made a bump in the crotch. When she looked to his face, he smiled at her and nodded to his wife. Carol was stretching, letting her shirt ride up completely over her breasts, the nipples hard and erect inside her crinkled areolae.

"Robert," Chris said when Carol resumed sitting, "we didn't get to bet on golf yesterday. Would you like to wager a little on cards? Make it more interesting?"

Robert caught Alyssa's eye. She widened her eyes at him. He

turned to Chris. "Sounds like fun, Chris. How much did you have in mind?"

"I was really thinking something other than money."

"Okay…what are you thinking?"

"I think we should play to five hundred points. The winner gets thirty minutes in the bedroom with the loser's wife."

Robert sat up straight. "Whoa, Chris. That's some bet. What makes you think that is okay?"

Chris held up his hands in a yielding gesture. "Easy, Robert. I don't mean to offend. Carol told me you two are trying an open marriage. You guys know I enjoy Carol sleeping with other men. It's clear she wants you, and Alyssa is one of the few women I would want other than Carol. I thought I would move things along. We don't have to. Sorry if I misunderstood."

Robert shook his head. "You moved things along all right. I'm not offended, and I knew Carol would probably try to get at me today, though I expected a little more subtlety. I'm not sure Alyssa and I are at the point where I'll literally bet her ass in a card game."

Alyssa's pussy pulsed in anticipation. She shifted her thighs to get some relief. *He won't treat me like property, but I want him to. Bet me like you own me, Babe, because you do.* "I'll do it," Alyssa said, looking at the table.

"What?"

"I said, I'll do it." She looked Robert in the eye. "Bet my body against hers. But raise the stakes. The losing wife submits to both the winners, not just the husband, and it happens here, on the table, not in the bedroom. How does that sound, you two?"

Carol sat straight up with her feet on the floor for the first time all game. "Oh, you gorgeous, dirty girl. If you wanted me to eat your pussy, you only had to ask." She looked at Chris. "Honey, are you sure? You have never done anything with another woman." A flush swept up from Carol's neck to her face. "It isn't fair for me to feel this way, but I'm jealous that you want her. I'm not sure I want to watch."

Chris leaned forward to take his wife's hand across the table. "Carol, I get jealous every time you are with another man, but it turns me on, especially when I watch. Today you can feel what I feel. You might find it turns you on. Of course, we might lose."

Carol thought a moment. "I guess I'll find out how it feels." She smiled at Chris. "There is no way we lose this."

Alyssa looked at Robert. "What do you say? This is within our arrangement, but it's also different. Are you willing to bet me against a chance with Carol? It is your call, Babe, and we will do what you say."

Alyssa glanced at Carol and Chris staring at Robert before turning her eyes to him. She held her breath as his lips pursed and waggled from side to side as he thought. She caught his eye and nodded almost imperceptibly. He exhaled with the hint of a smile. "Let's win this, Baby."

They all exhaled and smiled at one another, then became serious with the game. They sat still and forward, watching every card. The idle chitchat only resumed between hands. Each of them considered before making a play. After five hands, Carol and Chris were ahead 297 to 150. "Why don't you show us what we are going to win, Alyssa?" Carol taunted with a grin. "Slip that shirt off. The fire has us all warm, anyway."

Alyssa raised an eyebrow at Carol. "We haven't lost yet, but I'm game. Besides, when Chris gets a look at these perfect tits, he won't play another good hand." She whipped off the baggy shirt and jutted her chest out over the table.

Alyssa smirked back as Carol stared at Alyssa with her mouth agape and Chris stared, unblinking. "They are so perfect," Carol whispered under her breath. *I warned you.*

Robert adjusted the hard-on in his pants. "Jesus, Baby. You

are full of surprises." He looked at Chris. "Hey, buddy, have you never seen tits before?"

"None other than Carol's in a long time. Alyssa, yours are beautiful."

"Thank you, Chris." Alyssa looked at his crotch and noticed only a small bulge. *She said he couldn't satisfy her, but nothing?*

Robert dealt. He and Alyssa made their bid, but remained behind, 358 to 210. The next hand brought them closer, to 399–281. Robert and Alyssa had a strong hand next and drew to 439–371, but a decent hand for Carol and Chris would get them to five hundred first. Chris dealt. Robert bid five. Carol bid four. Alyssa bid low, meaning she would earn one hundred points if she did not take any tricks, but would lose one hundred if she took even one. Chris bid four.

Alyssa looked at Carol. "You had me show what Chris would win if you guys held on, and my tits have been out ever since. Why don't you show Robert what he gets if we win?"

Carol laughed. "There is no way you win, but I'll show anyway. Here are the tits you are going to suck, girl." She pulled off her shirt and threw it on the table. She hefted her breasts and pinched her nipples, shaking them at Alyssa.

"I am going to suck them indeed, win or lose," Alyssa said with a smirk, and she leaned down to lick the closest nipple. "Let's play."

The game proceeded slowly, with each player thinking before laying a card. They were all turned on, but they all wanted to be in control for the upcoming sex. After twelve tricks, Carol and Chris had taken seven and Robert had taken five. Alyssa had taken none.

"Baby, as long as you don't take this one, we win," Robert said to Alyssa.

"Chris, we have to give this one to her. He's right. If we take it, they win by two points." Carol leaned forward as Chris led the four of diamonds. Robert played the nine of clubs, keeping Chris in the lead. Carol played the six of hearts and grinned at Alyssa. "Come on, you have one diamond left. Take this one."

Alyssa grinned and laid the three of diamonds on the pile. "Woo-hoo! Epic comeback!" She high-fived Robert across the table, then looked at him. "Are you ready to put that cock to work, Babe?"

Robert smiled back at her, then looked at Carol and Chris. "I am, as long as our friends are still game for the bet. Guys, we don't have to go through with this if you don't want to. Our friendship is a lot more important than this little bet."

Chris looked at Robert. "Robert, she really wants you, and I want to see you take her. I meant it when I bet my wife. Please, enjoy her."

Carol returned Robert's look, stood, and removed her shorts. "I've wanted this a long time." She moved the beer bottles to the hearth and lay on her back on the low table. She looked at Alyssa. "Are you sure?"

Alyssa looked at her friend and then her husband. Her nipples were hard and ready to be touched, as they had been since she took off her shirt. Her pussy tingled, and she moved her thighs to rub the moist lips together. "Let's fuck her, Babe." She stood to remove her shorts as well and dropped them in her chair. She took Carol's hand. "Take off his clothes and lie back down."

Robert bent to let Carol pull the T-shirt over his head, then stood while she worked the tight pants down his legs. When his cock sprang free, she leaned forward to take it in her mouth, but Alyssa grasped her hair from behind. "Not yet. We get you for thirty minutes, not the other way around. Finish undressing him and lie down."

Carol did as she was told, and Robert stepped closer to her and fondled her large breasts. He pushed them together from the side, sliding his palms over them. They were heavy in his hands, even for their size. When he pulled and rolled her nipples between his thumb and forefinger, they slipped from his fingers as her breasts sagged outward. When he pinched her nipples again, he pinched hard and stretched her tits up from her body, making Carol moan.

While Robert enjoyed Carol's tits, Alyssa slipped to the end of the table and knelt between her friend's legs. She picked up Carol's foot and kissed from the big toe, through the instep, and up the inside of her calf to the back of her knee. She put down that foot and repeated the trip on the other leg. Carol's hips were writhing on the table, and Alyssa paused and winked at him.

Robert released Carol's breasts while he ran his hand above her belly, barely making contact with the fine hairs there. Carol's body responded with goose bumps everywhere. She moaned. "God, give it to me already!"

Robert and Alyssa smiled at each other and moved their hands and lips away from her erogenous zones, torturing their horny friend. Alyssa nipped a little skin between her teeth but stopped just short of her pussy.

Robert was kissing Carol's fingertips when he looked at Chris for the first time. He had removed his shirt, and had his hand down his pants, clearly rubbing himself. His mouth hung open. Robert made sure Chris's view was unimpeded by keeping Carol's body between them when he returned his focus to her. He kissed down the underside of her arm, along her armpit, then he turned upward across her breast to her neck, where he sucked hard. Carol inhaled in a hiss. Robert reached with both hands to pull her nipples again and kissed her earlobe before moving to her mouth, where he shoved his tongue in and wrestled with hers as she panted.

Carol hissed and started writhing and bucking. Her teeth

clicked with Robert's, and he moved to her neck, again sucking and biting, certain to leave a mark.

Alyssa squeezed his hand. "Feed her your cock, Babe. I'll get her pussy ready for you."

Robert stood. "Suck on this, Carol." She rose on her elbows and turned her head to engulf him. The angle wasn't ideal, but she took him to the back of her throat and licked the underside of his head. Robert moaned and returned one hand to her breast, cupping it.

Alyssa nodded, her head bobbing between Carol's legs. Carol grunted, and her throat strained as she appeared to have a small orgasm. Alyssa moved a hand from Carol's thigh. Carol writhed and grunted around Robert's cock until she tensed and tightened her sweaty thighs against Alyssa's head.

Carol pulled off Robert's cock to wail as a second, larger orgasm hit her. Her torso stiffened, making her breasts point at the ceiling while her abs rippled. Her head fell back, and if her eyes had been open, she would have seen Chris stand to remove his sweatpants. When Carol's legs relaxed, Alyssa stood. "She's ready. Fuck her good."

Robert kissed his wife as they switched places. Alyssa sucked one of Carol's breasts and grasped her husband's cock as he neared Carol. "Let me help you get that in, Babe." She hammered Carol's clit with the head of his cock before sliding the tip over, around, and between the open lips. She relented after a moment and placed the tip at her opening. "Give it to her." She pulled Robert's cock gently as he pushed into Carol's pussy with a moan.

Carol arched her back as Robert entered her. He leaned back and watched her face as he ground his cock inside her, looking for sensitive spots. Her breath caught as he touched her hard cervix and moved under it. Robert smiled at his wife. "Got it. Let's drive her wild."

He began rocking his hips, grinding the tip of his cock across her cervix, hitting the sensitive spots on either side on every stroke. Alyssa sucked Carol's nipple and used one hand to rub just above her clit, stretching and pulling the skin around it. Carol resumed bucking her hips and arched her back, pressing her pussy against Robert as if begging for more. Carol's body quickly returned to having another orgasm. As her body clenched, the noise she made seemed to combine release and pain. Her fingers entwined into Alyssa's hair, and her legs tightened onto Robert as he continued to grind inside her.

When she relaxed, Robert slid backward and began giving Carol long, hard strokes with his cock, still focusing on the spots he'd found earlier. Alyssa kissed Carol, then returned to sucking on what was becoming a raw red nipple. Robert saw Alyssa raise her head to look at Chris. He was wearing pantyhose, and his small cock was tenting them up where he held it in his hand, tugging it with two fingers. His belly rose and fell with his rapid breath. Robert could see why Carol would not be satisfied with his small dick.

Alyssa threw her leg over Carol's face. Alyssa's ass cheeks flexed and shifted as she ground her hips on Carol's face. Alyssa lowered her hips to pin Carol in place. The muscles in her back rippled when she raised her hands in front of her, letting Robert know she was pulling her own nipples as Carol ate her. God, his wife was gorgeous, even when he couldn't see her face.

Alyssa stared at Chris. "Your wife is loving my pussy. Watch her eating me while my husband fucks her with his big cock. She is coming over and over. Listen to her moaning into my cunt. She's going to make me come all over her pretty face. Do you like that?"

"Yes. Oh god, yes."

"Do you like seeing her face under my pussy?"

"Yes." Chris's breathing quickened.

"Do you like watching me play with my tits while she eats my pussy?"

Chris looked at her tits, blinked, and yelled as he came. Only a little of his semen oozed through the pantyhose. The rest ran down his cock on the inside of the hose. Her cheek rising revealed that she smiled at him while her ass still humped Carol's face. "Ooh, I like seeing you come. Are you ready to see me come?"

Chris's breath caught. "Fuck, yes. Come on Carol's face."

"In a minute. She has to eat me some more first. If you can get hard again, maybe you can play with me too." Alyssa dropped one hand from her breast to her pussy while her back and ass moved and flexed faster, clearly seeking her release.

Robert quickened his thrusts into Carol and lengthened them so he was coming almost all the way out, then bottoming out against her cervix on every stroke. Her hips rose to meet every one, grinding the top of her vagina against the tip of his cock. Her pussy clenched at him every time she came. She was moaning into Alyssa's pussy on every exhalation. Carol pulled and twisted her own nipples. Carol's skin flushed pink across her torso and up her neck as the time between orgasms continued to shorten. Her ass squished in a puddle of her juices on the table, and her legs alternated between limp and pulling Robert into her hungry cunt.

Alyssa's back and ass froze in a spasm as she came. She stuttered with her breath and leaned forward onto her hands as Robert watched her asshole open and close as her orgasm continued. Her body jerked a few times, then she rose off Carol, who was panting after another orgasm of her own. Alyssa looked at Chris. "Are you ready?"

Chris pulled his hard dick with two fingers through the pantyhose. "Yes."

"I'm going to suck her tits. You give it to me from behind."

"Oh god, yes." He stepped behind her.

Robert heard the pantyhose rip as Alyssa lowered her head to Carol's breast, and watched Chris's small penis enter Alyssa's pussy while she took on a puzzled look. When Chris's hips bumped her ass, her face changed, like she realized it wasn't a finger. He pumped for a few minutes before Alyssa raised her head. "Chris, do you like anal?"

Robert looked at his wife, who gave him an exasperated look and a shrug, then mouthed "little" to him. He nodded. Carol's head just lolled about. She had become too lost in her pleasure to speak.

"I've never had it," Chris said as he continued to pump into Alyssa.

"Run to the kitchen and get olive oil."

Chris left for the kitchen, and Alyssa returned to sucking and pulling Carol's breasts. When he got back, Alyssa looked over her shoulder. "Pour some in the crack of my ass, and work some into my hole with a finger. Go slow." He did as she asked. "Oh, that's good. Now add another finger, and then take that hand and lube your dick."

Chris looked at Robert with raised eyebrows. Robert nodded, and Chris looked down at Alyssa's ass. "I'm ready."

"Push your dick into my ass. Go slow." He put the tip on her sphincter and pushed. He slid in, her ass loosened by his two fingers. He bumped against her ass cheeks, and she moaned. "Oh yeah, Chris. Take a couple of slow strokes, then fuck me hard."

Chris stroked into Alyssa. Robert watched her cheeks ripple as Chris sped up. Alyssa must have bitten down tightly on Carol's nipple because the breast pulled back and forth as Alyssa bounced with Chris's thrusts. Chris yelled and buried himself against her, his cum obviously emptying into her bottom as he jerked against her. Alyssa looked at Robert, then said, "Oh, that was so good. That cum was just what I needed." She rose off Carol, leering at Robert.

Robert lifted Carol's legs over his shoulders, bent her in half, and hammered into her pussy. The position let him get his deepest into her, and he continued to hit her sensitive spot by her cervix. He was close to coming, and Carol looked at him through sleepy eyes. "Come in me," she sighed into his ear. Her request put him over the edge, and he roared and fired spurt after spurt into her, injecting it right on the entrance to her womb. After he finished, he ground his hips, trailing the tip of his cock across the top of her vagina and making her belly spasm in one final orgasm. He continued grinding until he softened and slipped from her pussy. His cock and a glob of cum trailed down to rest in the crack of her ass. "God, that feels sexy," Carol whispered as her ass clenched several times. "Stay there a minute." Her eyes closed, and Robert laid her legs to the side, then kissed her forehead.

Robert picked up Carol's limp body and placed her on the couch. He pulled the blanket on the back of the couch over her, then turned to Alyssa. "Want to go shower again?"

Alyssa nodded. "Yeah. I feel all oily." She caressed Chris's cheek. "Satisfied but oily. Thank you."

Chris smiled. "The pantyhose didn't bother you? Carol hates them."

"No, they didn't bother me. They were a little rough on my ass cheeks, but if they rev you up, go for it." She waved her hand around, indicating the scene of their activity. "Did all this turn you on? Is this the kind of thing you like?"

"It does turn me on. I know it is unusual for a man to get turned on by his wife's infidelity, but it keys me up. Getting to watch is better, and this was amazing. Thanks for letting me fuck you. You felt great."

"You felt great too. I'm going to go shower before I drip oil and…other things…on your floor."

"Yeah, right. Go ahead."

❧

Robert turned to Chris as Alyssa walked to the basement. "Are you sure this was good for you? I'm your friend, and I just fucked your wife unconscious."

"Oh yeah. I'm good with it. I came so hard. This was my own personal porno. Thank you for doing it, and for sharing Alyssa with me. That wasn't part of the bet."

"That was her choice, so when she was fine with it, I was too."

"Well, thank you anyway."

Robert went downstairs and pulled their clothes out of the dryer before entering the bathroom. Alyssa was rinsing the suds off her body. Robert's dick started to grow.

Alyssa smiled at him. "Not here, Babe, but soon. Let me finish up. I want to get the oil out of my butt."

❧

The four exchanged hugs at the door, then they exchanged kisses between the partners. Robert stiffened when Carol tugged his cock through his pants, and Chris palmed both Alyssa's ass cheeks. They all affirmed what a great time they'd had, then Robert and Alyssa ran through the rain to Robert's Suburban. Alyssa stared out the window without talking, then looked at her phone.

They had gone about ten miles when Alyssa pointed. "Turn down that road over there."

Robert wrinkled his brow but turned where she pointed.

"Now take that right."

Robert turned the big Suburban down a narrow gravel road. After a turn, he stopped at a red gate across the road. "What now, Baby?"

Alyssa smiled at him. "Get out." She opened her door and

ran to the front of the truck, unbuttoning her shirt on the way. Robert turned off the truck and got out, stripping off his shirt as well. Alyssa shucked off her shoes and pants, leaving her in soaked lingerie. She helped Robert remove his pants and shoes, then unsnapped her bra and pulled her panties off.

"I need you to take me right here, right now. I can't wait any longer." She bent over and placed her hands on the hood, presenting her pussy to him. He rubbed his head across her lips before sliding inside. Alyssa moaned as he pushed until he hit the top of her tunnel. He ground his hips against her to rub around her cervix. She pushed back against him, then started to fuck forward and back, slamming his abdomen.

"Yeah, Babe. Ram that cock inside my tight pussy. You own this pussy. Fuck it like you own it."

Robert thrust hard against her, using both hands to guide her hips back and forth on his cock. He looked at the raindrops on her back jiggle and pool as she moved, sliding down her skin. He reached with one hand to grab a handful of her wet hair and pulled gently, raising her head. "You want my cock? You dirty girl. You wanted me to bet this pussy in a game. This is my pussy. I decide when it gets wagered and when it doesn't. You would have let them ravage this pussy of mine. Maybe I should have you go without." He pulled out of her and held her hips.

Alyssa looked over her shoulder. "Oh, please, Babe. Give me some more. I won't be bad and bet my pussy in a game. Just look in my eyes and fuck me so you know I'm telling the truth." She stood and turned to face him, then leaned back against the hood and spread her legs.

Robert smiled and lifted his wife's hips as she grasped his hard cock and guided it to her wet opening.

She gasped as he shoved inside. "Oh god, fuck me. Fuck me

with that magnificent dick and come inside me. Fuck me and make me feel good, Babe. I promise I won't be bad."

Robert slammed into her, feeling the familiar spots inside her that drove her orgasms. He supported her weight as she arched her back, putting her upper back across the hood. She looked him in the eye and moaned. The rain splashed on her belly and breasts. It pooled in her navel and in the cleft of her pussy. Robert watched it run down her sides as her pussy gripped him, squeezing and releasing in waves. Even in the cold rain, a pink flush began in the center of her chest and grew up her neck to signal her coming orgasm, and she threw her head back to wail. After only a few more plunges, Robert's cock swelled, and he emptied into her, making her belly flutter as she gasped for breath. Alyssa flipped her body forward and threw her arms around his neck, clinging to him as she caught her breath.

"God, I love you." She kissed him and hugged him tight. "I couldn't wait any longer. I have been so horny for you. I have reclaimed you, Babe."

Robert chuckled. "I thought I was reclaiming you. And washing you off in the rain, apparently."

"You can reclaim me when we get home. I needed to reclaim you quickly after Carol. She is quite the slut. Plus, Chris didn't get me off, so I've been simmering for two hours."

"Glad I could help, Baby. Are you ready to get in and warm up?"

Alyssa laughed. "Yeah. This rain is cold."

They wrung out their wet clothes and put them in the back of the Suburban. They wrapped up in two blankets Robert kept in his car to drive home.

Alyssa laughed at Robert. "Don't get a ticket, Babe. The cops wouldn't find our attire appropriate."

"We can take the back roads and be fine. But I won't get a ticket."

Robert drove a while, then looked at Alyssa. "Chris didn't get you off?"

Alyssa huffed. "No. He has a short, thin dick. It felt like a finger. That's why I offered my ass, hoping I would feel fuller. It didn't work. He finished fast. I thought after he masturbated through the pantyhose, he would last longer, but I guess he was too excited from watching you pound Carol."

"I think he was too excited watching, and then fucking, you. I can see why he came quickly. I don't get the pantyhose thing though."

"Me either. I was worried he would try to fuck me through them and that the material would rough up my pussy, but he tore a hole instead. My butt cheeks are probably red. Thanks for fucking me so well back there. I almost feel like Carol did."

"Who knows? She might be so responsive and sensitive that she always passes out afterward."

"No, Babe. You gave her the fuck of her life. She will be back for more. You watch."

"We'll see. We still need to be discreet, remember?"

"Who will be more discreet than a woman whose husband condones her sleeping around?"

Robert thought a moment. "Maybe, but that also means she can talk without the typical consequences. I want to be careful."

"I know. I do too. But you can't tell me you don't want to come all over those big tits of hers."

"Come on, Baby. You know my favorite tits to come on are yours. They always will be. You don't need to feel uneasy about Carol's being a little bigger and heavier. I'll take yours over hers any day."

"Thanks, Babe. And I'll let you take them any day."

❧

Alyssa saw two flashes run from the living room into the back bedroom when she stepped into the laundry room from the garage. She turned to Robert and whispered, "I told you he would bring her here. They just ran to the back bedroom."

He chuckled. "Good for him. Sawyer is hot, hot, hot."

Alyssa dropped the wet clothes into the hamper and opened her blanket, flashing Robert. "Good for us. We don't have to explain why we are wearing blankets. Now you need to reclaim me, unless you don't think I'm hot, hot, hot." She yelled down the hallway to the back bedroom, "Clay, Sawyer? We are going to shower and nap a little before supper. We'll be in our bedroom for about two hours, okay?"

"Okay," Clay yelled back.

"Come on and reclaim me, Babe." She tugged Robert's blanket off his shoulders and ran giggling to their bedroom. Robert ran right behind, slamming the bedroom door behind him. He tackled her onto the bed and worked his cock into her still-wet pussy. Alyssa yelped with every hard thrust and wailed with her first orgasm.

13

MONDAY, MARCH 15, THE NEIGHBORHOOD

"Come on my tits, Babe!" Alyssa yelled to Robert when she felt his cock swelling inside her, revealing his impending climax. Robert stroked twice more, then pulled out and let Alyssa jump off the bed to kneel on the floor before him. She presented her tits under his cock with both hands.

Robert jerked his cock and grunted as his cum splattered first on Alyssa's cheek, then on her tits as he aimed to cover both white orbs. Even after they'd fucked three times the night before and once this morning, he gave her a big load that dripped off her nipples, onto her thighs. Alyssa dragged her finger across her left breast and lifted the cum to her mouth to suck it off.

"God, Robert. I've had so much sex since Friday, and I just can't get enough. I'm horny all the time. I couldn't get home fast enough today after work to fuck you before dinner. You just gave me three orgasms, and I want more right now."

Robert laughed. "It's a good thing you are going to Jessica's after dinner. You will have lots of energy to repay her, any way she likes."

"Yes. I can't wait. What she did for us…we could never repay her. If she wants me all night as the quid pro quo, it's a small price to pay."

Robert raised an eyebrow at his wife. "Like you will mind pleasuring her beautiful body all night and having her tongue inside you, giving you orgasm after orgasm."

Alyssa thrust her pussy forward, rubbed her clit with two fingers, and leered at Robert. "Oh, I said we couldn't repay her, not that I would hate trying." She bit her lower lip and inhaled. "God, go get dinner out of the oven, or I'm going to fuck you again."

❧

Alyssa kissed Robert at the front door and pulled his hand under the hem of her short dress, letting him feel her wet, bare pussy. "I love you, Babe. I'll see you in the morning."

"I don't like the thought of you fucking someone else all night, but we owe Jessica a lot. Enjoy, and tell Jessica 'thank you again' for me." Robert stuck his finger in her pussy and held her possessively while he kissed her again. "Remember our deal. Be back in the morning in time for me to reclaim you before work."

"Oh, I will." Alyssa pulled Robert's hand out of her, licked the glistening finger, and walked out the door, giggling as she walked three doors down and across the street to Jessica's house. Before she rang the bell, she looked back to see Robert silhouetted in their front door, watching. She rang the bell, then waved to him when the light from Jessica's foyer spilled out the open door.

"Good evening, Alyssa, come on in." The busty blonde

stepped aside to let Alyssa pass close by her into the foyer. "Would you like some wine?" She shut and locked the door.

"Sounds great." Alyssa followed Jessica into the kitchen. Two glasses sat beside a decanter of wine on the counter side of the island, opposite the sink. Alyssa leaned against the counter while Jessica poured.

"I saw Robert watching. Is he being protective as you walk down the street, or is he afraid I will try to steal you away tonight? I am younger than he is." Jessica grinned and handed Alyssa a full glass.

Alyssa laughed. "Yep, that's Robert. The Great Protector." She took a sip. "Honestly, our agreement is that we always come home at night—no overnight stays. He knows this is different, but he still wants me beside him in bed. It makes me love him even more."

"You are lucky, Alyssa. He's a great husband."

"I'm lucky you are such a good friend. To let him use you to punish me for cheating in Houston? That was more than I ever would dare to ask. He asked me to say thank you again. Our marriage would have ended if it weren't for you."

"I was glad to help you. After he gave me those orgasms on your kitchen table, I wasn't just helping you. I was wet for a week."

"No way. After what your ex used to do with you?"

"Oh yeah. Even after Mister Kinky. Robert made me feel amazing. I wore out a set of batteries in my vibrator that week. I joked about stealing you away, but I might try to steal him away too. Would you guys come as a package deal?"

Alyssa smiled. "Steal us both away? Maybe we'd let you." Alyssa sipped her wine. "Robert aside, I'm yours all night. I just have to be home for a reclaiming before he goes to work. What did you have in mind?"

"Getting right to business, huh? I'm not in a hurry. Finish your wine. We can chat a bit, relax and drink a little, then see where we go from there."

Alyssa drained her glass in four gulps. "Whatever you want. Just know that I've been wet all day thinking about getting between your long legs again." She stood with her feet apart and slipped a finger under her dress and into her pussy. She pulled the wet finger out and offered it for Jessica to taste. Jessica smiled and engulfed the finger, sucking it and rubbing her tongue on it as if it were a small cock.

Alyssa grabbed Jessica's jeans-covered ass and pulled her body close for a kiss. Their tongues danced with each other as Jessica felt Alyssa's tits through the tight dress. Jessica pulled the top hem of the tube dress below Alyssa's tits, then sucked on a nipple. Alyssa moaned, unfastened Jessica's jeans, and slipped her hand inside.

"No panties? You were ready too." She slid a finger along Jessica's slit, spreading the wetness from her lips to her clit, then circling the hard button. Jessica's hips jumped as her knees buckled with the sensation. When she regained her legs, Jessica pulled the top of Alyssa's dress down her body, revealing her flat stomach, then her flared hips. The cool air hardened Alyssa's nipples, the tightness feeling almost like Jessica had tweaked them, they were so sensitive. Tiny static crackles flickered inside her breasts, in search of a connection.

Jessica kissed Alyssa's navel. Alyssa moaned when the warm tongue filled her little divot, anchoring a spot just inside the skin for her pleasure to accumulate. Her flickering breasts connected to it, and her stomach tightened. Jessica revealed Alyssa's shaved pussy, finally letting the thin dress drop to the floor from just above Alyssa's knees.

Naked before Jessica, Alyssa's legs quivered around weak knees as she awaited what would come next. Jessica kissed Alyssa again, cupping a breast and pinching the nipple with one hand while slipping the other to her ass, kneading and pulling her cheek. Cool air tickled her exposed anus, making her Kegel muscles clench and sending a shiver up her spine.

Alyssa moaned into the kiss when Jessica pinched her nipple hard enough to buckle her knees again and turn the pain into bolts of pleasure flying from her abused nipple to the storm brewing behind her navel. Alyssa recovered enough to push Jessica's jeans over her hips. When they were midway down her thighs, Alyssa broke the kiss and bent, then crouched, to pull them off over Jessica's bare feet. *So beautiful. Love the toe ring.*

Before she stood, she kissed Jessica's mound and pulled both ass cheeks apart, rubbing them and dipping her hands so her pinky fingers brushed the lower lips of Jessica's pussy from behind. Jessica's hand gripped Alyssa's hair, pressing her mouth against Jessica's hips, but Alyssa pushed back and stood, grasping the hem of Jessica's shirt and pulling it over her head. She smiled. "I want to see all of you too."

She and Jessica kissed, pulling nipples and fingering each other. They pressed their bodies together, using their hands and arms to pull ass cheeks and backs. The pressure built a dull ache that Alyssa wanted to both end and last forever.

Jessica pulled back. "Climb on the counter and lie back."

Alyssa used the stool to climb onto the countertop. The granite was cold on her ass, and she jumped when she laid her back on it. She stayed down on the third try. "That's cold! Warm me up."

Jessica placed Alyssa's thighs on her shoulders and licked only the puffy outer lips. The broad strokes warmed Alyssa's entire pussy, which did from below what the crushing of her breasts had done from above. The powder keg of pleasure in her belly accumulated with each touch.

Jessica pushed Alyssa's thighs upward, tilting her hips and

opening her cheeks from front to back. The warm tongue left a wet trail around her anus, then proceeded up and beside her pussy, above her clit, then down the other side, starting the circuit again. The saliva cooled in the open air, so Alyssa chased Jessica's mouth with her hips when she slowed in the curves, seeking to reduce the contrast.

On the fourth trip around, Jessica dipped her tongue onto Alyssa's nether hole, making it distend and retreat, and the cool air touching inside her made Alyssa yelp. Jessica then licked straight up the center of Alyssa's lips, not stopping until she flicked the hard clit. The sensations inside her belly roiled, compressed, and needed only a spark to start the explosion. Alyssa moaned deep in her chest and pulled her nipples straight up as her climax smoldered. Jessica pulled back and sneered at Alyssa as she clutched the air near Jessica's nose, trying to pull the wonderful tongue back onto her needy clit.

"Not yet. Tonight you are mine, so you don't come until I let you, understand?" Jessica moved beside Alyssa's breasts and took Alyssa's chin in her hand. "Hmm?"

"Oh, I understand. Please get back down there. I was so close. I'll do whatever you want, just let me come." Alyssa cupped her pussy, wriggling her fingers inside to finish her orgasm.

"Oh yes. You will do whatever I want. But later." Jessica pulled Alyssa's hands from her pussy. "I'll make you come like you won't believe; just do as I say."

Alyssa threw her hands up and let them fall on her stomach. "If you say so, just hurry. I'm about to explode."

"Not yet, you aren't." Jessica sucked a nipple and flicked it between her tongue and the roof of her mouth. Alyssa whimpered, then whimpered again when Jessica treated the other nipple the same way. Jessica pulled off and licked Alyssa's pussy a few more times from bottom to top. She pulled back when Alyssa's breath quickened.

Jessica reached into a nearby glass, pulling out an ice cube. She pressed it on Alyssa's clit, and her orgasm exploded. Juice ran down her ass to puddle on the countertop. The noises Alyssa made rumbled in the kitchen, echoing off the hard floor and walls. Her legs tensed and stood out from her hips, her toes separating with the strain. Her hips rocked once, then again, in quick jerks. Jessica pulled the ice off her clit and replaced it with her warm mouth, sucking the sensitive button hard, not letting it recover. Alyssa's hands pushed against Jessica's forehead, seeking relief, but Jessica remained latched on, driving Alyssa higher. Jessica slipped two fingers into the juicy opening and curled them upward, pressing on Alyssa's G-spot, rubbing it again and again while never releasing her screaming clit.

Alyssa's second orgasm brought her legs tight around Jessica's head, her heels pressing on Jessica's back. Her hands pulled Jessica's hair as she fought to shove the blonde's face farther into her sex. Alyssa held her mouth open in an *O*, but she stopped breathing and squeezed her eyes closed as her body struggled with the sensations.

When Alyssa's legs relaxed, Jessica resumed her assault on the older woman's clit and rubbed the inside of her vagina with what felt like three fingers. Alyssa's hands cupped her breasts with what energy she could muster. Her pussy felt another orgasm coming, and her abs tightened in anticipation. *I'm going to come, and I need to pee. Come first.* Alyssa rocked her hips down, pressing into Jessica's fingers when she held her breath. Her orgasm came fast, and a stream of fluid shot into the air from her pussy as Jessica pulled her head back. The girl cum splattered onto the counter-top, sounding like water being poured from a glass. Jessica curled her fingers upward a few more times, extending Alyssa's pleasure, but stopped when Alyssa went limp.

Alyssa woke to Jessica kissing her forehead and caressing her belly. "God that was good. I think I peed though. I'm sorry. I couldn't hold it."

"You didn't pee. You squirted. A big one too. I'm flattered." She kissed Alyssa, letting her taste her own pussy on Jessica's lips. "Come to the bedroom." Jessica helped Alyssa sit up and hop off the counter, steadying her as she stood on wobbly legs. She held her waist as they walked down the hall, then eased her onto the bed.

Candles provided the only light in the room. The air smelled of vanilla and cedar. The satin sheets were cool on Alyssa's side. She looked at her blonde neighbor and licked her lips. She envisioned licking down from the full breasts, across the flat tummy, down to the tight pussy and the downy blonde tuft above it.

"I hope you don't mind. I envisioned more of a seduction than what we did with Robert. It seems more fitting for two friends, don't you think?"

"You mean after you made me come all over your kitchen counters?"

Jessica laughed. "Well, yeah. After that. That was your idea though."

"True." She reached her hand to Jessica's cheek. "Now that I'm in your bed, why don't I take care of you?"

Jessica leaned in for a kiss. "That sounds great."

"Lie back." Alyssa stretched Jessica's hands above her head, then trailed her fingers down the insides of her arms through her armpits and down her sides, to her hips. She pulled them back up to circle Jessica's large breasts, which fell to the side, circling in closer and closer to the crinkled areolae and erect nipples. She rubbed across them and pinched them lightly before dropping her mouth to suck them in one at a time. She let her fingers slide down Jessica's belly in the ridge between her abs and obliques, then pulled them up again and repeated the trip when she noted a hiss of pleasure. She kissed down the center of her belly, pausing to dig into the tiny navel that rose and fell with each rapid breath.

As Alyssa kissed below Jessica's navel to her mons, she reached the inside of Jessica's knee and traced upward, stopping at the hollow between her tendons to jump to the other leg. Jessica's leg twitched as Alyssa touched a sensitive spot, and Alyssa smiled when she traced over it again.

Alyssa moved lower and spun so she faced Jessica's pussy from between her legs. She spread Jessica's outer lips with her ring and first fingers, then barely touched the ends of the inner lips with her middle finger, making Jessica gasp and writhe. Alyssa laughed and pulled her middle finger back, then tapped on her clit. Jessica groaned. She tapped again, then withdrew her hand. She waited until Jessica raised her head to look down at Alyssa before dipping her tongue to lap at the wet lips.

Jessica sighed, "That's it," and rolled her hips against Alyssa's face. Alyssa flicked her tongue over the inner lips, teasing them apart before inserting it between them as far as she could stretch. She swallowed the tangy juice and shook her head side to side before again lapping upward and flicking Jessica's clit with her tongue.

Alyssa wrapped her arms around the outsides of Jessica's thighs, holding them wide apart with her hands. She jumped from the inside of Jessica's thigh to the other thigh with long licks of the open, wet pussy as Alyssa passed across it. She released Jessica's left leg and pushed a finger into Jessica's pussy, sliding it around before adding a second. She turned her hand so her pinky knuckle rubbed across Jessica's crinkly asshole, and moved her mouth over Jessica's clit to suck and flick it.

Jessica's legs clamped onto Alyssa's head and hand as her body spasmed, letting out a long, low moan. Alyssa treated Jessica's pussy just as Jessica had treated hers, pausing for just a moment before resuming full stimulation in search of a second explosion. She reached her free hand to pull on a nipple but instead rubbed on the rolling belly when she couldn't reach the tall woman's chest. She felt Jessica's ass open, letting her knuckle tease the inside of her opening, and Jessica climaxed again. Her strong legs stretched across Alyssa's back and drove her breasts into the mattress, hard heels pressing just above Alyssa's ass. Alyssa continued rubbing and licking until Jessica shuddered and pumped her hips with a growl, then went limp.

Alyssa smiled and slid from beneath the smooth legs to crawl beside her lover. She brushed sweaty hair from Jessica's forehead, then cupped a breast as it heaved with each ragged breath. Alyssa kissed both closed eyes and waited for Jessica to recover.

"That was quite a first round," Alyssa cooed into Jessica's ear. "I love the way we've begun."

Jessica reached a tired hand to rub Alyssa's arm. "That felt like more than one round to me. You were amazing. When you rubbed my ass, I thought I would jump out of the bed."

"Glad you liked it. I can't wait to get a mouthful of you again." She leaned down to kiss Jessica.

"I taste good on you." Jessica smiled. "Why don't you grab those bottles of water on the nightstand beside you?"

They drank quietly, gazing at each other for a few minutes before Jessica rolled to the nightstand on her side of the bed. She rolled back with a couple of black satin ribbons in her hand. "Would you mind if I tied your hands and blindfolded you?"

Alyssa took in a quick breath, then exhaled as she recovered. *Holy shit, this went somewhere I didn't expect.* "Our deal was a night with you. I guess if that is what you want to do..."

"Yes, our deal was a night together, not restraining you or any bondage games. If you don't want to do it, we won't. If you don't have that level of trust with me, that is fine. Don't feel pressured."

"I don't feel pressured. What did you have in mind?"

"I got something to surprise you with, and I want you to be unable to see it coming or to grasp it. I just want to tie you loosely to hold back the impulse to reach for the blindfold or the surprise."

Alyssa smiled. *I hope the surprise isn't a car battery and nipple clamps.* "That's so sweet. Thank you for thinking enough of me to arrange a surprise, and to ask if I minded." She presented her wrists to Jessica. "How do you want me?"

"I will tie your wrists together and to the headboard, then blindfold you." Jessica beamed at Alyssa. "You are going to love this." Jessica arranged several pillows for Alyssa to lie on, raising her hips a few inches and remaining comfortable.

Alyssa lay back on the pillows, let Jessica tie her wrists together, and shook her head when asked if the ribbon was too tight. Jessica tied the other end of the ribbon to the center of the headboard, keeping Alyssa's hands above her head. Jessica then kissed Alyssa and asked, "Are you sure?"

Am I? What if she wants to pour hot wax on me or some other sadistic thing? Look at her smile though. She's been gentle with this. It will be all right. Alyssa swallowed, smiled, and nodded. Jessica smiled and wrapped the wide black silk around Alyssa's eyes and tied it behind her head. Alyssa felt the mattress shift beneath the pillows as she heard Jessica get up. She heard faint footsteps on the carpet, then the bedroom door closed.

Alyssa was cold when she heard the bedroom door open. "Jessica? If I'm going to be here a few minutes, could you cover me up, please? It's chilly when I'm not moving." Alyssa heard footsteps on the carpet again, perhaps heavier than those that had left the room. *No, that's just my imagination. She wouldn't bring anyone else in to fuck me while I'm tied up.* "Jessica, are you there? Jessica?"

From her right, she heard Jessica. "Shh. Everything is fine. We are about to begin. Lie back and enjoy."

Alyssa felt the mattress sink beside her leg, then soft hands pulled her ankles apart. She heard a creaking sound, but not from the bed frame. *That sounded like a big leather belt.* The weight shifted, telling her someone was between her legs. "Jessica, what's going on? Is there someone else here?"

Jessica answered from the direction of Alyssa's feet. "Why would there be someone else here? This is our night, remember?"

If someone else is here, this will get ugly. "Okay. Keep me tied, but I don't want anyone else here."

"Don't worry. Everything will be to your liking."

The mattress moved, and Alyssa felt hair tickle her thighs and stomach in circles around her pussy. She kept her legs still as soft fingers ran from her insteps to her knees and along the insides of her thighs before retracing their path again and then a third time. Alyssa's breathing accelerated, and her stomach pumped with each breath. The chill that had set in while she waited had been burned away by the heat building in her center, waiting to be released by a touch that refused to come.

This time, the fingers running up her legs reached her lips and pulled them apart. The hair rose off her belly, and a tongue snaked between her open lips to spread and wet her on its way to her clit. Alyssa bucked her hips and gasped at the sudden change in feeling. "Oh fuck yes. Eat me."

The tongue and fingers took their time spreading, teasing, and lubricating Alyssa's pussy. They built her close to orgasm twice, pulling back just as the blindfolded woman was ready to scream and come. *Not seeing is the best part. I don't know what is coming, but I like it.* The excellent pussy work resumed when Alyssa's legs stilled.

The mattress shifted when the tongue and fingers broke contact the third time. Alyssa felt something hard press her open lips. "Whoa! What is that?"

"Just enjoy your surprise, Alyssa. This is nothing bad, nor anything you wouldn't want."

It still sounds like Jessica is between my legs. But... The object slid into her with one big push, filling her. "Unh, fuck! That's a cock! Wait!"

The cock stayed where it was. Jessica spoke again. "I promise, Alyssa, this is not anything that violates your agreement with Robert or is outside of what you and I wanted to do tonight. Enjoy the sensation, and I think you will thank me for it." She waited for Alyssa to respond. "If you want me to stop, say so, and I'll release you."

Alyssa didn't respond. The cock in her cunt pulled slowly backward, brushing her G-spot on the outstroke. Alyssa pulled against her restraints. "Wait. Don't pull out. Go some more, exactly that way."

The cock pushed back into her, again rubbing over her G-spot and making her quiver. As the cock sped up going in and out of her, a thumb pressed her clit and moved around and over it. Alyssa moaned and began to buck her hips in time with the thrusts of the cock inside her. She managed to get the tip to rub the sensitive area beside her cervix, and she came, wailing and pulling the cock deeper by wrapping her legs around the thighs between hers.

The cold sensation on the inside of her thighs made Alyssa jump. The cock was all the way in her, pushing against the top of her vagina, making her orgasm grow and linger. The cold broke her concentration, but another wave of pleasure made her abdomen spasm, and she refocused. Her orgasm faded, and the cock slid out of her, releasing a flood of wetness. As her juices ran down her ass, she let out a final whimper, then let her legs sag to the side as she tried to catch her breath. The mattress shifted again as the body between her legs climbed off, leaving Alyssa sweaty, panting, and tied in the quiet room.

Soft lips kissed Alyssa's, and two hands ran up her neck to the knot behind her head. The blindfold was released, and Alyssa blinked against the rush of light in her eyes. The knot around her wrists was untied, and she felt the ache in her triceps and back as she lowered her arms. She reached for Jessica's face with both hands. "You didn't think I would recognize my husband's cock?"

Jessica smiled. "On one thrust?"

"On the way out. Nobody touches my G-spot like he does. Where is he?"

Jessica laughed and reached under the pillow. "Right here." She held up a latex dildo that was an exact copy of Robert's erect cock.

"How did you get that?"

"I asked Robert to help me make it as I planned for tonight. It took two tries, but if you recognized it by feel, we must have done a good job."

Alyssa smirked. "And just how did you get him hard? He and I will have to talk about this."

Jessica laughed. "I didn't touch him. Well, only with the materials. We put some porn on the TV, and he stroked to get hard while I put everything together. I hope you don't mind that I borrowed him."

"How did you fuck me though? I felt legs when I wrapped around you."

"I used a strap-on harness."

"That was the cold part. Buckles?"

"Yes." Jessica giggled. "It even has an attachment on the inside that rubbed my pussy while I fucked you with it. I came so hard with you. I had to hold in a scream so you wouldn't know it was me."

"Can I fuck you with it?"

"I thought you'd never ask."

Alyssa knelt on the bed so Jessica could help her strap in. "Give me that inside attachment."

Jessica handed Alyssa what looked like a rubber stegosaurus back, rounded with wide spikes coming up from it. Alyssa held it to her nose, then licked between two of the spikes. "It tastes like you. I can't wait to put my girl cum on it too." They fastened the dildo into the harness, attached the pleasure attachment on the inside, and buckled it onto Alyssa's hips, tightening the thong between her ass cheeks.

Jessica lay back on the pillows Alyssa had just vacated and smiled at her guest. "Come fuck me, you minx."

Alyssa stood beside the bed and walked to Jessica's head. "Suck me first. Make me hard and wet so I can fuck you right, you little hussy."

Jessica laughed and sucked most of the dildo into her mouth, slathering it with her saliva. She clamped her lips around the fake cock. The base pushed against her clit, telling her Jessica was pushing back with her mouth. When Alyssa moaned, Jessica began to move her head from side to side, making the strap-on harness ride up and down Alyssa's pussy.

"That's enough. Lie back and spread your legs." Alyssa moved between Jessica's legs. She grasped the base of the dildo and tapped the tip on Jessica's clit before rubbing it up and down her lips, continuing until Jessica was spread open and glistening. Alyssa positioned the cock and slid into Jessica, not stopping until she pressed their hips together. Jessica purred deep in her chest, and

Alyssa ground her pussy on the wonderful inside attachment. *I can't feel where this is hitting. I want that G-spot and that cervix.* Alyssa continued to grind her hips and watch Jessica's face for a clue about her sensitive places.

Bingo! Alyssa sneered at Jessica when she struggled to breathe, and she imitated the movement over and over, making the blonde yelp on each stroke. As Alyssa stroked, she grew more forceful, enough to cause Jessica's pendulous tits to bounce in circles in time with their thrusting. Alyssa hammered into Jessica's hips, feeling the leather strap pull across her asshole when she withdrew and the wonderful soft grinding of the internal attachment every time she bottomed out in Jessica. *This thing will indeed make me come.* She sped up and lifted Jessica's legs to her shoulders, mimicking a position Robert used on her, and leaned forward with every stroke. Jessica wailed as the rubber cock continued to hit all the right spots.

Alyssa watched sweat drip off her body onto Jessica's belly, then reached with one hand to smear it around while she kept fucking. *Thank god for those glute exercises. This is wearing me out.* The internal attachment was driving her clit to scream, and Alyssa watched Jessica's eyes roll back into her head. Alyssa pinched a nipple and pulled it, stopping that tit from bouncing while the other one jiggled on. Jessica blew a long breath out her mouth, then locked her legs around Alyssa's hips, pulling her in and pushing her clit over the top into her own climax. Both women held their positions, grinding their pelvises together, reveling in the pleasure the toy was giving both of them. As their bodies calmed, Alyssa pulled out of Jessica, detached the harness around her waist, and sucked the entire dildo into her mouth, cleaning it and swallowing the copious juices on it. She turned the harness around and offered the inner attachment to Jessica, who licked it clean, smiling and moaning her appreciation.

They adjusted the pillows and lay down beside each other. Jessica kissed Alyssa. "Do you mind if I keep him?"

"Him? Robert?"

"Well, the part of him that can stay here. I was going to give it to you, because it is your husband's cock and it doesn't need to be anywhere but your house, but it feels so good inside me. Would you mind if he stays here?"

"I'll make you a deal. If we can get together and play some more, you can keep Robert Two."

"You want to get together again? This isn't a one-time thing to repay a favor?"

"I like you, Jessica. I regret that we didn't get to know each other sooner, but I really enjoy being with you. I would feel so bad if this were a one-time thing. Of course, if you would prefer not to get together with me or Robert or both of us…"

"Oh, Alyssa." Jessica squinted above a broad smile. "I like being with you two also. You are so beautiful and sexy, and Robert is a wonderful lover. I'm glad we connected lately, and I'd love to keep getting together."

They embraced, and a hug became a kiss, and a kiss became a grope, which became a steamy sixty-nine…

14
TUESDAY, MARCH 16, HOME

ALYSSA KISSED JESSICA one last time at the front door. "We need to get together again soon. I had a great time."

"Me too. Come back anytime. I hope you get through the day. Sorry for keeping you awake most of the night."

"Don't be. We slept for, what, about three hours? I'll make it through with some coffee."

"All right. See you soon?"

"You certainly will, and not just for sex. Get some sleep. I have to go see Robert."

Alyssa hustled up the dark street and crept into her bedroom. She jumped when the bedside light clicked on. "Welcome home, Baby. I missed you last night."

"Hey, Babe. I didn't mean to wake you." She looked at her pillow and laughed. "She said it took two tries to get it right, but that one looks right too."

Robert held up a silicone replica of his dick with a bow on it. "I thought you would let her keep hers. You can use this one when I'm not home."

Alyssa dove on the bed beside her husband and took the dildo. "I love it. I love you." She slapped him on the shoulder with a smile. "We are going to have to talk about you letting strange women make casts of your cock though."

"Yeah. I think we can sell them, don't you? Half-price if you help with the molding?"

"You dog. You had probably better focus on making love to me. Although, since I have been fucking your rubber dick, do I still qualify for reclaiming?"

Robert patted her ass. "Maybe, maybe not. But you always qualify for making love. Why don't you take off that dress and get under the covers with me?"

Alyssa stripped off her dress, diving under the covers and wasting no time in sucking Robert's cock. She got him hard and raised her head. "The rubber one is a good replica, but I want the real thing to come inside me, Babe. Please, take me back into your bed and love me right."

Robert smiled at Alyssa, her face hovering over his cock. He gripped her shoulders, pulling her body up to lie beside him. "I can do that but not yet." He kissed her neck and down her chest to her breasts, where he kissed across and around them before sucking first one, then the other, nipple into his mouth and biting lightly. Alyssa chirped, and Robert continued his descent toward her pussy, stopping to lick her navel. He worked down her lower abdomen and dipped his tongue into her pussy, which was open and wet. "You taste like Jessica, and it seems she got you warmed up."

"We didn't sleep much, but it's you who has me warmed up. I'm ready for you now. Make love to me, please."

Robert smiled and licked his wife's slit from bottom to top, then sucked her clit and flicked it with his tongue. Alyssa pulled at his hair the way she did when she was ready for him to give her his cock, but he pushed her hands to her tits and ate her until her hips bucked and ground against his face, splashing her nectar out and down her ass. He lined up his cock, thrusting it all the way in and making Alyssa arch her back and cry out. He ground his head on the hard nub of her cervix, taking time to hit the sensitive tissue around it, making Alyssa's vagina clamp down on his hardness. He waited until she clamped her legs on his thighs and her chest flushed red before he withdrew and began fucking her in earnest. His long strokes made her breasts bounce and her head nod as he moved her up the bed with his hips.

Her legs dropped, bent, beside him, so he reached with both hands to grab and spread her ass cheeks, tickling her sphincter with his fingertips. He changed his thrusts, shortening them and stopping about halfway into her.

"No. Fuck me hard. Fuck me all the way, Babe. Fill me up." Alyssa pleaded for the stimulation she needed.

Robert laughed. "You want all of me?"

"Yes, god, yes."

You want me to keep fucking you hard?"

"Oh, please."

"You want me to come in your pussy?"

"More than anything."

"That dildo couldn't give you that, could it?"

"No," she groaned.

"You like feeling the cum jet inside you?"

"You know I do. Please."

"I'll only give you my cum if you are mine. Are you mine?"

"Oh god, Babe, I'm yours. I'm always yours. Please fuck me."

Robert rammed to her depths and ground against her. He resumed fucking her hard with long strokes, adding a dip at the end to flick his cock over her cervix on each stoke. Alyssa grabbed his shoulders and pulled with her hands while she rolled her hips. They both moaned with every collision inside her. Her chest flushed red again, and her belly puffed with each rapid breath. He dripped sweat onto her body as he pounded and pounded her dripping pussy. He gave one final hard thrust, pressing hard on the end of her vagina, and fired inside her. Her orgasm burst, and Alyssa clenched with her hands, legs, and pussy, milking the rest of the cum from his cock before she settled.

Robert remained atop her, his cock buried inside, and bent to suck her left nipple. He sucked in the entire areola and pressed the hard nipple between his tongue and the roof of his mouth, rolling it up and down with the pressure. Alyssa's pussy tightened around his cock again. "Oh fuck, that was good." Alyssa panted twice before continuing. "You made me come just by sucking my tit with your dick in me." She smiled at her husband. "I've never done that before, but I want more."

"That was good, Baby. You had more energy than I expected you to."

"Me too. Jessica and I only slept a little, but I'm so horny for you, I can't get enough. You just made me come three times, but I could go again right now. I want you so much."

"I like the way you think. I'll need a minute to firm up."

Alyssa laughed, then groaned as Robert's cock slipped from her pussy, trailing down her ass and taking a glob of their cum with it. "Jesus, you have no idea how good that feels. I love the feel of your cum dripping out of me and your soft cock against my ass. I want you again."

I'm glad you like it, Baby. I'll give you some more tonight

after that meeting about graduation at the school. You remember we have that, right?"

"I remember." Alyssa looked from side to side, acting devious. "Do you think we could slip away from the meeting and find somewhere for a quickie? The library or a stairwell? That would be sexy."

Robert laughed. "We could, my bad girl. We'll let Clay take all the notes we need."

"That's a date. Are you hard yet?"

Robert tapped his soft dick against her still-open pussy. "Not yet, Baby. It's only been a minute. Not that you aren't hot enough to keep me hard all the time."

Alyssa rolled her eyes. "I hear you, but I guess we need to get ready. If I don't get out of bed, I'm going to fuck you all day."

"That sounds great, but we need to pay bills. We'd better go to work." They headed to the bathroom, fondling each other as they started the morning routine.

"Hey, Baby. What's going on?" Robert said when he answered his phone.

"I have been so horny all day. I actually went to the bathroom and let you fuck me earlier."

"Shit, Alyssa. You have your door closed, right?"

"Yes, of course."

"And just how did I fuck you?"

"I brought my present to work because I was so horny."

"You called just to tell me that?"

"No, but I thought you would want to know. I called because I won't be home for dinner before that meeting. We have a couple of franchisees in from out of town, and Doug asked a few of us to take them to dinner after work."

"At one of your restaurants? Don't you all get that enough?"

"No, the Embassy Suites across the street. The chef there is really good."

"Oh. I'm glad he's good, because I'm not confident you will provide excellent dinner conversation as tired as you must be. Will you miss the meeting at the school too?"

"I wouldn't dare," Alyssa laughed. "I plan on sneaking you away and having my way with you. I'll just go for drinks and leave before dinner. I'm too horny to miss seeing you."

"Are you sure? It's okay if you need to stay."

"No. I'll be exhausted. I'll meet you at the school, you can give me a naughty quickie, and we can go home to sleep."

Robert laughed. "I'm going to hold you to it. I'll see you there. Love you."

"Love you, Babe."

15

TUESDAY, MARCH 16, EMBASSY SUITES

Alyssa looked past her coworkers to the three tall men talking at the hotel bar. She made eye contact for about the tenth time with the dark-haired one. *That hot guy from the bar keeps eyeing me. His friends aren't bad either.* She closed her eyes in a long blink. *Jesus, Alyssa, get control of your libido.*

"Alyssa, what do you think?" Her coworker Jeff looked at her, waiting for an answer, and Alyssa blushed and shook her head.

"I'm sorry, Jeff. I zoned out there for a minute. What did you ask?"

"I asked about designing some training for our chefs beyond items on our menu. Do you think we could do it and build some skills to use later?"

"Oh sure." Alyssa spun her wedding rings with her thumb while she thought. "We could do that. We could bring them in over a few months in shifts. I take it you are thinking beyond the omelet test?"

The franchisees laughed. "That is just to get hired as a cook. We are thinking the ability to expand the menu for private events. Maybe even some of the more advanced Escoffier techniques."

Alyssa laughed. "Escoffier is past my kitchen skills. You will need to find someone to train it. I just coordinate."

The rest of the table started discussing chefs they knew who might be available to train.

Jeff leaned over to Alyssa. "Alyssa, are you ill? You seem to have zoned out a lot tonight."

"I didn't sleep well last night, and two glasses of wine and two shots of tequila haven't helped. I'm about to leave, anyway."

"Can't stay for dinner?"

"No. I have a meeting at Clay's school." She looked at the people around the table. "I have to go, everyone. You all enjoy dinner." She looked at the bar as she stood. *He's not there. Too bad. I wanted to see his big body one last time.*

Alyssa left her coworkers and headed to the restroom, a little unsure of her footing. *Wow. This is affecting me more than I thought.*

She opened the door to the restroom and froze. The tall man from the bar stood in the middle of the room, stroking a huge cock and shooting cum all over the face and tits of the redheaded waitress who knelt before him. The cock was almost as long and thick as a can of tennis balls, and the load of cum kept flying out of it, spurt after spurt, covering the woman's face with thick white ropes that dripped onto her full tits and then to her skirt. The man looked at Alyssa and grinned.

Alyssa stood still, unable to look away from the glorious cock and the cum-covered waitress. Her free hand cupped her breast and rubbed it through her blouse and bra. Her nipples hardened, and her pussy tingled. Her stomach fluttered, and her feet stepped farther into the restroom on their own. Her focus narrowed. All she could see was the cock; the two people around hardly warranted her attention.

Alyssa reached the couple and wrapped a hand beneath the giant cock, squeezing the last drops of cum onto the waitress's tits and wiping the opening with her finger, then tasting the juice she gathered. She stroked the cock, cradling it from below because she couldn't wrap her hand around it, astounded it was still hard and throbbing in her hand. Alyssa bent to lick the tip, then stretched her mouth wide to suck the head. She pushed it to the back of her throat and gagged as she pulled off.

"I want this inside me," she said, looking at the tall man's leering smile. *God, perfect teeth too. He's too good to be true.*

"Are you sure? It's big," the man said and pointed to the waitress. "She thought she wanted it inside but then offered a blow job when she saw it."

"I want this inside me. We'll make it fit."

"Let's go to my room. You can make noise there. You are going to scream."

The man stuffed his hard member down his pants leg and buttoned up, then took Alyssa by the waist to lead her out. "Room 1854, if you still want some after your shift," he said to the waitress as he left her on the floor. They turned away from the bar as they exited, moving to the elevator. On the ride up, Alyssa rubbed his cock through his pants. He reached under her skirt and slid her panties aside to finger her soaked pussy. They got to his room and kissed while he retrieved the key from his pocket. They stumbled into the suite. He closed the door and shoved Alyssa's back against it. He kissed her hard, shoving his tongue deep into her mouth and tearing her blouse open, then shoving her bra cups below her tits to rub them while her buttons bounced on the tile floor.

Alyssa unbuttoned his pants and dove her hand inside his boxers, grasping the engorged shaft but unable to pull it free. She pulled her hand out and used both hands to push his pants down his legs, then knelt to slide off his shoes and finish his pants. She opened her mouth and sucked the purple head while she unzipped her skirt. As she rose, she slipped the skirt and panties down her legs, dropping them on the floor in front of the door. She gripped the big cock and pulled the man attached to it farther into the room. She bent forward, her hands on the back of the couch, supporting her body. She spread her legs a bit and looked over her shoulder. "Come on."

The man finished removing his shirt and tie. He stood naked behind Alyssa, his giant cock aiming at her glistening pussy. He parted her lips with his fingers, pulling them wide and inserting first one thick finger, then a second and pumping her cunt with them before spreading his fingers inside her and pumping some more.

Alyssa groaned deep in her chest as he stretched her and spread her juices on her lips. She ground her hips against his fingers and hung her head between her arms. As he moved, she matched him, enhancing the full feeling his fingers provided. He withdrew them at last. Alyssa whined and looked over her shoulder. He stepped closer to her and rubbed the big head against her open hole before pushing it inside.

Lightning pulsed up Alyssa's body as the cock stretched her beyond what she could endure. Her pussy lips felt like they would part at the top and bottom of her slit, and her clit buzzed from the taut skin around it. He paused to let her finish screaming before pushing farther in. She wailed when he pulled back. The juice he pulled out of her rolled down her thigh. She felt his hands on her hips and braced for his next thrust. He got farther in, and she felt every inch. Every spot in her pussy was alive with pressure. He filled her from side to side. She felt her legs quiver as an orgasm rushed forward inside her. He pulled back and shoved back in again, reaching the end of her and pounding her cervix along with the rest of her vagina. She screamed, and her orgasm buckled her. Strong hands held her hips up, and she felt the giant cock inside her pull back and refill her again and again. Her head hung low, and her nipples hardened as her body turned the sensation in her cunt into orgasm after orgasm, using the liquid to keep itself protected from the huge invader.

When Alyssa's arms gave out, she felt his hands maneuver her sideways over the couch. Her tits and face pressed into the seat cushion, and her hips rested over the padded armrest. The huge cock never left her wrecked pussy, and once she was pressed into the couch, his thrusts resumed. The rough upholstery burned her skin everywhere it touched as her body rocked from his rough fucking, but she focused only on the pleasure coming from her stretched pussy. Alyssa heard a constant, low noise in the room and had to pause before she realized it was coming from her mouth. When Alyssa felt his hips press against her ass, his cock pressed against her guts. Her mind began to slip in and out of awareness as the sensations overwhelmed her. She felt a gush of fluid spray out of her pussy, down her legs, to her feet, just before the first hot spray of cum hit her inside. Spurt after spurt filled her, squeezing out of her pussy past his cock and joining her cum on the floor. The warmth and pressure inside her swamped her brain, and she blacked out.

❧

Alyssa woke in the hotel bed to the sharp pinch of the tall man pulling her nipple with his teeth and rubbing her pussy. Her body was already nearing orgasm as he flicked her clit while spreading her outer lips. She looked down at the big hard cock lying across her thigh, and reached the head with her hand, rubbing it. "I'm ready for more."

The tall man looked up at her and smiled. He climbed atop her. Her pussy stretched and popped as the head slipped past her lips, the skin stinging and burning as it neared its limits. Alyssa's body crackled with energy that flexed her neck and drove the back of her head into the pillow.

She hissed a breath as he pushed farther in. Her walls, battered before by the huge cock, gripped it as it returned to them. The cum he'd deposited a few minutes earlier squished and flowed down her ass each time he withdrew. He sped up, and she pulled at his sides. When he bottomed out inside her, she came with a shriek, feeling her own wetness spread over her lips and thighs. She held him still with her hands as her cunt spasmed around his cock, then said, "Don't stop fucking me," before it calmed.

The swirl of his hips that massaged the top of her vagina with the tip of his cock made Alyssa jerk her shoulders forward. The entirety of her vagina stretched, ached, and roiled with his huge member demanding space she could not give. The pleasure filled her core and sought a release.

Alyssa didn't get far past one orgasm before she began another. She fought for breath as her belly tensed and spasmed. She heard a continuous whine, but she didn't realize that it rolled from her own throat, her ability to speak usurped by the pleasure. After a few minutes, her legs went limp and her arms sagged into the mattress. "Keep going. Don't stop," escaped her lips before she slipped into a frenzied fog on the heels of yet another release.

Her brain was overwhelmed with sensations from her body. Cocks entered every orifice.

Yes, fuck my ass too.

Hands fondled, pinched, stretched, spanked every part of her. Lips sucked, teeth bit. Cum filled her and rained on her face and body, eventually covering her eyes and sealing them closed.

So warm. Cover me.

She was pounded and lifted, flipped and rolled. Whenever the sensations stopped, she grasped into the darkness around her until she found another hard cock to replace it.

Don't stop.

She couldn't think. She lost track of time. Her only thought was of the next orgasm. She realized that this was no longer a question of what she would enjoy, but a question of what she could endure.

And she loved it.

More.

⁕

The tall man, Dave, kept fucking Alyssa, just like she asked. He grinned when he heard her phone ring, stop, and ring again. He rammed into her faster as it dinged, indicating several incoming texts. He smiled again when he heard the door open and his companions enter the bedroom.

Dave flexed his cock inside her and bit her nipple. Alyssa's eyes flew open as her pussy squeezed his cock in pulses up and down his shaft. She wailed and gripped onto his shoulders. He rolled her over without pulling his cock from her and began thrusting into her from below. Her body bounced with his motion, but her legs were limp beside his. He supported her with his hands on her tits, pinching her nipples and pushing her body upward. When she didn't open her eyes, he asked, "Do you want more?"

Alyssa nodded and whispered, "Yes, more. Fuck me more."

Dave felt the bed move and looked up to see his friend Chuck naked and standing beside him, tapping his erection on Alyssa's lips. She opened her mouth to take it in. Chuck's dick was long but not thick, and he eased in until she gave a small gag, telling them the cock had hit her throat. A few of his inches remained outside her mouth. Her body slumped against Dave's hands, mauling her tits. "Don't make her puke, Chuck."

"She's doing this, not me." Alyssa's head bobbed as she sucked the cock in her mouth until Dave saw her chin touched Chuck's balls. "Fuck, I'm in her throat. The bitch took all of it." Dave slowed his bumping from below so she didn't bite his friend.

The last of Dave's companions, Joe, retrieved Alyssa's phone when it rang. Laughing, the blond man pressed her thumb on the home button, unlocking it before stepping back from the bed. Moments later he returned.

"We have another frantic husband situation, gentlemen. About thirty minutes ago, the first texts arrived asking where she was. He's called twice. It seems our slut here missed a meeting at her kid's school to be with us."

Dave laughed. "Well, we need to make sure spending time with us is quite memorable, don't we?" He stopped fucking Alyssa and slapped her ass cheeks hard several times. "There's a souvenir." He moved a hand to her chin and shook her head when Chuck pulled his cock back. "Do you want a memorable time, baby? Do you want us to fuck you all night?"

Alyssa nodded. "Mm-hmm. Fuck me. More."

Dave released Alyssa's head to Chuck, who again filled her throat with his cock. "Let's give her some memories, boys. You know what to do." He resumed flexing up into Alyssa. The bed shifted around his legs as Joe climbed on behind Alyssa.

Dave heard Joe laugh and the sound of Alyssa's camera click as he felt Joe's cock in her ass from inside her pussy. Alyssa's eyes shot open, then closed again. Her body stiffened momentarily, then sagged back onto his hands. Even with Chuck in her mouth, Dave would swear she was smiling. Joe's cock pressed against Dave's as he worked farther into her ass. Joe's balls bumped against his just outside Alyssa's pussy.

"Picture time, guys," Joe cackled. The three of them remained still while Joe snapped several pictures from different angles. "She's going to love these. So will her husband." The sound of the phone landing on the bed was like a starter's pistol, and all three men fucked into Alyssa hard as they laughed.

Dave noticed Alyssa stiffen and slacken. He heard her moan. He looked over her shoulder at Joe. "This bitch may be the most responsive we've ever had. She won't stop coming. Maybe we take her with us. Just not all the way home."

The three of them laughed without any pause in their movements. Alyssa's body shuddered.

Dave knew her orgasms wouldn't stop as long as they kept her stimulated. He smiled. He loved making women overload on his cock, believing he ruined them for anyone else. There was no way they could remember a night with him and his companions and be satisfied with their husbands again. He smirked at Alyssa. She would remember him forever, pictures or no.

The three men continued to fuck her. Joe came first, shooting once in her ass, then pulling out and painting her back and ass with cum. Chuck came next, shooting across the side of her face from hairline to jawline and coating her eye. He put her left hand around his cock, accentuating her wedding ring as Joe photographed Alyssa's cum-covered back and face.

Dave's huge cock swelled as he neared orgasm, and he stopped moving so Joe could get a closeup of him stretching her pussy. Dave rolled Alyssa onto her back and pounded into her, drawing another deep groan from their insatiable slut. He pulled out to spray cum onto her. The first spurt landed between her tits, followed by a couple on her belly, with the final ropes deposited on her gaping pussy. Despite it being his third of the night, his huge load coated her body in white jizz. Joe laughed and took several pictures from a couple of angles.

Alyssa lay still as the three gathered at the foot of the bed. Joe opened the text strand from Robert. He attached a photo of all three of them in Alyssa. He wrote, "She isn't finished yet. Stop calling," and hit send. The phone rang immediately, and Joe sent it to voice mail. The men laughed, and Joe switched back to the text strand. He attached a photo of Alyssa lying on the bed covered in their cum, wrote, "We will send her home in the morning," and hit send before turning the phone off and returning it to Alyssa's purse.

Dave lay beside Alyssa and stroked her clit. She jerked but didn't open her eyes. She mumbled, "Fuck me more," and he motioned for Chuck to climb onto her. The three companions fucked Alyssa for the next couple of hours, mainly one right after the other but once double-teaming her, shooting their cum inside her and on her body and face.

They let her drink water and vodka from the minibar between fucks. Her body alternated between limp and spasming in climax for the entire time. She mumbled, "More," between sessions, stretching her arms out for the next man when one finished with her. Joe took more pictures, showing her flushed body covered in handprints and bite marks, her face caked with cum.

Dave took a final turn with her about one in the morning, fucking her mercilessly, pounding her into the mattress with his giant cock as she spasmed and groaned beneath him. He left his final load deep inside her gaping, ravaged pussy. He lay in the bed beside her while she slept, idly rubbing her clit and chuckling when her body jerked with her small releases. His two companions showered and dressed, then he did the same. The men packed their bags and departed for their early flight, leaving Alyssa snoring, uncovered, on the bed.

WEDNESDAY, MARCH 17, EMBASSY SUITES

ALYSSA WOKE TO the incessant beeping of the alarm clock. Dazed, she couldn't open her eyes and fumbled with her hands, reaching to the noise and feeling the clock, pressing buttons until the noise stopped. The crust on her eyes cracked when she touched it with her fingers. She rubbed and picked at it until she could open them to take in the dark room. A sliver of light fell on the bed from between the curtains, and a glow came from beneath the bathroom door. The blue numbers on the alarm clock read 3:49.

Alyssa sat up and tried to step out of the bed, only to fall back from the pain in her legs and pelvis. Her inner thighs felt like she had spent the night doing splits, and her pussy hammered her brain with a deep and growing soreness, from her lips up into her belly. Usually after a big cock or a hard fuck, she felt open and a little stretched around her lips. Now she actually hurt. Her lips felt they had been pulled too far apart, her walls ached like overused muscles, and the top of her vagina throbbed like it had been punched repeatedly.

After a moment, she noticed a similar, duller pain in her ass and reached her hand to gingerly touch herself. Her fingers traced the wetness from her pussy to her ass and down her thighs a few inches. In the dark, she couldn't tell what the fluid was. She turned on the bedside light. *Thank god it's only cum, not blood. I have to pee. This is gonna hurt.*

Alyssa sat up. She was prepared for the pain below, but her breasts jiggled and felt like they had been pulled off and put back on. On that realization, her swimming head made her vomit onto the bed. *I'm drunk too. This keeps getting better.* She slid to the edge of the bed closest to the bathroom before trying to stand. Her legs wobbled, but she stayed upright by bracing against the wall. She opened the door and lurched to the sink, catching herself on the countertop, then she spun her ass around to sit on the toilet. Her legs protested, but her pussy screamed at her brain as the urine flowed out of her, further inflaming the irritated skin around it. Alyssa rested her head in both hands to collect her thoughts as the cum dripped out of her opening.

What happened to me? I was leaving for Clay's school, and I saw that cock coming on the waitress. I had to have it, and then I don't remember. I just needed to keep coming. I couldn't stop. I couldn't think. I don't know how many there were, but at least three. I actually had one in each hole, and I don't even know their names. At least the big one didn't go in my ass. Could they have drugged me? No. They weren't at our table, and I chose to come to this room, and I wanted to keep fucking. This was all me. Shit.

Alyssa spun off the toilet to vomit again, this time getting the acrid liquid in the bowl. She let her head slide down onto the seat and rested for a few minutes. When she stood, she flushed and shuffled to the sink. She stared at the mirror. Her hair was disheveled and matted with cum on one side. Red friction burns showed through the cum on her left cheek, both shoulders, and across her hips above her mound. Both breasts had burns as well, and the white skin was tinged red with the beginnings of bruises across them. Her flat belly had dried cum across most of it, except the portions lower down that were still wet and dripped to mix with the cum on her pussy and legs. She turned to see red handprints on her ass and cum between her cheeks. She looked herself in the tired eyes, then hung her head. *I need to get home. I don't know if Robert will come get me, but I'm going to ask.*

Alyssa staggered into the living area of the suite to find her purse on the table by the door. She had dropped it on the floor when the tall man brought her in. She opened her phone and hit the home button to unlock it. When it didn't respond, she pressed again. *I didn't turn this off.* She held the power button, and the Apple logo came up. *Shit. This isn't good.* The home screen came up, and she saw only four text notifications but eight calls. *They turned it off.* "Goddammit! Those fuckers!"

Alyssa opened the text app first. There were three from her coworkers asking where she was or telling her that Robert was looking for her. At the top was an unopened message from Robert reading simply, "Go to hell." Alyssa's eyes welled up before she touched the message preview with her finger. Above Robert's reply, the screen was filled with a picture of Alyssa, sprawled on the bed and covered in cum, captioned, "You can have her back now." Alyssa screamed and fell to the floor, bawling.

❧

Alyssa didn't know how long she had been crying, but both the carpet and her face were wet with tears, drool, and snot. She wiped her face against the couch, wincing at irritating the burn on her cheek. Her hands shook as she picked up her phone to look at the text strand. She could hear the pain and concern in Robert's texts, first searching for her, then pleading for her to call, then demanding to know if she was all right and to let her talk to him. Those requests were met with half a dozen pictures of Alyssa fucking the men, their faces, of course, not showing.

Alyssa drew her knees to her chest before she dared to listen to the voice mails, which followed the same pattern. The last one had come in at 12:19. Her phone showed 4:36. She rested her head on her knees and wept until she realized she was cold. She crawled to the bedroom and pulled the bedspread off the unused bed to wrap up. She held her phone. *Call or text? Which is worse? If I call, he doesn't have to look at the pictures.* She hit Robert's number.

The call rolled to voice mail, and her phone dinged with a new text at the same time. *He doesn't want to talk to me.* She opened it and read through her tears.

"Is this you?"

"Yes, Babe."

"Are you all right?"

"No. I need you."

"Did they rape you?"

Alyssa thought a moment. "No."

A long minute elapsed before the reply. "Where are you?"

"Embassy Suites across from the office. My car is there."

"On my way."

Alyssa moved to the bathroom and started the shower. *At least they left a clean towel.* She got in when the water warmed, and washed the cum off herself. The scuffs on her face and body burned, but she stayed under the water, hoping it would wash away what she had done. *I fucked this one up.* Her tears went down the drain with the water.

Alyssa ran the towel over her hair, then pushed her fingers through it. She looked in the living area for her clothes. Her skirt and blouse were there, but her panties and bra were missing. *Goddamn. They took my fucking underwear.* Alyssa pulled her skirt up, fastening it into place. She slipped on the blouse but noted as she tried to button it that either the button was missing or the buttonhole was torn. She slapped the wall and tied the shirttails together under her boobs. *Either show the abs or show the boobs. Damn it.* She stepped in front of the mirror. *Wet hair. Bruised and scraped. Shirt tied together. No underwear. Can barely walk. Just another whore leaving the hotel at five in the morning.* She sat on the couch with her purse, drinking the last bottle of water. Her phone dinged.

"I'm in the lobby."

This is gonna suck. Alyssa limped out of the room to the elevator. When she arrived in the lobby, she didn't see Robert.

"Over here," he said from a table close to the restaurant.

Alyssa moved toward him, then stopped when she noticed her overnight bag beside him. She looked to see the sadness in his face, took a deep breath, and joined him at the table.

"Are you sure they didn't rape or drug you?" Robert asked in a low voice.

She hung her head. "No. They didn't force me to do anything. They were on the other end of the bar from where the waitress picked up our drinks, so they couldn't have drugged me there. I think they gave me alcohol while I was in the room, but I got there on my own."

He touched the red mark on her face. "Are you hurt?"

Alyssa shook her head. "Not really. Ashamed, scared, broken-hearted, but not hurt." Alyssa looked up at Robert. "Babe, I'm sorry. I haven't figured out how everything happened—"

Robert held up his hand. "Now isn't the time. You broke our

agreement about an open marriage last night, and you did it in a very hurtful and frightening way." He slid a key card packet across the table to her. "I got you a room so you could clean up, sleep, and think. Clothes and toiletries are in your bag. I moved your car to the hotel deck, but it was in the company lot all night, so your coworkers know you didn't leave when you told them you would."

He started to say more, then stopped himself. He looked into her eyes. "Look. I haven't slept tonight. I'm calling in sick to work. Now that I know you are safe, I'm going home. You call in sick and stay here, or go in, or whatever is best for you. When we have both rested and thought, we can talk about what happened." He stood to go.

"I love you," Alyssa said, not looking up from the tabletop.

Robert stopped moving. He opened his mouth to speak, closed it, then did it again. "I want to believe that." He left.

Alyssa sat a while, staring at the table. When the staff began to prepare the restaurant for breakfast service, she picked up the key and went to the room to sleep.

Alyssa woke about noon when the thin ray of sunlight seeping through the curtains landed on her eyes. She sat up in bed, letting the covers fall into her lap. *At least I'm sober. My body hurts.* She climbed out of the bed, retrieved the bottle of Advil Robert had been thoughtful enough to pack, and swallowed four with water. She went to the bathroom and ran hot water in the tub, brushing her teeth while it filled. The heat stung her skin when she stepped in. The water lit up the upholstery burns on her body when she sat, making her twitch before settling in up to her neck, quelling the pain with her mind. After a few minutes, the irritation in her skin faded and the hot water began to work on the soreness in her legs, pelvis, and breasts.

I lost control. I couldn't get enough sex. I just wanted orgasm after orgasm, and I couldn't think of anything else, or even notice anything else. Even when I couldn't open my eyes, I still begged for cock. Why? I hadn't slept much the night before, so I was tired. Maybe I wasn't drunk when I left the bar, but I had downed three, maybe four drinks? Too many to be clearheaded. There were empty airplane bottles by the bed when I woke up, so I had more in the room.

I was horny too. Sex all weekend. God, since Friday, I fucked Bryce, Summer, Robert several times, Chris, Carol, Jessica, and even fucked the dildo I brought to work yesterday. I couldn't get enough. Even then, I fantasized about the guys at the bar and was leaving to fuck Robert at Clay's school during the meeting. Did it make it hotter that it started in public? Maybe.

Then there was that cock. If I hadn't gone to the ladies' room and seen that monster pumping cum all over that waitress, I would have left. I couldn't look away from it. I didn't even know I walked toward it until I had it in my hand. It was not as long as Paul's in Houston, but it was thicker. It felt so good; I came so hard and so often. I couldn't get enough, and I barely noticed the other guys when they came in and fucked me, until I wanted them to keep going. I'm not even sure how many there were.

And I never noticed the shit with my phone.

She spoke to herself out loud, letting the harsh acoustics of the tiled room add weight to her thoughts. "So let's review, Alyssa: Because you were tired, drunk, and horny, you fucked at least three men, maybe more. You have an open arrangement with Robert, so that isn't the worst thing in the world. Oh, but to fuck them, you missed Clay's meeting about graduation, you reneged on your offer to have exciting sex in the school with your husband, you did all this without calling to let them know you were safe, and you let the men fucking you take pictures of it and text them to your husband with captions. Clearly outside the open arrangement you have with Robert. Fucking wonderful." She slapped the water and swallowed a sob.

"There is one more thing, Alyssa. Your open arrangement requires that you let Robert reclaim you when you get home, and your pussy is so battered that you dread having sex with the man you love. That is, if he'll even have you. You're covered with bruises, bites, and burns from other men. Nice way to seduce your husband. Jesus."

Alyssa closed her eyes to think. *I need to understand why I did this before I talk to Robert.* She leaned her head against the back of the tub. Alyssa's eyes popped open, and she moved to get out of the tub and dry herself. Her body groaned at her, and she stayed stooped a moment before straightening. *Shit, I still hurt all over.* She dried off and grabbed her phone.

17

WEDNESDAY, MARCH 17, HOME

Two hours later, Alyssa texted Robert. "Can I come home?"

"If that is what you want."

"I'm afraid, but I will see you soon."

She pulled into their garage thirty minutes later. Robert met her at the door. "Let's take a walk."

"Babe, my body hurts. Can we sit and talk?"

"I hurt too, and we're going to figure it out before you come back in the house. We'll go slow. Hold my arm."

"Let me put on my sunglasses. I'm hungover." Alyssa held his arm with both hands and limped beside him down the driveway and up the sidewalk. Robert didn't speak until they reached the neighbor's yard.

"You stood us up last night. Want to tell me what happened?"

Alyssa shook her head. "I don't want to, but I probably have to."

"You owe me that."

"I know." She walked a few steps in silence. "I binged on sex. Once I started, I couldn't think or control what I was doing. I got so turned on, I didn't think about anything but continuing to fuck, having nonstop, mind-breaking orgasms. I didn't realize more men had joined us in the room until they were inside me, and I was so worked up that I didn't care." She dipped her head, then stopped walking and turned to Robert. Her bottom lip quivered, and her chin tightened. "I didn't hear my phone, and I didn't know what those assholes were doing with it. I wouldn't have let that happen. I'm so sorry they took pictures and texted you."

"I know you wouldn't. But it did happen, and it was terrifying. Do you know if they took any pictures with their phones?"

Alyssa's stomach dropped, and her knees buckled. She gripped Robert's arm for support. The entire neighborhood made no sound—no birds, no cars, no people—as she recovered her legs. "Shit. I didn't think about that. I don't know. I hope not. They took my bra and panties though."

They resumed their slow walk down the street. Robert's arm flexed and relaxed under her hands. Alyssa looked up to see his neck and cheek flushed red. "You said you couldn't stop once you started. What got you started?"

Her stomach quivered with butterflies. "I had drinks with Jeff, Amelia, Doug, and a couple of franchisees, just like I told you. I didn't go looking for anything. I wasn't lying—"

Robert stopped walking and held up his hand. "I know. I called them looking for you, remember? They told me you had left in time to get to the school." He looked down at her with—pity? Condescension?—softening his face around his eyes. "You will have to figure out what to tell them, you know."

Alyssa stiffened her back. "Yeah, but they don't matter if I can't work things out with you."

"That's true." He looked at the clouds gathering in the sky, then back to Alyssa. "You left the bar on time, yet never left the hotel. What happened?" He resumed their walk.

"I wondered that too."

Robert's bicep flexed again. "Um, weren't you there?"

The butterflies in Alyssa's stomach got angry and solidified in her chest, ready to burst out of her mouth. *Smart-ass.* "Of course I was," she spat with more venom in her voice than she intended. His hand clenched into a fist. She covered her mouth with her hand. She took a deep, calming breath. *Easy. He's defusing his anger with sarcasm. He's protecting you from what he really wants to say.* She steadied her voice. "I'm sorry. I know what physically happened. What I couldn't understand is how I lost my direction. No matter how I thought about it today, I couldn't figure it out. I called Janice Walker, the crisis counselor from Houston, remember?"

His hand relaxed, followed by his arm. "Go on."

Alyssa sighed in relief, knowing she had pushed to the limit. "She said sometimes people engage in binging behavior, especially when they are tired, or drunk, or stressed in some way. I was exhausted, and a little drunk, and do you remember how horny I was the entire weekend?"

"I remember. You planned to sneak me off for a quickie at the school. I was looking forward to that, actually." He looked away from her, but she noted the flush still in his neck.

"I was too. I'm sorry, Babe." She squeezed his arm and rested her head on his shoulder as they walked. "Ms. Walker told me I probably got triggered and started a sex binge, like an alcoholic blackout. She said I was in the mood for sex, and my judgment was impaired by the alcohol and lack of sleep. She said one more thing too. She thinks I might have been aroused that the encounter started in public. She thinks I may get turned on by that."

Robert turned to look at her with pursed lips but kept walking.

He wants to roll his eyes, but he's fighting it. Please believe this is the truth. It's the best I can explain it. Alyssa watched his face as they walked, letting Robert guide her direction.

Robert faced forward again. "Say that I buy this line about impaired judgment and horniness. What triggered you between the bar and the front door?"

Here is the hard part. The nervous pit in her stomach pulled her heart lower in her chest. Whether he believed her or didn't, how could he trust her ever again? "I went to the bathroom before I left, and the hot guy from the bar was in there coming all over the waitress's face and tits. He had a cock the size of a tennis ball can. I was mesmerized. I walked in and told him I had to have it in me without even thinking. It was all downhill from there."

Robert rolled his eyes. "This is pretty damn hard to accept. You just see a dick, and you fuck until you black out?"

Alyssa stopped walking and turned Robert to look in his eyes. "Maybe. She made it sound like a perfect storm kind of thing. I know it sounds far-fetched, but it's all I can understand."

"It doesn't sound so perfect to me. Our open marriage still means the family comes first, we're safe, and we maintain discretion. You violated all those rules. How can I trust you?"

Alyssa hung her head. *It's as bad as I feared.* She fought back a sob, unable to speak until her chin stopped quivering. "You can't. I can't trust myself right now."

They walked a while in silence. As they neared the lake at the bottom of their street, the sky lit up with lightning concurrent with a huge clap of thunder, startling Alyssa. "That was close. I don't think I can get back up the hill to the house before it rains." *Please don't leave me here.*

"Let's go to the gazebo, then." Robert pointed to the lakeside gazebo about a hundred feet off the road. Alyssa limped as quickly as she could, and they got under the cover just as the bottom fell out. "We can wait here until it passes."

Robert sat on the bench along the side latticework away from the rain.

Never before had Alyssa been afraid to ask her next question, but the cold dread in her chest made her start and stop twice before she got the words out. "Babe, can you hold me in your lap?" She waited, watching her husband's face. He didn't flush red. *He's not mad that I asked.* Only Alyssa would notice the imperceptible amount that his eyes narrowed and the twitch downward in the corners of his mouth. *He's considering it. He hasn't considered it since our first date. Please.*

He nodded, and Alyssa sat on his lap. Her sore bottom nestled perfectly into place, the way it always had. Her side fit against his belly, and her aching breast lay on his shoulder. Except for the pain that every touch caused up and down her sore body, Alyssa was home. A low hum came up her throat as she stroked his hair.

Robert wrapped his arms around her waist and gave a squeeze. "This open marriage thing isn't working too well, is it? Maybe we should call it off."

I knew this was coming. Don't give up yet, Babe. She kissed his head. "Maybe. We knew we had a lot to learn and would make some mistakes. Until last night, it worked pretty well, didn't it?"

"We got lucky with Summer and Bryce. Last night's pain was worse than all the pleasure from our other encounters combined."

Alyssa hadn't thought he would weigh things so harshly. "You think so?"

Robert pulled back to look at her face. His eyes were wide and his eyebrows high on his forehead. "Did you see those pictures? In our text strand?" He shook his head and returned his gaze to hers. "We have had fun playing outside, but last night, when you left Clay and me alone without calling, when I thought you were in real trouble and I couldn't get to you, it was horrifying."

He thought I was being hurt. I assumed he at least knew I was safe, even though the texts they sent were cruel. She had forgotten just how protective he was, even when he was angry at her. *He would have been climbing the walls if he thought they were hurting me.* "I'm so sorry, Babe. I didn't mean to put you through that."

"I understand that, but when Find My iPhone showed that you were at the hotel, and I got those texts, I knew I couldn't help you."

Had he given up on her last night? *God, no.* "You knew where I was and didn't come get me?"

"Alyssa, that hotel is eighteen stories tall, with forty suites per floor. That's…720 rooms. You hadn't checked into one, and the only identification of the men with you were pictures of their dicks. You were stuck where you were until they decided they were done with you. I thought—" He shuddered a breath. His chin quivered below tight lips. He took a deep breath and let it seep out before trying to speak again. "It hurts that you wanted to be there, but at least you didn't need me to rescue you while I sat idly by."

Alyssa squeezed his shoulders. "I did need you to rescue me, from myself."

They held each other, neither hearing the storm rage.

Robert broke their silence. "So we should end this experiment?"

We can still make this work. Think. He wants me safe. "You said things had gone well until last night, and I fucked that up royally. If we could prevent incidents like last night, do you think we could still make it work?"

Robert rolled his eyes. "Maybe, I just don't know how to prevent episodes like last night. I won't go through that again."

A wall of rain soaked their backs when the wind shifted.

They moved to the other side of the gazebo, where the seats were already soaked. The wind swirled, blowing in from alternating sides. Alyssa and Robert embraced in the center of the floor to avoid the worst of the blowing rain, with little success. Alyssa pressed her body against Robert's and looked up at him, silently enjoying the pain from compressing her breasts against him. *I'll take this pain any day if he will stay with me on this.*

He's the protector, the level head. Let him have control. "What if we shortened my leash?"

"What?" He pushed her shoulders back far enough to look in her eyes.

"What if we shortened my leash? Instead of being completely open, what if I had to call you for permission to be with someone else beforehand?"

"Wow. Even today, you damn well want this."

I do, and I want you to want it too. "Babe, I know last night was awful, and I feel it today. I also know how good we can feel if we do this right. I want to make our marriage as wonderful as we deserve it to be." A bright flash of lightning followed instantly by a huge boom made Alyssa jump. Robert's arms tightened around her as she buried her head in his chest.

The smell of lightning hung in the air. Robert sighed. "Last night sure as hell wasn't wonderful. It wasn't even awful. It was worse than that."

Alyssa looked up as tears spilled down her cheeks. "If you want to stop, I promise we'll stop. But if last night was as bad as it gets, maybe we find a way to have the good without the bad."

Robert's hands flew out in an exaggerated shrug. "Jesus. You know that never happens."

"It's about keeping me in control. If I call you for permission, you keep me in control."

"Alyssa, I thought you said calling would ruin the mood?"

Alyssa nodded. "Exactly. If I call you for permission, we slow things down and keep me thinking straight."

"You think if we call each other, we can still make an open marriage work?"

Alyssa felt hope welling in her chest. *You're close. Follow me, Babe.* "No. I think if I call you, we can make an open marriage work. You don't need to call me, Robert. I have never, in all the years I've known you, worried about your judgment."

The scorn that had been on his face melted into surprise. "Really? Never? I make mistakes all the time, just like everyone else."

Alyssa smiled. *There you go. Use that judgment of yours. See that the imbalance makes it safer and better because you have control.* "Robert, do you know what you're like when you're drunk? You're more conservative and measured than you are when you're sober. No, Babe, I never worry about you losing track of what's important."

"Don't you want me to call you anyway, just to keep things fair?"

Alyssa shook her head to stifle a smile. "Absolutely not. I'm the one who needs a dose of reason now and then, not you. You are the one I count on to help me think clearly. You are the one person with my best interests at heart. If I have to call you before I play with someone else, I won't hurt you again."

Robert stood quietly looking at the rain enveloping them. "You make some sense. What if you lose your mind before you can call?"

It was Alyssa's turn to watch the rain while she thought. "Then we immediately go back to a traditional marriage, or you can toss me out, your choice."

He kissed the top of her head. "All right. We'll give this one more try. Alyssa, if you hurt me like you did last night, or if you hurt Clay, I don't think our marriage will survive it."

Alyssa gripped him tightly and buried her head in his chest. "I'll never hurt you again, Babe. You will keep me from hurting you. From hurting us." Alyssa raised her lips to his for a kiss. They kissed for long seconds. Alyssa looked out at the rain. "I can't even see the lake, it's raining so hard."

"I can't see the Morrison's house, either, Baby," Robert added, referring to the neighbors immediately beside the common area by the lake.

Alyssa smiled. "That's the first time you've called me Baby since yesterday. Does that mean I can come home?"

"I guess it does."

"You have something to do first, remember?"

"What's that?"

"Reclaim me. Make love to me and wash away the other men with your cock and your cum."

"Baby, I don't have the giant cock that the one guy had, but I still will hurt you, based on how you're limping around. We'll wait."

"No, Robert. You bring me back home the right way. I meant it when I said I would endure any pain for you to reclaim me. Even if it hurts so much I cry, please, please, make my body yours again." She looked at him and smiled. "Besides, doing it in public really does turn me on."

Alyssa pulled her wet T-shirt over her head, then dropped her bra on top of it. She stepped out of the tennis shoes she had worn home. She winced as she bent to push her jeans and panties over her hips and down her legs, holding Robert's arm as she stepped out of them, kicking them on top of her shirt. She retreated two steps, stood in front of Robert, and opened her arms to him. *Take me, Babe.*

Robert straightened, and he looked away from his wife, turning his head up and to the side. The skin of his face flushed red, and his lips tightened to a thin line. His fists clenched and relaxed.

"Babe?"

Robert silently watched the rain. His body looked poised for a fight.

"Babe, say something, please?"

Alyssa waited until the hope and excitement that had helped her strip without any pain evaporated, letting the aches flow again along with the fear she had lost her husband only seconds after keeping him.

Alyssa dropped her arms and her head. She sat cross-legged on the floor and put her face in her hands. After a moment, she felt a hand on the side of her head.

"Does all that hurt?"

Alyssa looked up at Robert. His face had paled, and the corners of his eyes and mouth had relaxed. *He hurts for me. Just another way I hurt him.* "Yes. It is no more than I deserve though." She dropped her head again to look into her lap.

He caressed a red mark lightly with his thumb. "Did they hit you?"

She put his hand over his, pressing it harder against her breast but swallowing the gasp that the soreness forced through her chest. "No. They fucked me hard. The burn marks came from the couch upholstery. I think my boobs are so sore because they held me up by them when I was coming too much to stay upright. I told you I couldn't think. I was having orgasms one right after the other."

"I thought it might only be your face."

I turn him off. Alyssa looked up at Robert. "Am I too ugly for you to want me?" She took a ragged breath. "Am I too used?"

Robert knelt and moved his hand to her chin to command her eyes. "You will never be ugly to me. You were used, but I still want you. Do you still want me, even though I would never do to you what they did? Even though I won't hurt you to make you pass out from orgasms?"

Alyssa's pussy throbbed, warming and lubricating for what she now knew would come. What she needed more than anything in the world. "Oh god, Robert. I always want you. You do make me pass out from orgasms, but you don't hurt me afterward. I love what you do to me. I've always loved it. Please take me." She reached for his face, pulling it to her raw, bruised breast. He kissed the burn, giving a little lick between his lips as he did. She winced but held his head in place. He kissed her again and began to move slowly across her breast, kissing every raw and red part of it before moving to flick her nipple with his tongue. She reached for the hem of his shirt, and he pulled his head back to let her pull it off, then he kissed her other breast just as he had done the first.

God, that stings, but I want more. She pulled his head up to kiss him again and reached for the buckle of his belt. She opened his pants and pushed them down as far as she could reach.

He stood and stepped out of his deck shoes, then removed his pants.

"Thank god you don't wear underwear."

His cock pointed straight at her, and she leaned forward to engulf his length. She caressed his balls with one hand and pulled his ass toward her with the other, letting the head of his cock slip into her throat with a swallow. She swallowed twice more, letting her throat muscles ripple along his head before pulling back and catching a breath.

Robert pulled out of her mouth and placed a hand on her shoulder, easing her onto her back. He knelt between her legs and leaned forward to kiss the burn marks on her hips while kneading her inner thigh with one hand. He switched hands and thighs back and forth after only a few strokes on each side.

Through it all, Alyssa kept her hand in his hair, holding his head on her body, not letting him see her grimace. She took her breaths in gulps, holding it while he kissed the stinging burns on her soft skin and gasping when she couldn't hold it any longer. His hand worked the sore muscles in a way that would help tomorrow, she knew, but was excruciating today. He released her thigh and moved his finger along her opening. She bucked her hips, trying to get him inside. "Yes, open me, Babe. Get me ready for you."

Alyssa released Robert's head as he pulled his finger from her. He leered down at her, then tapped on her clit. The pain of tapping her sore button and the pleasure of knowing her husband was the one tapping clashed inside Alyssa, making her yelp and arch her back. His cock notched into her opening and eased in. Her walls ached as his hardness parted them. Her lips, still inflamed from the night before, stung at being parted again. *Thank god I'm so stretched out. That fucking hurts.*

Robert leaned back. The head of his cock pressed against her front wall, and Alyssa moaned. *How can it hurt this much and feel this good?* He maintained that angle and stroked in and out of her, the angle hitting perfectly to drive Alyssa's building orgasm. Her cervix ached and rejoiced at the bump of his cock on every stroke, and her body spasmed when he tapped her just right. He curled forward to suck her nipple and flick it with his tongue. Her right nipple and pussy shared a connection, and she felt her opening squeeze his cock while she moaned. His constant suction and continued flicking of her nipple shot electric ropes between her tit and pussy with each passing minute.

Alyssa's noises morphed into a long whine coming from behind her nose. She stared at Robert's face, even as her body writhed. She rolled her hips as best she could to feel him on each side of her pussy, timing it to let him hit her G-spot and cervix on every stroke. *We get off hitting those.*

Her hands pressed into the painted floor as she moved. She could feel the hard wood pressing on her tailbone with every pounding stroke Robert pushed into her. *Just another bruise. God, He's making me come.* Alyssa drove her hips into her husband as the orgasm rolled her belly and made her stop breathing. Her body tensed as she came. Robert had stopped thrusting while she climaxed, but resumed fucking her as hard as he ever had when she gasped a breath.

Hot tears rolled down Alyssa's cheeks, and she gritted her teeth until her jaw muscles cramped. Despite the pain in her pelvis, she clutched at his hips, pulling him into her again and again. She focused on making him feel good, making him feel like the only man who pleased her, even though every move-ment—every time his hips collided with hers, every time his cock tapped all the best parts of her vagina, every time she felt him—pain reminded her of what she had done and that she needed to make amends. She clenched her pussy on his hardness, squeezing, hoping he felt her tighten when she felt him swell.

He pulled out of her and jacked his cock over her. His first shot landed warm and wet on her neck and trailed down between her breasts. Spurt after spurt landed on her chest. Robert bel-lowed while he covered her breasts and belly. His final drops fell onto her open pussy.

"Look at you. You are covered in my cum. You are mine again."

She looked at him through her tears. "Are you sure, Babe? You didn't cum in me. I missed that."

"I wanted to come on you this time. Maybe because they did. I wanted to override them."

"You overrode them the moment you answered my call this morning. Nothing those guys did would ever be better than you."

"Even nonstop, mind-breaking orgasms?"

Alyssa grimaced. "That hurt you. I shouldn't have said that."

Robert leaned to kiss her. "We decided to explore so we could feel new things. It gives me something to aspire to." Robert rose onto his knees and moved beside her. "Are you all right, Baby? I didn't want to hurt you."

"I've never felt better." She wiped her eyes and winced when she pulled her legs together. "It will be a slow walk back up the hill though."

"Maybe we can get a ride. Here comes a truck." The rain had stopped. They scrambled to dress, Alyssa skipping her underwear in favor of speed, laughing the entire time.

Alyssa saw three workmen get out of the truck and walk toward the lake. They elbowed each other and pointed not so subtly when they noticed she was wearing a wet T-shirt with no bra. When they passed on the sidewalk, she smiled without raising her head from Robert's shoulder. "Hi, boys. Do I have something on my shirt?" She laughed as the men blushed and muttered noncommittal responses as they hurried by. She held her wadded underwear in her hand as she ambled up the hill, clinging to her husband. "I love you, Robert. I won't hurt you again."

Robert sighed. "You will, but I'll love you anyway."

18

FRIDAY, MARCH 19, ALYSSA'S OFFICE

WHEN ALYSSA RETURNED to work on Friday, her coworkers dropped by her office to check on her. They received various versions of, "The Uber I called had an accident, and my phone was in the car while they took me to the hospital. I'm sore, but I'm fine. I'm sorry that you were all so worried after Robert called you. Thank you for checking on me. Next time, no drinks before the school meeting, ha ha."

Amelia came in and shut the door. She eased toward Alyssa's desk like she was unsure of something, rather unlike the confident, decisive fixer Alyssa relied on when something in the training kitchens went awry. Alyssa was curious what could put this young woman on her heels.

"Alyssa, you have always been kind to me. The other women aren't."

Alyssa's curiosity grew. "Oh, I wouldn't say that."

"I would. They talk behind my back and shoot me dirty looks when they think I'm not looking. You never do. Thank you for that."

"You're welcome. You're young, bright, and beautiful; you will get some sniping from the other women." *Is she being bullied?*

"It doesn't happen to you, and you are all those things."

"Aw, I'll thank you for bright and beautiful, but I'm certainly not young anymore."

The young blonde looked at Alyssa's desk for a second. "You still look it." She sat in the chair across from Alyssa. "Can I ask you a question?"

"Sure. What's on your mind?" Alyssa smiled just a bit, anticipating answers.

"Why don't they call you slut like they do me?"

Alyssa gasped. "What did you just say?"

Amelia put her hand over her mouth. "That didn't come out right. I'm sorry. Please let me try again."

Alyssa delivered her practiced stern scowl. *This isn't for effect.* "I think you'd better."

"You are just as beautiful, bright, and successful as anyone here, but the women call me names, not you. Why don't you get the same jealousy?"

"I see. Yes, that is better phrasing but not completely acceptable."

"I'm sorry about that. I've struggled with how to ask you that. I guess I should have thought a little more."

"Uh-huh. Well, I don't want to hurt your feelings, but if I were to guess, they call you names…" Alyssa paused to make eye contact with Amelia. "Like slut…" She paused again to let Amelia look away. "Because you talk about your sexual exploits at the office. I know it's only with a few people, but it gets overheard. Anyone who is jealous of you will use what they overhear to sully your reputation."

"It should be just fine for me to date around. I'm not married."

"That's true. You should date around; sow some wild oats until you find the right guy. Maybe you should only talk about it away from the office." Alyssa knew how to help both of them. "I tell you what, if something happens, good or bad, and you can't wait to tell someone, come to me. We'll close the door, and you can tell me all about it." She smiled at the young beauty. *There should be lots of stories to keep me revved up.* "And stay clear of Doug. He has a reputation for going after the ladies, and he talks."

"I don't interact with him much. I'm too low on the totem pole. How do you stay clear of him? He's your boss."

"He and I came to an understanding not long after I started. I let him know I was happily married and if he came onto me again, I'd sue him and the company into bankruptcy."

Amelia looked up and to the left, and her eyes narrowed the way they always did when she thought through an issue. Her face cleared, and she looked at Alyssa. "Are you not happily married now? I, um… I wasn't going to tell you this, but I feel like I want to help you too. I saw you Tuesday night. I was headed to the restroom when you went to the elevators with a tall man. You were all over each other."

Dizziness swept over Alyssa even as her stomach sank through the floor.

Amelia leaned forward and put both hands on the edge of Alyssa's desk. "I would never say anything. You are always so nice. I thought you should know you were seen though."

Alyssa swallowed. "You didn't tell Robert when he called looking for me?"

"No. I wouldn't want someone telling a boyfriend if I was with another man, so I didn't think you would want me to tell your husband."

Alyssa forced a thin smile with her lips, knowing it was belied by sad eyes. *Not even as discreet as you tried to make it with that Uber story.* "Thank you for protecting me. It's what a friend would do. Next time, though, if Robert is looking for me, feel free to tell him everything you know. If he needs me, then I need him to find me, whatever the circumstances."

Amelia's eyes widened. "Really? Even if you are with another man?"

"Yes. I'd prefer that to not happen, but when my family needs me, I want them to find me. We will deal with the consequences later."

"So why didn't you answer your phone when he called you?"

I have to trust her to keep my behavior to herself, but she only needs to know enough so she knows I trust her. "It's a long story, but let's say I regret I was incapable of answering."

"Wow. I don't want to pry, but is your husband okay with you sleeping around?"

"That's between him and me. You don't need the burden of keeping my secrets."

"I see. Maybe we can swap secrets sometime, if the offer for private conversations still stands. You won't hear me talking about dates in the open office anymore. You will see that I can keep my mouth shut."

"Your discretion will help you, Amelia. My offer to listen is still open. I think we are going to be good friends. If there is a way I can help you, just ask."

"I'm glad I came by, and I'm glad you are all right."

"Thank you."

Amelia left Alyssa's office before Alyssa unclenched her abs. *Oh fuck. If she saw, who else did?*

⟲

After lunch, Doug walked into Alyssa's office and closed the door. "Hey, Alyssa, are you still holding up this afternoon?"

"I am, Doug, thank you. What's up?"

"I came to talk about our deal. It seems the terms need to change."

"What deal, Doug? I don't know what you're talking about."

He leered at her. "The deal where I don't have sex with you."

"I don't think we ever had a deal about having sex. We had a deal about you not sexually harassing me, and that hasn't changed. You say one more word, and things will get ugly fast."

He nodded. "Just hear me out a moment, then I'll leave if you want me to. I believe we are coming to an arrangement. You see, I noticed you were a little drunk Tuesday night, so when you left, I followed just behind, hoping you might stumble and I could hold your ass while I helped you to your car. Instead, I saw you walk in on a huge cock and a girl with cum all over her, and a minute later, I saw you walk out with the owner of that cock."

It had to be Doug. Shit.

"Now, I didn't tell Robert what I saw when he called, and I think you want me to keep it that way. The question is, What are you willing to do to keep things quiet?"

Alyssa looked down at her desk. *He can't hurt me by telling Robert, except Robert will be angrier that I was seen. He could spread it around the office. Shit. Think. How do I get out of this?* She spun her wedding rings with her thumb.

He moved around her desk to stand close beside where she sat in her chair. "Alyssa, I am waiting, but you need to respond. The price of my silence goes higher the longer you wait."

She looked up at him and smiled. "What did you have in mind, Doug?"

"I think you took two days off because he wrecked your pussy pretty good, so a blow job for today sounds fine. I'll start fucking you next week, and every week for as long as you want my silence."

She smiled. "That seems like a high price to pay. What if I don't like it?"

He unzipped his fly and fished out an impressive, fully hard cock. "I think you'll like it."

Not as big as Robert, but not bad. I think I know how to handle this. "Let me make a quick phone call and I'll give you my answer."

He nodded, and she hit the speaker on her desk phone, twirling a lock of her hair as she dialed. Robert picked up on the second ring. "Hey, Baby. You never call my office line. What is going on?"

"Hey, Babe. I guess I wasn't thinking straight when I dialed." She waved her hand around as if she had a flighty moment, then she looked at Doug as she spoke to Robert. "You see, Doug is here in my office. He has a good-looking erection hanging out of his pants, and he just offered to not tell you about the man he saw me with on Tuesday night if I would suck him off and then fuck him every week that he remained silent." She smirked at Doug. "I wanted to get your opinion."

Doug tried to put his cock away but fumbled it. Alyssa tilted her head and then shook it at him. She wanted it out for this conversation.

"Is that so, Doug? You want to fuck Alyssa, but instead of just asking, you tried to blackmail her?"

Doug's mouth moved, but nothing came out. Finally, he managed, "Well, I don't think *blackmail* is a good term. I just offered an arrangement to help her with her situation."

"I see. And you have your penis hard and out of your pants as what, a visual aid?"

Alyssa envisioned Robert chuckling and shaking his head as he skewered her boss through the phone. She stifled a giggle.

"I didn't want her to feel like she wouldn't enjoy it."

"That was nice of you, of course. We wouldn't want her to make an uninformed choice. So, Baby, you know I trust you to respond appropriately to Doug's offer. What do you think you will do?"

Alyssa frowned and bit the inside of her lip. "I want to surprise him. Can I call you back after we negotiate?"

"Sure." The line went dead.

Alyssa looked up from Doug's softening cock to his face. "So tell me, since you know my situation so well, what exactly are you saving me from?" His look of discomfort grew the smug satisfaction swelling inside her.

"Look, Alyssa, maybe we can forget this ever happened." He tried to back away from her.

Alyssa grasped his cock and kept him close. She recognized an opportunity. "Where are you going? I thought we were coming to an arrangement." She smiled as he winced at his own words.

She stroked his cock a couple of times, getting it back to full hardness. Doug smiled. "You still want some of this?"

Same old Doug. Unable to think with anything but his dick, even after he gets in trouble with it. His choice. "I think we can come to an arrangement. Let me give you a good-faith gesture. I've seen you. It's fair that you see these." She unbuttoned her blouse to her skirt and opened the front clasp of her bra. Her breasts were blue and purple, and the burns had scabbed over, but she presented them to him, hefting them in her hands.

"You like it rough."

"Sometimes. Usually not this rough."

"They are sexy anyway." He stood in front of her chair. "You ready to suck me and let me come on those?"

"Not entirely," Alyssa breathed. She leaned back, holding her tits, moving them together. "For now, I'm offering you a visual aid like you offered me. Jack off for me, come on these tits you have lusted after. Once you clear your sex-addled brain, we can finish negotiations."

"Goddamn. That sounds good to me." Doug unbuckled his belt and opened his pants, letting them fall to midthigh. He stroked his cock with his left hand, slowly at first, then accelerating. Precum leaked from the tip that he smeared onto his shaft, lubricating it so his hand made squishing sounds as he stroked. His right hand squeezed his balls, and he groaned. The head of his cock swelled, and its purple color deepened.

"Shoot on my tits. Come for me." She leaned forward until her tits were under his blurry hand. He groaned as the first shot splashed on her chest. He jacked and moaned under his breath until the last few drops fell onto her cleavage. "Stay right there." She pulled out her cell phone and took a selfie of her cum-covered tits and Doug's cock, faking a disgusted look as she snapped the picture. She put the phone away and smiled up at him.

"I'm glad things are different than they used to be with Robert and me. Now that your head is clearer, are you ready to negotiate? About how many times you get to fuck me?"

"I think so. I think we can start with a fuck today, don't you?"

Alyssa smiled. "Let me call my husband for his permission." He smirked and moved his hand along his cock. She hit speaker again, dialing Robert's cell phone.

"Hey, Alyssa."

"Hey, Babe. I called your cell this time," she giggled.

"Yes. I'm glad. You know my office line is recorded."

"I do indeed, though I think Doug is just learning that, based on his dick going limp." She leered up at Doug.

"So what did you decide you want to do, Baby?"

She stared at Doug. She hardened her lips and furrowed her

brow. "Well, can you just listen a minute while I negotiate with Doug? He needs to know that you and I have no secrets."

"I can, and we don't, Doug."

Doug backed up from Alyssa. With his pants down, he stumbled, recovered, and stood still.

Alyssa pointed at Doug and leaned forward. "Doug, you heard that our last call was on a recorded line, and you admitted to trying to blackmail me for sex. You're the one who is fucked here. I could ruin you, here and anywhere else you wanted to work. You and your family would starve. Because I feel sorry for your wife, I'm going to offer you a deal. Interested?"

"Yes. What do you want? I'll give you a raise, a big one. You need more vacation too?"

Alyssa frowned. "Doug, Doug, Doug. What you're going to do for me is to stop harassing all the women in this office. You are going to be the model employee. You aren't going to talk about the women with the guys, you aren't going to proposition the women, you aren't going to leer at the women. If I so much as see a wink from you, the tape goes straight to HR, and then it goes public. Do you understand?"

Doug hung his head. "I do."

"I think you should thank me for the opportunity to improve yourself."

"Thank you for the opportunity to improve myself."

"There. I think we have indeed come to an agreement, and I look forward to seeing your improvement. You probably want to start by pulling up your pants."

Alyssa pulled some tissues from the box on her desk and wiped off her tits, then waved Doug toward the door he was almost sprinting for. "Please shut that on your way out, Doug." She spun her chair away from the door until she had rebuttoned her blouse, then spun back around and picked up her phone.

"God, Babe. That worked perfectly. Do you think we could actually get the recording of the call?"

"I don't know. We could subpoena it if there were ever a suit, I guess. You sounded intrigued by his cock. What happened?"

"I wanted more evidence of how he is. I didn't know if we could get the phone recordings, so I got him to go a little further. I didn't ask permission, but you said you trusted me. I hope you don't mind. I was trying to do a good thing."

"What did you do?"

"I didn't touch him. I opened my blouse and let him jack off on my tits, then I took a picture to add to the evidence if we need it. I looked thoroughly disgusted when I snapped it." Alyssa held the phone with both hands, as if she were praying. "Please say you're okay with me. You heard what I did. I helped everyone in the office." She held her breath, waiting for him to respond, envisioning his head flushing red as she did. She had to exhale before he spoke.

Robert chuckled. "Jesus, Alyssa. To tease a guy and then threaten his family…that's harsh, even if you do have noble motives."

Alyssa patted her thigh, clapping with one hand. "I did it for us, too, Babe."

"Really? How so?"

"We didn't make love last night. You didn't want to hurt me. I understand, but now you have to reclaim me when I get home, and I can't wait." Alyssa twirled a lock of her hair and smiled.

"I should have known, Baby. If that is what you want, you only have to ask, you know. You didn't have to expose yourself to that sleazebag to have me."

"I know." She dropped her voice to a husky whisper. "But now it is a guarantee. Nonetheless, get ready for tonight, mister."

"I will. Everything else okay?"

"Yes. I might have a new playmate for us but not soon. She needs to earn some trust first. That's all I had. See you tonight. Love you, Babe."

"Love you."

19

SATURDAY, MARCH 20, HOME

Alyssa woke to a finger tracing the seams between her ab muscles and dragging across her belly. She kept her eyes closed and smiled. "That feels good, Babe," she whispered. "Keep going."

The fingers traced her belly again and again, getting as high as her rib cage and as low as her hip bones but avoiding her bruised breasts and burned hips. The touch remained light, barely skimming the skin, sometimes one finger, sometimes as many as four, but never straying and never applying pressure. She felt the sheet lift where the touch was, and it returned to her as the hand moved away, almost making her feel like there were two hands on her.

Alyssa squirmed, rubbing her thighs together to pressure her moistening pussy without disrupting what the wonderful fingers were doing to her. She arched her back just enough to feel the sheet drag across her hard nipples, sending shocks into her pussy. *God, this is wonderful. I need some slow lovemaking today.*

She reached for where she thought Robert's cock would be. The hand left her belly long enough to catch her wrist and slide it back to her side. The light pats on the back of her hand sent a clear message to leave it there, then it returned to her belly. Alyssa sighed as it continued to tease her. Alyssa kept her eyes closed, enjoying the enhanced sense of touch that blindness created.

"Go further. I'm ready."

The hand broadened its track, brushing the underside of her breasts, then drawing a straight line to her mound, not quite reaching her clit, before withdrawing to her navel. The fingers continued to tease her as her breath sped up and grew shallower. Her belly began to rise and fall, increasing the pressure she felt when she inhaled, but the fingers stayed away from her breasts and pussy.

"God, please, do more."

"Shhh."

The fingers drifted to her breasts, circling them. Her breath caught when they touched her scabbed-over burns, but she smiled after getting over the shock. The fingers traced inward to the edge of her areola before pulling along her side to her thigh and back up on the inside, feathering their touch across her puffy outer lips and up the middle of her belly, back to her breasts. On the third pass of this track, the fingers circled deep into the areolae and teased the tips of the nipples, and as they reached her pussy, two fingers spread the outer lips while a third dipped between the inner lips, dragging from the base of her opening, to her clit.

Alyssa's hips were moving more now, and when the fingers parted her lower lips the second time, she closed her legs on the hand and thrust forward to press her clit onto the finger as her orgasm began. The hand clamped down on her pussy, pressing into her clit and stroking her lips. Alyssa's voice strained with a sound that came from deep in her chest. The noise continued until she ran out of breath, when her body stayed tense and her face reddened.

When she finally inhaled, her legs and head fell back onto the bed as she panted.

"Be quiet, woman."

Alyssa gasped. *That's not Robert's voice.* Her eyes popped open, and her head jerked to the voice. She took in Robert's smile and smiled back. "Why did you change your voice?"

"I thought you might want a fantasy about someone else doing this."

"Oh no. Only you do this so well, and I don't need to fantasize about anyone else." She grasped his hard cock. "Make love to me, Babe. I need you."

"We went hard last night. Are you sure?"

"Yes, but go slow. I want to feel your love even more than I want to feel your cock."

Robert climbed between her legs. She kissed him as she felt his cock slip between her parting lips. He slid in, spreading her open as her walls clutched against him. She pulled him forward, not letting him stop his slow progress until her cervix felt his tip. He moaned into her mouth and ground his hips. She felt him everywhere inside.

He slid back until his tip was barely parting her lips, then pushed in again. His slow pace gently filled her and eased back, dragging her lips with his shaft, stretching them so she felt even fuller than she was. He gripped her breast, holding it and rubbing the nipple with his thumb. Robert broke their kiss and pulled his head back. She looked into his eyes as she enjoyed his slow lovemaking.

Alyssa caressed Robert's back with both hands. "God, you make me feel good, Babe. Keep going." She squeezed her pussy on his cock as he stroked evenly at the same pace. His slow movement pressed on her G-spot as he moved forward and back and around her cervix when he bottomed out. The warm, soft pleasure that had accumulated so slowly while they loved each other filled that spot behind her navel and began to overflow.

Alyssa's face flushed hot all the way down through her chest. She pumped her hips against his and pulled his hips into her as she came around him, pushing him over the edge. He pressed harder into her, and spurt after spurt painted her deep inside. Alyssa pulled his face to hers for a long kiss. "I love you, Robert."

"I love you, too, Alyssa. Was that the gentle loving you wanted?"

"God, it was perfect. You make me feel so loved. I can't get enough of this feeling."

"I can't either. Want to just stay here all day?" He flexed his cock inside her.

Alyssa giggled and squeezed her pussy in response. "I'd love to. You make me so horny, I could make love to you again right now. But you have golf, and I have a few errands to run before supper." She felt his soft cock slip from her lips and drag down across her asshole, followed by a stream of their combined cum. Her throat opened in a moan. "Unh, you have no idea how sexy that feels. I really could fuck you right now."

"I appreciate that, but that particular feeling is because I'm not prepared to give you a second ride."

"I know, but I love it, and it keeps me horny."

"I could skip golf today."

"No, you need to go. You need to see how Bryce is handling what happened last weekend."

"I was hoping to avoid him for another week. I could go with you on your errands."

"Nope. I need to run these errands alone. You can't come with me. Golf instead."

"Okay. Then I need a shower. I don't want to golf smelling like sex. Want to join me?"

"Thought you'd never ask."

20

SATURDAY, MARCH 20, AROUND TOWN

Robert bent over his open trunk removing his golf shoes.

"Here are your winnings." Bryce threw a twenty-dollar bill into Robert's trunk.

Robert turned. Bryce had been his normal self during golf today, if a little calmer than normal. Robert wondered if that was about to change. "Bryce—"

Bryce put his hand on Robert's shoulder and smiled. "Easy, Robert. We're good." He patted Robert's shoulder with his fingers. "Logically, I should hate you. I mean, absolutely fucking hate you. You fucked my wife, she wants to divorce me, and somehow it's my fault. I'm going to get killed in the divorce. She has pictures, so I guess it is actually my fault."

Robert directed his muscles to relax. He felt his shoulders lower.

Bryce shrugged and shook his head. "I don't hate you though.

196

We've been friends for a long time, and I don't want this to end that friendship. We won't be as close as we were, but we are still friends on my side." He held out his hand.

Robert shook it. "I'm glad to hear it, Bryce. I'm actually very sorry things played out the way they did."

"Me, too, but I'll be happy with Candace. She's not as hot as Summer, but she likes girls and loves to share them with me. It's going to work out for both of us." He smirked, then straightened his face. "I want to warn you about Alyssa though."

"Warn me about what, Bryce?"

"Look, this isn't easy to say, but when I offered to fuck Alyssa in my bathroom, she didn't hesitate. I don't think it was her first time with another man. I'll speak from my own experience. Once I started cheating on Summer, even as great as Summer is, I couldn't stop. Alyssa may not be able to stop sleeping around on you. As gorgeous as she is, she will get every dick she wants. Be careful, Robert."

Robert looked at Bryce's face, trying to keep his own face impassive as he mentally recounted Alyssa's adventures outside their marriage and the knot in his stomach tightened. "Thanks for telling me, Bryce. I'll keep my eye on her. You really couldn't stop?" Robert wondered if Alyssa could stop if he asked her to.

"I might have been able to, but I never wanted to. It was a thrill. Now I'll be with a woman who wants to share that lifestyle. I hope that will work better. See you next week?"

"No, we will be out of town. High school reunion. See you the following week." Robert's phone rang.

"I'll let you go. See you in a couple of weeks."

❧

Alyssa looked at the short, sheer nightie. *Robert will love this on me.* Alyssa held up the other outfit. *And this one. I don't want to buy both. They cost too much.*

"You will make either one look spectacular."

Alyssa spun her head across the empty adult store to the man behind the elevated cash register platform. "Are you talking to me?"

"Of course. You have picked two of our bestsellers. A lot of women look at those two outfits, but very few would make them look as sexy as you will."

"You are very kind, if a little forward." *He's not hitting on me, just trying to get me to buy. He's too young and good-looking for me.*

"I don't mean to offend. I'm just trying to sell my product. But either of those will look great on you." He stepped down from the register and started across the store toward her. "Do you have any questions about them?"

Alyssa held up the leather harness outfit. "I think I understand how this works, but how do you get it on with the straps across the shoulders and the thigh straps?" *He's tall with good teeth. Wonder what he's packing?*

The tall man took the hanger when she offered it, and he pointed out the pieces of the harness. "The buckles on the back of the chest, waist, and thighs let you loop it over your head, then buckle in. These triangles go around your breasts, this strap around your waist, then these hang down to reach your thighs, leaving your pelvic area completely uncovered. It's a very sexy look." He handed it back to her. "Would you like to try them on?"

"I don't see any dressing rooms."

"Yes, we don't normally allow people to try things on, given the intimate nature of what we sell. I can see you are trying to decide, so I'll tell you that one of our video booths has a mirrored wall, and if you wanted to take those in with you to watch a video, I wouldn't stop you."

"Oh, I didn't come to watch the porn videos."

"I would never think you would. But the videos start when you enter. You have to pay me, then I unlock the door remotely. It will play while you change. You can watch it or not, your choice. It is the only place to try on the clothes."

"I only want to buy one, and I would like to see how they look so I can decide. How much for a booth?"

"It's ten dollars for twenty minutes. That's the shortest time we rent for."

Maybe I can watch the video a little bit too. I'm still horny from this morning. Alyssa pulled two fives from her purse. "Give me the mirrored room, then. Thank you for the consideration."

The cashier returned to the register. "Go straight back through that door beside you. Number four in the corner will be yours."

Alyssa stepped through the curtains and down the narrow hallway. The dim lighting made her stop after the bright fluorescents of the main shop. Her eyes adjusted, and she continued to number four and opened the door.

The video screen opened to a menu. Alyssa looked at the options: "Straight Couples," "Gay Couples," "Lesbian Couples," "Straight Group," "Gay Group," "Lesbian Group," "BDSM." She pushed the "Straight Group" button, and the screen lit up with a blonde woman kneeling in front of three men. *Will she take all three at once or one at a time? I'll see while I try these on.*

Alyssa stripped off her outer clothes, leaving her bra and panties on. She slipped the gauzy nightgown over her head and looked at the mirror on the side wall. The light from the screen caught in the gown, illuminating her body beneath it, showing her breasts and the gap between her legs. *Oh, that's hot. Will it show my nipples? My pussy?* She reached under the gown to remove her bra and panties. She saw the dark bruises clearly through the material, even in the low light. *I won't know until those go away.* She sighed.

As Alyssa put the gown back on the hanger, she saw the blonde on the screen riding one of the huge cocks while sucking another and jacking the third with her hand. Her grunts filled the booth. Alyssa stopped moving except to shift her right hand to her pussy. She jolted when she slid her finger between her lips. She pulled the finger to her mouth and sucked her juice from it, still watching the screen.

Alyssa took the harness outfit off the hanger and looped the top strap over her head. After the leather straps were situated around the edges of her breasts, she reached to fasten the upper buckle behind her back. *Not too tight. I don't want to be stuck in this.* She buckled the waistband and then attached the straps that went around her thighs, about the height of where thigh-high stockings would stop. She turned to the mirror. *Goddamn, that's hot. Everything is out in the air, but the straps make it look like it is restrained. It doesn't rub or pinch either. I have to get this.*

She hung the outfit on the hanger, then sat down on the bench just as the third man slipped his cock into the blonde's ass on the screen. *Fuck, that's hot. She has to feel so full. I wish I could remember how that felt.* Alyssa leaned against the wall and slid one hand to her clit and the other to rub her breast. *I'm in a masturbation booth, might as well use it as intended.* She pulled her hand from her breast to her open pussy to slide two fingers inside, and threw her head back as she raced to orgasm. She cried out as she came. When she raised her head, the blonde was disengaging from the men inside her, each hole leaking white cum.

The knock startled her. "Which one did you decide to get?" came through the door.

"Oh, um, I'm still deciding." Alyssa stood and put her bra on, adjusting her still-sore breasts in the cups.

"You want both, don't you?"

"Yes, but I don't want to spend that much. I'll decide before I check out."

"I think there is a special that would allow you to get both. I'll need to come in and check the tags."

Uh-huh. I think I know that special. He has me thinking though. Alyssa slipped her panties up before reaching for the door and sticking her head out, keeping her body behind it. "What would you need to see?" She looked down. *That's a big erection in his pants.*

"I need to see how badly you want both of them." He rubbed his cock through his pants. "They are our bestsellers, and sometimes they go on special, depending on the buyer."

She looked back to his face. He was smiling at her. "I think I know what you mean." *I promised Robert I would call. Here is the first test.* "Give me a minute to make a call."

"A call?"

"Trust me, and wait right there." Alyssa called Robert.

"Hey, Baby. I was just talking about you."

"Good things, I hope."

"Nothing to worry about. What do you need?"

"Well, you know how you are helping me use good judgment? I'm calling for your help."

There was a pause and the sound of a car door closing. "You are still horny from this morning?"

"Yes."

"And someone is there who you want to help you with that?"

"Yes."

"Is it someone we know?"

"No. It's the cashier at the lingerie store."

"Is she hot?"

"He is. And his cock looks big. I think he wants to fuck in exchange for some outfits I'm looking at."

"Alyssa, that sounds a lot like selling yourself for clothes. Is that really what you want to do?"

"When you put it that way, I don't. I am really horny though. I just tried on outfits in front of a porno. I need to get fucked."

"Where are you?"

"I don't want to spoil the surprise about what I got for you."

"Alyssa, if you want to fuck when you are like this, you have to tell me where you are in case you lose your mind again. Where are you?"

"Oh. That makes sense. I'm in the adult bookstore just up from the mall. You remember where we bought that vibrator a few years ago?"

"I do. That explains how you tried on outfits in front of a porno. Do you really want this guy?"

"Yes. I'm dripping, and jilling off didn't get me what I needed."

Robert sighed. "Go ahead. I'm going to come by there in an hour, in case you lose control. Be done by then."

"Oh, I will be. Thank you for helping me, Robert. I think you'll like what I'm getting for you. Love you."

She hung up and went to the door, sticking her head out again. "Nobody else knows we are in here, right?"

"I locked the door and put the closed sign out. It's just you and me."

Alyssa opened the door and let the cashier come into the booth. The menu on the video screen came up.

"I set it to play again so we could have some light. Why don't you do the group sex again? It seemed to really get you off."

"How do you know that?"

He pointed to the ceiling. "We have cameras in all these, just like everywhere else in the store. I watched you. How do you think I knew just the right moment to knock?"

"Fuck. Are there recordings?"

"Of course. They feed into the office."

"We will have to erase this."

"Glad to. Now why don't you put that harness back on, and if you fuck me, I'll let you have it and the nightie for the price of the nightie."

"Those outfits are for my husband. I'll fuck you for both of them, but not wearing something I'm getting for him."

"You're worried about sharing the outfits but not your pussy?" He shrugged. "It's not the strangest thing I've seen. Take off that underwear." He pulled his shirt off and unbuckled his pants, letting them drop to the floor. He stepped out of his shoes and the pants in one motion.

Alyssa removed her panties but left the bra to protect her tender tits.

"Take that off too."

"They are bruised. Didn't you notice that on the camera?"

"I saw they were dark. They look perfect, and I want to see them. You still want both outfits? Take it off, or we have no deal."

Alyssa removed the bra. *I'm not doing this for the outfits. I'm just letting you think that.* "Be gentle with them. They hurt."

"I'll be gentle. Now kneel."

Alyssa knelt in front of him and sucked his long cock into her mouth. The faint smell of his sweat hit her when she had taken him to the root, the tip just entering her throat. She bobbed a few times, and he reached down to gently rub her breasts. He pulled them up, getting her to stand.

He kissed her nipples, then turned her to bend and lean against the video screen, her face just an arm's length away from its sights and sounds. This time, a redhead lay across a hammock with a big cock in her pussy and another in her mouth. The men alternated thrusts, swinging her between them. Her legs were supported by the man in her pussy, who controlled her direction with them.

Alyssa felt the cashier's cock between her lips slip through her opening and continue to press forward. Wet as she was from her previous orgasm, he didn't stop sliding forward until his hips hit her ass cheeks. His length pressed against the end of her channel, but he wasn't thick enough to stretch her out. He felt good in her needy pussy. Alyssa moaned and pushed back, increasing the pressure on her pelvic floor. He pulled back and slowly stroked in and out of her, gradually picking up speed and shortening his strokes. Alyssa pushed back on every stroke, pressing his cock into her and building yet another orgasm. She reached with one hand to strum her clit while she fucked.

The redhead in the video captivated Alyssa. She thrust back onto the real cock between her legs in time with the redhead swinging in the video. *I wonder what it is like to feel two at once? I can only remember feeling overcome with orgasms. Maybe another time.* She squeezed her cunt on the cock inside her. Her mind blended the reality she felt and the fantasy she saw, and she came hard, squirting some juice on the floor of the booth. She pulled her hand off her clit to let it desensitize.

His cock started to swell. Alyssa looked over her shoulder. "Don't come in me."

"I'll come on your tits, then."

"Oh yeah. Dirty. Just say when you're ready."

He stroked hard into her, withdrawing his full length and slamming back in for a dozen more strokes, then grunted, "Now," as he pulled out. Alyssa spun, knelt, and jacked his cock toward her tits. The first shot splashed off her chest onto her chin. The next few hit her tits hard before the final drops fell to her thighs.

She looked up. "Oh, that was good. You have a nice cock."

"You have a nice pussy too."

Alyssa stood and dressed in silence, remaining topless. He dressed as well.

"Do you have a bathroom?"

He led her through the back storeroom to a half bath, where she washed the cum off her tits before donning her bra and shirt. He was waiting when she came out.

"Let's ring these up and we will get you on your way."

"We need to delete the camera records."

"We will right after I sell you two outfits for the price of one."

They finished the transaction and walked to the office behind the video booths. The camera system occupied one wall, with multiple screens, each with a DVD drive below it. She saw the feed from booth four, where the redhead was receiving two loads of cum on her face. The cashier popped the DVD out of the recorder and handed it to her.

"Thank you. I wouldn't want this to be seen."

"Neither would I. My wife would kill me." He popped out the DVD from below the image of the register and handed it to Alyssa. "Take this too. She owns the store and would be even madder if she saw the discount I gave you."

Alyssa laughed and slid the discs in her purse. "These are safe with me." As she turned to leave the office, she saw the inside of booth four through the one-way mirror. There was a fresh load of cum on the wall beneath it. She turned to the cashier.

"Some days, I love my job. You looked really sexy in those outfits. Your husband is lucky."

Alyssa rolled her eyes.

He walked her to the door, unlocked it, and turned the sign to open. "Please come back, ma'am. It was a pleasure doing business with you."

Alyssa got into her car just as Robert pulled up beside her and rolled down his window. "Thanks for coming to check on me, Babe. I just finished up. Feel like meeting me at home and making me yours?"

"Yes I do. I've been hard as a rock ever since we talked. I hope you are ready."

Alyssa sat in her car for a moment, pretending to refresh her makeup. *He is upset with me, even if he acts excited. Did I really fuck that guy for some clothes I didn't want to pay for? It was exciting, but that was the location and the videos and because it was taboo, not because he was a great lay. I'm not getting out of this open marriage what I thought I would. I'm acting like an everyday, run-of-the-mill slut. I don't want to be one. But what do I want?*

She backed away and drove home by habit, doubts about her own behavior dominating her thoughts.

21

SATURDAY, MARCH 20, HOME

"Go take a shower, Baby, then meet me in the kitchen. I'll start dinner." Robert patted his wife on the ass as he nudged her toward the bedroom.

"I won't be long." She smiled.

"I'm counting on it." Robert prepped a roast and got it in the oven. He cut broccoli and asparagus into a pan for roasting and seasoned them, setting them aside for later. As he finished the salad, Clay cut through the kitchen on his way out.

"Bye, Dad. I'm going out with Sawyer. I'll be home later tonight."

"Okay. Have fun. And be careful with her; she's good for you."

Clay rolled his eyes. "I will."

Robert pulled some candles out of a cabinet and set them around the kitchen before lighting them. He had just closed the blinds in the kitchen windows when Alyssa strode into the room, wearing the harness outfit. She stopped and looked at her husband. "I thought I would surprise you, but you have beaten me to it. I love the candles. Why aren't there any on the table?"

He stepped to her and gripped the harness between her breasts. "Is this what you fucked that man for?"

Alyssa recoiled a little. "Yes, but only you get to fuck me in it. Are you upset?"

Robert shook his head. "I just want to know how hard I have to reclaim you. Why don't you lie on the table?" He led her to the table and hefted her hips to sit on the edge before nudging her chest to lie back. He pulled a chair to sit between her legs, and she put her feet on the back of the chair behind his shoulders. He looked at her face. She was looking up and to her right, as much away from what he was about to do with her pussy as possible.

Robert kissed his way up her thighs, slowing his progress by switching from one side to the other to build her anticipation. As he neared her pussy, he opened her inner lips with his fingers. Her hips remained still when he licked from her ass to her clit and back down again. He repeated the trip slowly several times before stopping to suck her clit between his lips and squeezing it.

With her pussy wet, Robert slid two fingers into her and curled upward to find her favorite spots while he flicked her clit with his tongue in time with his finger motions. His fingers turned and curled until a soft gasp broke the silence. He smiled and continued to rub that spot. He applied more pressure with his fingers and his tongue until Alyssa's hips rolled with his motions. He felt her juicy slickness replacing the watery feeling of his saliva.

Robert picked up his pace, wanting Alyssa to come soon. He added rubbing around and across her ass hole with his other hand and was rewarded with another gasp, then a series of low moans.

Her hips were bucking against his face, and her belly tensed each time she exhaled. He peeked up at her tits to see the pink flush between the purple bruises. He pressed hard with both hands and his tongue three more times as she bucked against him.

He pulled his hands out of her, moving quickly to grab the leather straps that extended between the waistband of the harness and the thigh wraps and pulling them down, holding her still and open. He latched his mouth onto her clit, pulling her hood back with his teeth and flicking it against them with his tongue hard and fast.

Alyssa wailed as her climax burst from her. Her body curled upward. Her hands pressed Robert's head into her screaming sex. Her legs strained against his strong hands to squeeze his head and curl up to her chest. The flow of pussy juice exploded onto Robert's chin and onto the table. Robert continued to flick her clit against his teeth, extending her spasms. After a few moments, he released his hands, allowing her to finish tucking into a ball of quivering flesh, and he stilled his mouth to let her recover.

Her body shuddered a few more times before she released his head from her hands and legs. Robert rose from her hips to look down on his wife. She lay back on the table panting, legs splayed open for him, and her gaze focused on the wall to her right.

"I see I still have some work to do," Robert said as he sat down in the chair to her left.

"That was so good, Babe. I loved it."

"But you aren't mine yet. You are still thinking about him, aren't you?"

"Yes. No. Well, not really him."

"Who, then?"

"I'm thinking about me."

"And you can't do that and look me in the eye when we talk?"

She turned her head to his slowly. She smiled at her husband behind watery eyes. "I fucked a man for a five-hundred-dollar piece of lingerie. I thought I could expand our marriage. Instead, I've become a whore."

Robert patted her belly and left his hand there, caressing side to side while she fought her tears. "Have you, really? I don't think so. When we talked before you fucked him, you didn't want to get the discount, you wanted to fuck. You were horny. You know we have the money to buy that outfit. Did you do it for the naughty thrill of it?"

"Maybe. Being in a dirty video booth, trading my body for something, fantasizing about a porno while he did me from behind? Yes, all that made it more exciting." She looked away again. "I thought about it when you pulled up in the parking lot, and on the way home. When you asked me if this was the outfit I fucked him for, what I had done devastated me."

"Clearly I have more work to do to reclaim you."

"Reclaim a whore?"

"Reclaim my wife. My adventurous, creative, sexy, horny wife. Baby, if you are worried about becoming a whore, then you aren't one. I'm not advocating that you blow the bag boy for groceries, but how we spice up our life together is between us. If you want to get a thrill that way sometimes, and you stay within our agreement, you are enjoying life, not being a whore."

"Thank you, Babe. I still don't like what I did."

"Okay. You don't have to like it, and you don't have to repeat it."

"I think I should throw this outfit away."

"Hmmm. If you feel that strongly about it, you should. You look absolutely lascivious in it. You just walked into the room and I was hard. I like it and like you in it."

Alyssa brightened and turned back to her husband's gaze. "You do? It doesn't make you think of me fucking another man?"

"It makes me think of fucking you."

"You say the sweetest things." She smirked at him. "You haven't fucked me yet though."

"When I'm done, this outfit will be a souvenir of when I ruined the kitchen table reminding you whose you are."

"That could take a while."

"The roast cooks for another three hours."

She raised her arms to him and rested her feet on the edge of the table. "That should be just long enough."

Robert smiled and stood. He positioned his cockhead at her opening.

"Take me, Babe. Make me yours."

He plunged into her wet, open pussy until his balls rested on her ass. Alyssa groaned as he spread her walls with his cock. He pumped her fast, with long strokes, and she matched him with her hips, rising to meet him. The staccato clicks of buckles hitting the table joined the slapping of their bodies bumping together.

Robert rubbed the head of his cock across her cervix on almost every stroke, making sure he touched the sensitive area around it. Alyssa's eyes rolled and her mouth grimaced into an *O* as her body flexed when her back arched. Robert kept pumping into her while she spasmed.

Robert looked down at her body, and he felt pain when he saw her damaged breasts and chest. He slowed his movements and wondered what else hurt her.

Alyssa gripped his arm. "Pull my nipples, Babe."

"Are you sure?"

"Yes. Pull them hard. I want to come again."

Robert reached for her breasts while he continued to pump her pussy but slowed, making Alyssa's breasts easier targets. He cupped them from the side, stopping them from bouncing, and caressed them as he moved his finger and thumb beside each nipple. Alyssa clenched her jaws as if anticipating the pain to come. Robert pinched them gently.

She slapped his arm. "Pinch them hard, Babe. Pull them. I want to feel it deep inside. Make me come."

He squeezed hard and pulled the nipples away from her body, hammering into her pussy as he did.

Alyssa screamed and her back arched as he pulled. Her pussy clenched around his cock. She writhed on the table, her head moving opposite her hips. Robert buried himself in her. Her cervix fluttered back and forth across the head of his cock as she spasmed, pushing him over the edge. He grunted as he filled her with cum. They ground their hips together for long seconds as their orgasms wound down.

Robert lifted his wife's leg and placed a soft kiss on her calf. He put it down on the table and did the same with her other leg. "I love you, Baby. Are you mine again?"

Alyssa looked him in the eyes. "Always, Babe. God, I love you." He pulled his cock from her pussy, releasing their combined juices to drip down her ass. She sat up and wrapped her arms around his neck. "That was so good. Only you make me come like that. Thank you."

"Are you sure I didn't hurt you?"

"Oh, you did, and it was so worth it. It made the orgasm bigger." She kissed him. "Babe, I'm yours. You pleasure me, hurt me, whatever, just keep loving me."

"I'll always love you, Baby." He brushed her sweaty hair from her face.

She moved his hand to the harness between her breasts. When he gripped it, she smiled. "Take me wherever you want, Babe. We still have two hours."

22

SATURDAY, MARCH 27, HOME

"I'm giving him another half hour, then I'll call Sawyer's mother to see what she knows." Alyssa paced the family room floor, wringing her hands.

"He's an hour late. That isn't awful for being on a date." Robert sat on the couch, his eyes following her like he was watching a tennis match.

"But his phone still shows in the middle of the lake. What if there's been an accident?"

"Baby, if there had been, they would have called already. Practice ended at seven thirty, and he and Sawyer were going out. You know sometimes that app doesn't update for hours. We don't need to worry yet."

"Okay, Mister Calm, why haven't you gone to bed?"

"Fair enough. I want to see him get home. I also want to

make sure you stay calm. You know what can happen when your judgment is impaired, like when you are fatigued and emotional."

Alyssa frowned. "That isn't fair. Well, it's fair, but it is awfully soon to make a joke out of what I did. Besides, if I go into a sexual frenzy here, aren't you the beneficiary?"

"I guess I am, until you wear me out, then old Mr. Reynolds had better look out." Robert grinned.

"Hmm. I hadn't thought of him. A wild night with our eighty-four-year-old neighbor sounds exciting. You should feel threatened." Alyssa plopped down on Robert's lap, laughing. "I'm not so tired that you need to worry. I know you will help me, anyway. I called, didn't I?"

"You did, and it worked fine. I'm always here to help you." Robert rubbed her hip. "See, now you aren't worried about Clay. I'm helping you now."

"I'm still worried; I can think about two things at once."

The garage door opened. Clay stepped into the laundry room and stopped when he saw his mother approaching. "Um, hey. I lost my phone."

Alyssa gripped him in a hug, then stepped back. "Do you know what time it is? Do you know how worried we've been?"

Clay looked at the clock. "Oh. I didn't know it was almost two. I'm sorry."

"You couldn't use Sawyer's phone to let us know where you were?"

"Mom, I didn't know it was this late, so I didn't realize I needed to call."

"Clay, we love you, and we like Sawyer, but over an hour late with no call is not acceptable. And you lost your phone? You have had a bad night, young man."

"No, it was a great night." His broad grin faded when he met Alyssa's eyes.

"That's it. You are grounded."

"Come on! I was an hour late. You missed my graduation meeting and didn't even come home that night, and nobody yelled at you!" He shoved past her into his room and slammed the door.

Alyssa sagged against the wall with her hands over her mouth.

Robert pulled her to him and walked her to their bedroom. He sat her on the bed. "Why don't you lie down and try to sleep. I'll go talk to him and be back in a few minutes."

Alyssa sat still. "It will be a while before I sleep, Babe." She looked up at him. "I didn't think he knew I never came home."

"Me either. He is a smart kid, though, with a good sense of fairness. I'll be back."

True to her word, Alyssa lay awake beside Robert until after four o'clock before exhaustion closed her eyes.

❧

Alyssa was cooking bacon when Clay walked into the kitchen the next morning. "Hey, honey. Want some breakfast? I'll make you an omelet."

Clay looked at his mother and nodded as he got a cup of coffee from the pot. "Mom, I'm sorry for what I said last night. I shouldn't have."

"No, you shouldn't have, but you weren't wrong. I apologized to you for missing the meeting, but I didn't know you were as upset as you were."

"Dad told me that what occurred that night was between you and him. You looked like you had been in a wreck. Are you all right?"

"Dad is helping me with it. I'm going to be fine. We'll be fine. Did my appearance worry you?"

"Yeah. That and the limping around for two days. There was nothing wrong with the cars, so I knew you weren't in a wreck, but you didn't talk about it, so I just worried." He flushed red. "Was it from some other guy?"

It was Alyssa's turn to blush. "The things we talk about around here. But since you know, yes, it was."

"Do you like being hurt, Mom?" He gave her a worried look.

"No. I liked the way I felt when it was happening, but afterward I hurt. When I realized I had missed your meeting, well, then I really hated how I felt. That is what Dad is helping me with."

"This is weird, Mom, but is there anything I can help you with? I can't take you being hurt. I'll worry every time you aren't here."

She pulled his head down to kiss his forehead before wrapping him in a hug. "Thank you for worrying about me. There isn't anything you need to do for me except be your typical, wonderful self. I'll be all right, and I won't give you any more reasons to worry." She squeezed his waist again before returning to cooking. "Speaking of worrying about each other, I worried about you last night. What happened?"

"I lost my phone."

"It shows up at the lake. Swing by there this morning and get it. What else?"

"Sawyer and I got some dinner, then you know, we hung out some, drove around. Sorry I lost track of time."

"When you and Sawyer are, you know, hanging out and driving around, you are using protection, right?"

"Mom!"

"Clay, honey, you just asked me if I like being hurt during sex. I can make sure you aren't putting a baby in that pretty girl. So?"

He rolled his eyes. "Yes, we are using protection. We don't want a baby either."

"Good." She smiled at her son. "And if you are going to be late, let us know so we don't worry. It isn't that we don't trust you to be out, it's that we want to know if you need help somewhere."

"You have to do the same for me." He smiled at her.

Alyssa closed her mouth after a moment. *He got me with that one.* "Well played, Clay. If I'm going to miss one of your events, which I don't plan to do, I'll call. My curfew is between your dad and me though. Fair enough?"

"Fair enough."

"I think, since we understand each other a little better, you can come off the grounding I gave you last night."

"Thanks, I'll let Sawyer know we are back on."

"Tonight you have to be in early. Remember you are staying with Grandma and Grandpa while Dad and I go out of town. They're old, and can't wait up for you, so make your hanging out and driving around quick."

He blushed again. "We will. I wouldn't want Grandma mad at me. She's tougher than you and Dad.

Alyssa laughed. "She's mellowed since I lived with her. You're lucky. Here's your omelet."

23

SATURDAY, MARCH 27, REUNION HOTEL

Robert felt Alyssa hug him from behind. He had been staring out over the city from their hotel balcony railing while she showered.

"What's on your mind? You've been quiet all afternoon."

He squeezed her arms with his. "It's nothing. Just thinking about something. I didn't mean to worry you."

"Babe, I know you better than that. You've been gazing off this balcony at nothing for almost an hour. If you don't want to talk about it now, that's fine. I'll be here when you do." She held her position for a few seconds in silence, then released him to go back into the room.

"Wait," Robert said, almost to himself. "I really dread tonight."

"Why? This is your reunion. You get to visit old friends. Tell me."

"I want to see my old friends. There's a reason I haven't been to the other reunions though. Yes, there were always other events that conflicted, and there were some invitations I ignored. But there was a reason for that."

Alyssa leaned on the railing beside him and hooked her arm through his. "Go on."

"I don't want to see them."

"Them, who?" Alyssa turned Robert's face to hers. "Just tell me. All of it. Let me help you."

"You remember me telling you over the years how my high school girlfriend, Dawn, broke my heart? How I didn't have any long-lasting relationships after her until you?"

"We didn't talk much about it, but I remember."

"She didn't just break my heart. One of my friends stole her away late in our senior year. I was humiliated. That's why I've never been back. I thought I could go this year because I haven't thought about them in a long time. Today, though, I've thought about facing everyone."

"Why would it be a big deal? They will be there with their spouses, and you will be there with me. You'll probably laugh about it together."

"They will be there together. They are married. If Billy is like he used to be, he will broadcast it, especially if I am nearby. He likes to let everyone know how great he is. How good an athlete he was, how successful he was with girls. He's a loud personality, and he likes to demean other people to show his importance."

Alyssa's breath caught in a sob. "Do I not make you happy? Do you wish you were married to her instead of me?"

"Oh no. No, Baby. I didn't mean it that way. I wouldn't trade you for the world, and I am proud to have you with me tonight. I just mean that Billy will love having some fresh meat to berate in front of everyone. I don't look forward to that."

"Do you think he might have grown up a little since high school?"

"That isn't what I hear. Apparently, he peaked in high school. He comes to the reunions and relives old times. He also likes to hit on all the pretty wives and girlfriends."

"Do you think he will hit on me?"

"Most certainly. Very publicly, if he can."

"I see. Is he handsome?" Alyssa squeezed Robert tighter as he jerked to face her. "Shit, that didn't come out right. I'm not interested. I only want to understand."

"He was. He's tall, and he went to college on a football scholarship. They say he has gone to seed and that his chest and shoulders have sunk into his belly. I haven't seen him, so I don't know. You will have to decide for yourself. You didn't sleep much last night, and you were up early, so I'm watching your judgment."

"Oh, I don't plan on using our open marriage arrangement tonight. Not at all. I'm your arm candy tonight and your horny slut when we get back to the room. Sound good?"

"Well, it wouldn't be very discreet if you did use it, even if we are out of town. And I like your plan, especially for when we get back here."

"If only we had a little more time, we could play," Alyssa said, stroking Robert's cock through his pants. "Instead, let's get ready and then show your classmates what greatness looks like."

"Greatness looks like you in that little slinky dress you bought," Robert said as he patted her ass.

"In it or out of it?"

"I like the way you think," Robert growled.

⇜

"Robert! You came!" squealed the buxom blonde woman jumping up from her chair at the registration table in front of the ballroom doors.

"Tanya! It's good to see you!" She and Robert embraced for a moment before Robert said, "You remember Alyssa?"

Tanya beamed at her and squeezed her as tight as she had Robert. "Yes! Hey, Alyssa! I'm so glad you are here!"

Alyssa smiled and returned the hug. "It has been so long since we saw you and Burt at the school. How is everyone?"

"Everybody's good. It's hard to believe we are empty nesters now." She glanced around. "But we kind of like it," she whispered, smiling devilishly. She stepped back to the registration table. "Come here and we will get you signed in. Let's catch up after everyone signs in. And you'd better save me a dance or two."

"You always light up when you talk with her," Alyssa said as they walked into the ballroom arm in arm.

He squeezed her hand to reaffirm that he was with her and no one else. "Yes, you know I had a thing for her for a long time. Mainly, she's been a good friend to me for almost thirty years. I've always liked Burt too. And they like us. Of course I light up."

"I'm just teasing you, Baby. I look forward to catching up with her too. Let's get a drink. I'm going to need it with all this nineties music playing."

"Agreed. Bar's over there."

They walked across the room toward the bar, greeting a few people along the way. As they approached, Alyssa felt Robert's arm tense. She looked to see a tall man at the bar, leaning down to whisper into a woman's ear. Alyssa saw him grab her ass before she swatted his hand away and left the bar. The large man shook his head, then looked up. His face brightened when he saw Robert. "Robert! How's it hanging?"

"Shit," Robert said under his breath but kept walking to the bar. "Good evening, Billy. Everything is good with me. How is it with you?" He turned to the bartender. "A merlot and a bourbon on the rocks, please."

"Everything is always great with me, Robert." He turned his gaze to Alyssa and smiled with perfect white teeth. "And who is this lovely lady?"

He recovered from going to seed. And great teeth. Damn, he looks good. Alyssa squeezed Robert's arm and let him introduce her.

"This is my wife, Alyssa. Alyssa, this is Billy."

"Pleased to meet you, Alyssa." He smiled and took her hand, bending to kiss it. "Any friend of Robert's is a friend of mine."

"Nice to meet you as well." She let her hand linger in his before pulling it back.

The three of them chatted at the crowded bar for only a moment. Robert looked back and forth from the bartender to the tables across the room while barely speaking. *He wants to get out of here.*

Billy leaned toward Alyssa. "Perhaps you would like to dance while Robert waits on the drinks?"

He is aggressive. Put him off. "Not now. I need to let Robert introduce me to his old friends. Maybe later."

"Robert can't introduce you to anyone while he waits at the bar. You might as well enjoy dancing while nothing else is going on."

Robert put his hand on Billy's chest and raised his voice. "Billy, she said no."

Alyssa squeezed Robert's arm. *Shit. Now I have to dance with him or Robert looks like a possessive jerk.*

Billy smiled and patted Robert's arm. "Easy, Robert. I was just asking her to dance. Nothing else. I'll leave you two to your drinks."

Alyssa looked up at Robert. "You don't mind, do you honey? Like he said, it's only one dance with one of your old friends."

Robert's head reddened, and Alyssa gently rubbed the arm she held while he withdrew the other from Billy's chest. "I guess not. Go dance one, then maybe the drinks will be here."

⤥

Alyssa took Billy's elbow when he offered it, and they hustled to the half-empty dance floor. "Walkin' on the Sun" was playing. Billy managed to keep his hands on Alyssa's waist, twice turning her away from him so he could grind on her ass. *Robert wasn't kidding. He is making a show of it.* His hands slid to her hips. She pulled them back to her waist and looked over her shoulder. "My husband wouldn't like that."

"I didn't hear you say you didn't like it. Besides, Robert shares everything with me. He always has."

"I didn't say I didn't like it. I also haven't seen him share anything with you in the twenty-three years we have been together." The song ended, and "How Do I Live" started playing. "Let's go get our drinks."

"They haven't come yet, see?" Billy nodded toward the bar. Robert was speaking with a short woman with curly brown hair but looking alternately at the bartender, the woman, and Alyssa. There were no drinks in front of him.

Alyssa made eye contact with Robert and raised her eyebrows. He frowned, then returned to his conversation.

"He's talking with my wife, Dawn, see? She can keep him company while you and I get better acquainted."

"Okay. One more dance. Then I will need a drink." *Boy will I. This could be a rough night. And a hot one.*

Billy wrapped his arms around Alyssa's waist and slid one

hand to her butt cheek, pulling her against his body as they swayed to the music. *Just for a moment. He's hard.* Alyssa finally pulled his hand back to her waist. "Maybe you are getting ahead of yourself."

"I think you are right there with me. You enjoyed that."

"I'm not saying I didn't, but this is a room full of people who know we aren't married to each other. So watch your hands."

"I see." He spun her around so her back was to the wall of the ballroom and danced her slowly toward the edge of the floor. When they had no other dancers behind her, he reached both hands to her ass, kneading and pulling her cheeks. He slid one hand down to the short hem of her dress and tickled her hamstring as he raised it. He leaned down to nibble her neck.

Fuck, what is he doing? I can't believe it. Just then, the song ended. "I'm getting my drink. Thank you for the dance."

"Enjoy your drink. We can dance, or something, again later."

Robert tried not to stare as he watched Billy lead his wife onto the dance floor and begin grinding on her within the first few seconds. He had put her in this position by snapping at Billy. She'd had to dance with him or embarrass Robert by making him look insecure.

Alyssa could take care of herself, but he wasn't taking any chances with Billy. Alyssa moved his hands off her hips just as he took a step to go interrupt them.

"Don't you do it again! Don't you show up after twenty-six years and do it again!"

Robert took his eyes off the dance floor to face the woman who hissed those words in his ear. "Dawn? Hey. Um, do what again?"

"Give him your lover, you asshole. Don't you do that to me." Dawn's blue eyes blazed up at him beneath her pinched forehead.

Robert looked at his ex-girlfriend. She didn't look drunk or stoned, but she was talking nonsense. "What are you talking about?"

"You just handed him your wife, and he can't keep his hands off her. Don't you give her to him. Is that some kind of a thing between you two?"

Robert didn't like Billy's hands either. In fact, he wanted to break every bone in them, but he wasn't going to let that become anything more than an anger-fueled daydream. Unless Billy fondled his wife some more. "Dawn, I'm at a bit of loss. They're dancing. We're in public. What are you talking about?"

"You gave her to him, just like you gave me to him. Is she a bad lay too? Did you give him a title to her like you did with me?"

Robert eased back from her until his back touched the bar. She was upset at him, and they had not spoken in over two decades. Not since she'd left him for Billy. "Dawn, calm down. You aren't making sense." He swiveled his head toward the dance floor. Billy had Alyssa close against him and his hands low behind her back. Robert needed to retrieve her, but he had hamstrung himself with his earlier aggression.

Dawn pushed his chest. "You don't remember? Surely you do, since you are doing it again."

Robert looked at Dawn, then again for Alyssa's silver dress, thinking it would stand out, but it didn't. "Really, Dawn, help me here. Please."

She reached into her purse and handed him an old, dog-eared piece of paper. "This."

Robert unfolded the paper and saw, in his handwriting, "Billy, I'm giving her to you. I hope she rides better for you than she did for me. Robert." He scanned the dance floor, then read the note again. "Okay. What does this have to do with you?"

She snarled at him but kept her voice low. "You gave me to Billy, you dick. He showed me this paper at my house and told me you were done with me and I was his. He said if I stayed with him, he'd teach me how to be good at sex the way you didn't."

"What? That note went with that skateboard I gave him. It didn't roll right for me, and he said he could fix it, so I gave it to him, and left that note with it because he wasn't home when I dropped it off." He looked at his former girlfriend. She had never been a rocket scientist, but he thought she had more sense than to believe that story. Then he remembered that she had been quite insecure in high school. "You thought I gave you to him? Like I could even do that? And you bought it? Surely you got past that before you agreed to marry him."

The color drained from Dawn's face, and she began to lean. She placed her forearm on the bar and closed her open mouth. "He told me that note was about me. He even offered for the two of us to call you to confirm it. I didn't take him up on it. I went along because I was ashamed. I'm more ashamed now. I need to go." She took the paper and folded it as she headed toward the restroom. Robert watched her and shook his head, then turned to see Alyssa coming from the dance floor, straightening her skirt.

⌁

Alyssa saw the bartender bring the drinks and the dark-haired woman hurry away. She reached down to settle her skirt just as Robert made eye contact with her. His head reddened, and she saw the anger in his eyes from thirty feet away. *Shit. Perfect timing. Time for that drink.* She kissed Robert on the cheek and swallowed half her wine in one gulp.

"Of all the people in here tonight, him? What the fuck, Alyssa?" Robert growled in her ear. "And you let him under your skirt after knowing him for ten minutes? After everything I told you?"

"I didn't have much choice after you barked at him. Everyone here would think you were a jerk if I hadn't danced with him." She kissed his ear. "I'm sorry, Babe, but I did it to protect you. Besides, I needed to size him up. And no, he wasn't under my skirt. He just tried to raise it a little. Do you trust me?" She leaned back from his ear to look him in the eye.

"Sized him up, did you? Was his cock bigger than mine? I know you felt it grind against your ass and your stomach. Did he meet your expectations?"

"Robert. You know I would never hurt you again. We're through all that. Please trust me."

Robert softened his tone and leaned closer to her ear. "Alyssa, a month ago, you were in Houston breaking my trust repeatedly. We're recovering, but seeing you dance with him, that jerk of all people, the way you did, makes me doubt you. What are you doing?"

"I'm still working on it. You need to let me do what I am going to do, for both of us."

"Both of us weren't dancing." Robert nodded to the dance floor. "Look at him. He's got yet someone else's wife, grinding on her and pawing at her tits. She can't get away fast enough. Is that what you want?"

"That isn't what I want, but please let tonight play out. Know that I'm doing it for you, and that I love you." Alyssa gulped the last of her drink and signaled to the bartender for another. "When that drink comes, let's go catch up with Tanya and Burt."

"That sounds fine." Robert and Alyssa stood quietly, Robert watching Alyssa, Alyssa looking toward the dance floor where Billy was dancing and groping another woman who seemed more amenable to it than the last one. Alyssa frowned. The bartender set the wine down by Alyssa. "Let's go," Robert said as he took her elbow and steered her toward a table.

⚜

"Woo-hoo! I love the way you shake it on the floor, Babe!" Alyssa spun into Robert's arms to strains of "Unbelievable."

"It's because we took dancing lessons after we got married. You remember how rough we were before." Robert smiled at his wife and pulled her close as the song switched to "I Could Not Ask for More." He bent to her ear. "We should go dancing more often. Put those lessons to use."

Alyssa leaned back to look at his face. "I'd love that, Babe. Let's find the time."

"Clay will go to college in August. We will have an empty house and a lot more time." He cupped her ass. "Of course, there are better ways to use the empty house."

Alyssa slid a hand between them to cup his crotch. "You squeeze my ass like that, and we'll find a way to use a dark corner. I'm horny, Babe."

"Mind if we cut in?" Billy tapped Robert on the shoulder. He stood with a blonde-haired woman. "You remember Lori, don't you, Robert? She has been waiting to catch up with you." He offered Robert Lori's hand as his other hand snaked onto the small of Alyssa's back.

"Oh, hi, Lori. Good to see you. Maybe we can dance in a minute? My wife and I were just discussing something."

Alyssa patted his chest and stepped back. "It's all right, Robert. We can finish our conversation later. Billy can entertain me while you two catch up." She stepped into Billy's arms to sway to the music, drifting away from Robert.

❧

Robert leaned down to Lori after he missed what she said as if the reason was the music and not because of his focus on Billy and his wife across the floor.

"I'm glad you came, Robert. We've missed you at the other reunions." Lori danced closer to him so he could hear her over the music. "When I told Billy I hadn't spoken with you yet, he stopped trying to fondle me and made a beeline across the dance floor."

Robert scowled at his old friend so she would read his sarcasm. "How nice of him to bring you over."

Lori laughed. "Yes, and it's nice to have a dance partner who knows where my waist is. My husband will appreciate it." Her smile faded. "Are you sure you want him dancing with your wife? Billy is notorious for bad behavior at these things, and he's already worked her over to the edge of the floor."

Robert spun her so he could see across the floor. "Damn," slipped out under his breath. For an instant, he considered crossing the floor, grabbing Alyssa, and leaving, not caring what anyone said or thought. He must have tensed, because Lori hugged him tighter.

"Don't make a scene. He's an ass and not worth it."

He looked down at Lori. She nodded and relaxed her grip when he sighed. "It's no secret that he and I left school on bad terms, but she is a grown woman, and you heard her offer to let us catch up. Let's catch up."

Lori smiled and talked with Robert for that song and "Kiss from a Rose." Robert didn't hear much, but he did watch Billy grind and fondle his wife for the next seven minutes.

❧

Alyssa and Robert sat with Tanya and Burt and two other couples. Robert sat to Tanya's left, with Alyssa on his left. They had their backs to the bar, facing the dance floor. Alyssa participated in the conversation but continued to watch Billy as he danced with other women. His one willing partner was corralled by her husband, who took her out of the event. A few others stayed with him for a dance or two, only to depart hastily. He visited the bar frequently.

"Alyssa, I have to go to the restroom. Want to join me?" Tanya asked across Robert.

"Oh, um, sure," Alyssa answered as she stood.

Instead of the restroom, Tanya pulled Alyssa into an empty side room. "Look, I don't know what is going on, but you need to leave Billy alone. He really hurt Robert in high school. He thinks he's god's gift to women, but he isn't. The only thing you can do tonight is hurt Robert. Don't."

She's responding as I thought she would. Robert's friends were rallying around him already. Alyssa felt more secure in what she planned for tonight, knowing Robert had support. She worried about them getting involved too early, and she rubbed her sweaty palms together as she stood toe-to-toe with Tanya. "Tanya, thanks for looking out for Robert. I'm not going to hurt Robert tonight, or any night. I'll take care of my marriage and my husband."

"Letting Billy feel you up says otherwise."

Alyssa frowned to cover her relief. "I know what I'm doing. You don't."

"I'll just watch for now, but understand I'm here for Robert, not you."

More than you know. "I'm counting on it."

⁂

Robert worried when he saw Dawn approach from across the room just as Alyssa and Tanya left the table.

"Want to dance, for old times' sake?" Dawn asked him.

"Um, sure?" Robert stood and walked to the dance floor with Dawn.

They started the slow dance apart, like two people who didn't know each other. After a minute not talking, Dawn leaned in. "I'm sorry."

"Sorry for what?"

"I'm sorry for believing Billy all those years ago. I'm sorry for hurting you. I'm really sorry for not talking with you about it."

"Look, that was a long time ago. Yes, you hurt me, and Billy made it much worse, but I wouldn't trade what I have now for anything."

"Really? Because your wife sure does have the eye for my husband tonight."

"It appears so." Robert sighed. "She asked me to trust her, so I am, at least so far. What about you? Billy seems to be cutting a pretty wide swath through the ladies tonight."

Dawn choked back a sob. "He does that everywhere we go. He always has, all the way back to high school. I never had the guts to fight him on it. I felt so unworthy after you gave me to him."

"Look, I didn't…"

"I believe you. I can't believe I was so stupid then, and that I never questioned it through all these years. Shows what a crushed sense of self-esteem can do, huh?"

"You get embarrassed like this every year? Don't your friends or family help you?"

"They tried at first, but I was in college and put them off. We got married after graduation, and then, well, things just continued like they were. I didn't even question, and people pitied me but stopped trying to convince me I could do better."

"Look, we haven't talked in twenty-four years. I don't know you today, but you can do better."

"I know that now. I was so mad at you for bringing him another woman, a replacement, that I was going to fight for my place with him. When you told me the truth, everything crashed inside me. I've been such a fool, wasted so many years."

The song ended, and Dawn stepped back from Robert. "I'd better get to Billy's table. Thanks for the dance."

"Why don't you come sit with us. We can pull up a chair, and you know everyone there. We all used to be friends. We can catch up, and you can have a little time to think."

"You sure? I don't want to intrude. And I don't want Billy near your wife."

"Come on. I've invited you, so you aren't intruding."

"What about your wife?"

"I don't want him near her either."

❧

Over the next few minutes, Alyssa, Robert, Dawn, Tanya, Burt, and a few others talked around their table. Alyssa paid special attention to Dawn, leaning in close to whisper about her situation with Billy. She wanted to know how well they got along, how they went out with friends, how they got along with their daughter. Dawn seemed relieved to discuss how Billy often ignored her and belittled her. The receptive audience and alcohol combined to loosen Dawn's tongue, though she kept her voice low and leaned in so only Alyssa and Tanya could hear. *He does what he wants, and she lets him. Even when she's there, just like tonight. Her ego is crushed. This makes things even better.*

"Excuse me, ladies. I need another drink," Alyssa said as she rose and headed to the bar. She asked the bartender for another merlot. *Another couple of these and I'll be drunk.* Before the bartender returned, she felt the hand on her back that she had anticipated.

"Are you having a good time, Alyssa?" Billy whispered in her ear as his hand slid to her ass.

"I am. Your wife is quite forthcoming. You sound like the real man in your house. And I told you before, my husband wouldn't like where your hand is."

"I am the man in my house, and everywhere else I go. I have been ever since I first held a football." He squeezed her ass and left his hand on her cheek. "And I notice you only tell me that your husband doesn't like where my hand is, never that you don't."

"You're right. I haven't said I don't like it."

"Thought so. Why don't we dance again while he fixes your drink?"

"Lead the way."

Billy led Alyssa to the far edge of the floor, near the wall. The music slowed, and Billy pulled Alyssa against him with one hand on her ass. As he pushed against her, his other hand reached up to grasp her breast, his fingers clutching at the low neckline. Again, he leaned down to kiss her neck. *Jesus. Is he really doing this here?* "Easy there. The floor is too well lit, and too many people are watching you, Billy."

He dropped his hand to her waist but kept one on her ass. "Maybe we could go somewhere not as well lit, and I could show you just how much man I am."

"Hmm. Interesting that you say that. I can feel how much man you are pressing against my belly. What about our spouses?"

"Dawn won't care. Maybe I'll even bring her along. I did

once before. As for Robert, well, how could he be upset? He's been losing girls to me since high school, and I'll let him have you back in the morning."

"Let's see how the evening goes. For now, I need that drink." Alyssa moved Billy's hand from her ass and walked to the bar, where her merlot was waiting.

❧

Robert watched Alyssa go to the bar and Billy make a beeline for her seconds later. He felt his face get hot as the large oaf grabbed his wife's ass, and his teeth ground together as Billy walked her to the dance floor. He moved to stand when he lost sight of the pair on the far side of the dance floor. "Do you trust her?" Tanya whispered as she gripped his knee to hold him in place. "I don't know what she is doing, but I listened to her talk with Dawn. She was most interested in how badly he treats her. Does Alyssa like bad boys?"

"I don't know. I wouldn't think so, but she has been different since a recent trip to Houston. She's a lot more adventurous."

"Would she leave with him?"

"I don't think so, but I'm not sure. She's more unpredictable lately."

"Don't let her. If things get ugly, you have friends here. She can't get out without going past us, so sit tight for now and talk with Dawn. Y'all are having a tough night and could both use a friend."

"I'll do that, but if she's not back in sight in five minutes, I'm going to find her."

"All right. I'll help you. For now, talk with Dawn."

Robert turned to Dawn, whose eyes were wide and mouth hung open. "What? Did I do something wrong?"

Dawn blinked and caught her breath. "No. I can see you love her. Really love her. I've never seen Billy look like you just did."

"Of course I love her. Just like Burt loves Tanya and Steven loves Maggie over there. All these husbands love their wives, who love them back. You shouldn't be surprised by that." He touched her shoulder lightly before moving his hand to the table. "You deserve better. I wish I could help you."

"You have already, a little. You told me the truth about how I ended up with Billy. Despite the shame at my own stupidity, I feel better."

"I'm glad you feel better. Maybe you can find that confidence you lost so long ago."

"Perhaps." Dawn closed her eyes and sat silent for a while. Robert watched her a moment, then scanned the room for Alyssa. She was leaving the dance floor, adjusting the top of her strapless dress, heading to the bar.

Dawn broke his concentration. "Robert?"

"Oh, um, yes?"

"Did you love me back then?"

Robert coughed to cover his surprise. He cleared his throat and took a sip of his drink. "That's some question. I didn't expect to have a heavy conversation tonight. I guess I did love you then. Your dating Billy sure hurt like I did. Did I love you the way I love Alyssa today? I wasn't mature enough to have done that then. Does that make sense?"

"Maybe. I don't know if I'm mature enough to understand. Maybe I will be, now that I see things differently." She looked around, then leaned to him. "I loved you too. At least, it hurt like I did when Billy showed me that note."

Robert didn't respond. He watched Alyssa laugh with the bartender and head his way.

❧

Alyssa slid into the seat beside her red-faced husband and kissed him on the cheek. She put her hand on his arm and bent close to Dawn. "Your husband is quite the character. He told me he had another woman join you two in bed. Is that true?"

Dawn paled and sagged into her seat. Her head fell forward, and her breathing stuttered. She nodded enough for Alyssa to see. "I see." Alyssa put her hand on Dawn's knee. "You didn't like it?"

Dawn leaned forward. "No. She tried to involve me, but he only wanted her. My humiliation overwhelmed me, and I went to the guest room after a while and stayed there until she left."

Alyssa shook her head. "What a waste. You should have had a marvelous time. Sharing, and being shared, is beautiful."

Dawn tensed.

"Do you want to try something extraordinary, Dawn?"

"Billy's all I have. He's all I've ever had, at least since Robert. And he's all I ever felt I deserved. I don't know what extraordinary is."

"I think you might like something else." Alyssa waited for Dawn to respond, then continued when she did not. "Would you like me to help you experience extraordinary?"

"What do you mean?"

"What you might be missing."

"I don't know."

"That's fair. You keep talking with everyone while I get more alcohol."

❧

Alyssa sidled up to the bar. "Gin and tonic, bartender."

"Yes, ma'am," he responded.

Billy arrived just after the drink, placing his hand on Alyssa's butt and pulling her against him. "Hello again. Want to dance? There is a dark corner just for us."

Alyssa leaned into him slightly and turned her head. *That's some strong whiskey breath. And that's his hard cock poking into my hip.* "I don't want to dance right now. I want a little liquid courage. Why don't you join me?"

"Another scotch, bartender."

The scotch appeared quickly. Alyssa drank her entire gin and tonic. "Bottoms up!"

Billy raised his eyebrows at her, then did the same with his scotch.

"Ooh. I love a man who can hold his liquor. Let's have another." Alyssa motioned to the bartender. "Another round just like that one, please." Her hand fell to rest on Billy's forearm on the bar. She smiled up at Billy. "You live in town, right?"

"Yeah. Why?"

"Well, after you told me about bringing a second woman into your bed, I asked Dawn about it. She was a little unimpressed. I asked her if she wanted me to show her something extraordinary. She's thinking about it. Would you like me to show her how to properly share a man?"

"Yes, show her. That's so fucking hot. You are one sexy woman. Way too sexy for Robert. Why do you need to know where I live?"

"She might not be comfortable at home. Too many memories. Did you get a room here at the hotel?"

"Nah. She can drive us home. She doesn't know how to party. I'll have you naked in the back seat."

The bartender set down the drinks.

Alyssa smiled. "It will be better if she learns here, where she can relax and feel good. Drink these, and I'll take care of it."

Billy leered at her. "You get the room. I'll get her, and we can get started."

"Down, boy. She needs to get comfortable with it first. Let the party continue a while. I'll keep selling it to her. At the end of the night, she'll be ready."

"If you say so, but I really want to fuck you soon. Robert won't cause any problems, will he?"

"He'll be fine with everything in the end."

"You sure? I don't want to fight him, but I will if I can get your sweet ass."

"Drink up and let me do my work." She downed her drink and let him drink his. She stepped away from Billy, crossed to the ballroom doors, and turned left.

✦

"Which way is the restroom?" Robert asked Dawn.

"Take a right when you go out the doors, then a little way down on the left."

"Thanks. I'll be right back." Robert held his breath as he struggled not to run out the doors to follow his wife. He turned left and saw Alyssa at the desk speaking with the clerk. He sped up but refrained from running. He reached Alyssa while the clerk typed. "What are you doing?" he hissed in her ear, grabbing her upper arm.

"Just a second, Robert." Alyssa smiled at him. She pulled his hand off her arm.

"How many nights?" the clerk asked.

"Five, please. Checking out on the first."

"Yes, ma'am. How many keys?"

"Two, please."

Robert walked away from his wife as Alyssa thanked the clerk for the keys and slipped them in her clutch. She caught up to Robert near the ballroom.

"Robert, wait. I know we said we didn't want to use our open privileges tonight, but I think it would be good for everyone."

"Good for everyone? Just who is everyone? You booked five nights. The rest of the month. You want to spend the rest of our open month with him? I can't bear that." He stepped closer to the door.

Alyssa grabbed his arm and leaned into his ear. "Robert, we can't talk about this with everyone around. I'm not trying to hurt you. I'm trying to help you. Will you please, please trust me?"

He leaned in close as well. "Do you hear yourself? You want me to trust you when you're drunk and you have been letting Billy Redwood fondle you all night, right in front of everyone? Friends have come to me and apologized for what he is doing. You asked me to trust you before, and I have let you do whatever it is you are doing, but you are asking too much. I am pondering using the ripcord."

Alyssa's body stiffened, and her mouth fell open. Her head shook almost imperceptibly.

Robert's teeth clenched as he noted her reaction. Whatever she wanted to do, she would do, even if he ended their open marriage right here, right now. Her eyes were pleading for him to back off.

Alyssa exhaled forcefully, but the muscles in her neck and shoulders revealed her stress as they strained against her skin. "Look, Robert, please don't think that way…"

At that moment, a group of people spilled out of the ballroom, laughing and stumbling, bumping Robert into Alyssa and knocking her backward. She stumbled, and he wrapped both arms around her back before she fell. "Jesus, Robert. You caught me so fast. You have the best hands. No wonder I always feel safe with you." She kissed him hard on the mouth for several seconds before he righted her.

Robert wondered if the kiss was just part of her plan to be with Billy tonight, if that was her plan, then discarded that thought. The look on her face when he'd caught her only showed itself when she was vulnerable and loving. It was the one she couldn't fake, and that she only gave to him. Whatever she had planned, she loved him. But he wondered how that love measured up against a new, exciting lover.

Alyssa gave him another soft peck when he righted her. "It would take too long to tell you what I have in mind, but I need about another hour to make this work. Will you trust me enough to let me help you?"

Nothing about the night felt like she was helping him. She was doing whatever she wanted, probably only for herself. Still, he knew she loved him, even if she had been off the rails lately. Robert knew she would act on her own. She might as well know the stakes. He didn't know if she cared or not at this moment. "I'm walking back in that room. I trust you while you are in that room. If you leave with him, our trust is broken. Forever. It goes well beyond ending our open relationship. Fair enough?"

Alyssa's mouth fell open again. She made eye contact with him, and her chin quivered an instant before her jaw clenched and she raised her head. "Fair enough. Will you escort me to the restroom and back? I've been drinking a lot and don't want to accidentally leave with anyone. I want you to see that if you don't know it in your heart."

"Just go," Robert said, sloughing off her hands and returning to the ballroom.

❧

Alyssa strode into the ballroom and across to the bar. "Another gin and tonic, bartender."

"Yes, ma'am."

"And one more scotch," Billy said as he walked beside Alyssa, placing his hand possessively on her ass.

"I got a room. Are you sure you want me to show your wife the many ways to share a man?"

"Fuck, yeah. I'm so hard thinking about it." He pressed his crotch against her hip.

"You are indeed."

The drinks came. Alyssa drank half of hers, then turned to go. "Let me finish this, then. I need about forty-five minutes."

Alyssa arrived at the table. She noticed Robert's bright-red face and kissed the top of his head before sliding into the chair beside Dawn. They all talked pleasantly for a while. As the conversation broke from one group discussion to smaller ones, she leaned to the pretty brunette and whispered, "Have you been thinking? Do you want me to show you lovemaking like you have never had? Are you willing to try something amazing?"

Dawn whispered in Alyssa's ear, "Are you sure? I can't hurt Robert, but I really want a better life than what I have now. Maybe trying a threesome again will make Billy love me again."

"Dawn, I can show a kind of love you can only imagine. You'll never again be satisfied with what you had before. Will you let me show you?"

"What about Robert? I hurt him so bad before…"

"Don't worry. Robert will be fine. We have an agreement."

Dawn's eyes popped wide. "What?"

"I'll explain later. Do you want to share a man?"

"If you think it will be good, and it's all right with Robert, I'll try it."

"Dawn, just stay with me and you'll be a different woman in the morning."

※

Alyssa, Robert, and the others at their table talked a while longer, still catching up. Only a few couples remained in the ballroom when Alyssa stood. "I'm getting another drink." She looked at the drinks on the table. She pointed to Tanya's empty glass, then leaned into her ear. "Stay here. There may be a scene."

Tanya tensed, then whispered back, "Remember what I said. If you hurt him, you can't run far enough away from me."

Alyssa smiled, then leaned in again. "Just watch."

"Bartender, a gin and tonic and a white wine, please."

Alyssa felt the now familiar hand on her ass. "You ready to leave? I'm ready."

"Yes. Give me ten minutes, then come to the table so we can say goodbye. Have another drink while you wait."

"One drink, then I'm coming over."

"Okay." Alyssa carried the two drinks to the table.

※

Alyssa set Tanya's drink down in front of her, then returned to her seat. She leaned over to kiss Robert's cheek, whispering, "Please remember I love you a lot, Babe. Please trust that this is good for you."

Robert reddened but didn't speak. Alyssa leaned to Dawn and whispered, "Things are going to get ugly in a minute. If you want to change your life for the better, agree with everything I say.

Don't lose your nerve. In ten minutes, everything will be over, and you'll be in for the best night of your life. Can you do that?"

"Okay, but how bad will this get?"

"Pretty bad, but it will be over quickly. Whatever happens, stay with me, and you'll be the big winner." *If she doesn't freak out. And Robert doesn't freak out. Fuck, here he comes, staggering all the way.*

Alyssa leaned to Robert, put her hand on his thigh, and licked his ear. "Ready to go, Babe?"

Billy stood behind her and spoke loudly. "Dawn, Alyssa, let's go. It's time to have some real fun."

Alyssa turned and smiled. "You mean you want me to show your wife how to share a man?"

"You know it, hot stuff. I want it so bad. Let's leave."

The thin crowd hushed and subtly moved around the table, waiting for the fireworks. Robert stiffened, but Alyssa pressed her hand into his thigh, telling him to stay put. Dawn shrank away from Alyssa and Billy.

Alyssa laughed and stood to face him. "Oh, you think that because I let you chase me tonight, I wanted to leave with you? Oh no. I gave the other women in the room a break from your slimy hands and your whiskey breath. More than that, I gave your sweet wife a pleasant evening with her old friends, even though you embarrassed her at every butt-groping opportunity."

"You cock-teasing bitch!" Billy pulled his hand back to slap Alyssa, but Robert grabbed his wrist as Burt and some of the other men around stepped forward.

The bartender said from behind Billy, "Sir, it seems you have had enough. You should leave before we have to call the cops."

"Never, ever come near us again, Billy," Robert said to the gasping drunk.

Billy glared at his wife and growled, "Come on, Dawn. Let's get out of here. It's no fun, anyway."

Alyssa stepped between Billy and Dawn, reaching behind her to hold Dawn's hand. "If your beautiful wife, whom you debased at every opportunity, will come with me instead, I will show her how a real man behaves. My man. A real man would never ask another woman into his wife's bed the way you just did." She turned to face Dawn. "Stay here. We can protect you from him. With any luck, you will feel confident enough to leave his abusive ass in the dirt. Your friends here will help you. Look around."

Dawn gripped Alyssa's hand as she scanned the people around her. The women nodded back at her. The men glared at Billy, as if daring him to interrupt. "I don't know what to do. I'm afraid."

"Take the chance you denied yourself for twenty-four years," Tanya said, gripping Dawn's shoulders from behind with both hands. "Feel your own strength. We are here to help."

Tears spilled down Dawn's cheeks as she took a deep breath and muttered, "Go home, Billy. I'm going to stay a while."

Billy flashed anger across his face, then stepped back. "You will come crawling back, Dawn! You know you will. You can't survive without me taking care of you. You are too weak to make it in the real world, you mouse." He strode to the door, alternating between strutting and staggering.

"He knows the cops sit just up the road waiting for drunks, right?" Burt asked the group.

"He should, they are here every year," answered someone behind them.

Alyssa turned to face Dawn and Robert. "Can I explain?"

"You had better," Robert replied. "You had me in knots all night with that show you put on. You could have given me a hint."

"I hated that part, Babe. It really kept him going though. I watched him, and when he wasn't hitting on women, he was watching you, grinning." She whispered in his ear, "I'll make it up to you. Remember what I promised you tonight." She resumed speaking to the group. "I couldn't tell you two my plan, because it just came to me when I saw how he behaved. I've seen his kind before, and he needed a lesson." She put her arm around Robert. "I figured I could get him drunk and it would be easy."

"How did you do that, Baby? I watched you match Billy drink for drink. You never drink more than a couple glasses of wine. How are you even standing?"

"I tipped the bartender a hundred to make mine with no gin and to double Billy's scotches. He didn't like Billy's behavior either."

Robert frowned. "Getting him drunk isn't much of a plan."

"I wanted to get him drunk, tease him, then very publicly stay with you and leave him hanging. I thought he would blow up and embarrass himself, just like he did. I assumed he had a bitch of a wife who let him do what he does at these things, and she could get embarrassed too."

Alyssa turned to Dawn and took both her hands. "And then I met you. I've seen your kind before too. Sweet girl, beaten down by some egotistical jerk, left with no hope. You talked about how he tricked you and kept you, like a toy in a closet. I decided to offer you a way out, if you would take it. I hope you're glad you did."

"Damn, girl!" Tanya exclaimed. "You could have told me in that side room, after I threatened you."

"No." Alyssa smiled and embraced Tanya. "You did exactly what I hoped you would. If this had gone to shit, I needed you to help Robert pick up the pieces. I wouldn't trust anyone else with that job, so you couldn't get involved. You have no idea how important a friend you are to him."

"Jesus, Alyssa." Robert shook his head. The crowd stepped back, moving to leave now that it was almost 2:00 a.m. and the excitement had died down.

Dawn stepped up with tears in her eyes to whisper to Alyssa. "So all that about showing me how to share a man, was that merely to entice me to let my husband leave?"

"Yes, I wanted to tip the scales." Alyssa pulled Robert's head to theirs so he could hear. "But the offer stands, if Robert wants to take it."

"Whoa, there, Baby. When were you going to ask me?"

"Are you saying you wouldn't want to heal some old wounds with Dawn? Perhaps in a loving, exciting, sexy way? With me there to help?"

Dawn looked at Robert. "I… I was ready to let Billy bring your wife home so I could be with her. I think I'd like it better with you, if you'll have me." She bit her lower lip and nodded at him.

Robert's body slumped, then straightened. Alyssa watched his eyes narrow, then relax. He blew a long breath up into the air, then shook his head at Alyssa. "This is what you meant about using our agreement tonight?"

Now he understands. His back relaxed under my hand. He's okay. She smiled at Robert. "Yes, Babe. I want you to show her how you make me feel. How a real man loves a woman."

"What about you?" Robert asked, nuzzling Alyssa's ear.

Alyssa took Dawn's hand and made eye contact. Dawn blushed and smiled. She nodded once, then looked away. "I can't wait to show her how a woman makes her feel. Oh, and I get to reclaim you, as always."

"You worked hard for this. Who am I to refuse?" Robert looked at both women. "Shall we?"

24

SUNDAY, MARCH 28, REUNION HOTEL

THOUGH THEY LEFT the ballroom discreetly, Robert strolled from the elevator to the room with a beautiful woman on each arm. He opened the suite door and allowed the women to enter before closing the door and locking it.

Alyssa stopped at the bathroom door. "No offense, but I need to wash his slime off before we make love."

"No offense taken," Dawn replied. "I feel like I should to, but it will take more than one shower."

"You'll get there." Alyssa caressed Robert's cheek. "Babe, why don't you and Dawn get more comfortable? I'll only be a minute." She closed the bathroom door and started the water.

"I wish we had talked about all this years ago." Dawn stepped close to Robert and wrapped her arms around his waist. "All that time wasted."

"Maybe, at least about that stupid note." Robert pulled her

247

against him. "I don't think we could have helped you until this moment. I'm glad we did." Robert bent to kiss her upturned mouth. Tentatively, she kissed back. Robert lingered over the soft kiss for almost a minute before fluttering his tongue against her lips. She opened her mouth to receive him and sucked his tongue before extending her own, circling and wrestling with his. Their necking intensified, their hands drifting lower to rub and knead the ass cheeks they grabbed. Robert slid one hand to Dawn's hip before tracing up her side to cup her breast and thumb the nipple through the dress. Dawn moaned into his mouth and moved one hand between them to grasp his hard cock through his pants, stroking it in time with his nipple teasing.

Robert brought his hands to the back of Dawn's neck, released the clasp on the back of her dress, and pulled the zipper down to the middle of her ass. His hands slid up over her bare back, where he pulled the dress off her shoulders and down her arms. He let it drop, and it pooled atop her hips. His hands chased it down, and Dawn wiggled her hips, together getting the dress to the floor. He stepped back and stared at her, taking in smallish breasts; flat, toned stomach; and slightly flared hips, all encased in a skimpy black lace bra and panty set. Her fit legs were adorned with stockings and high heels.

She held out her arms and looked at him. "Am I still pretty?"

"No. You aren't pretty. You're beautiful. Anyone who tells you otherwise is blind." Robert stepped toward her, but she put a hand in his chest, stopping him.

"My turn." Dawn put both hands on his chest, then moved them up and under the shoulders of his jacket, pushing it back and letting it drop to the floor. She pulled his tie back and forth, loosening it. "There is no sexy way to do this. Sorry."

"Anything a beautiful woman in lingerie does is sexy. Keep going."

The tie out of the way, she moved to his shirt, leaning to kiss the newly exposed skin after opening each button. When her hands reached his waist, she unbuckled his belt and opened his pants. She knelt before him and pulled the pants over his ass and down his legs. "Oh. No underwear?"

"Never."

She kissed his cockhead while she untied his shoes. He raised his feet one at a time while she removed shoes, socks, and trousers. She stood to kiss him, following with, "You look better than you did in school."

Robert kissed her, his hands sliding under the back of her panties to stroke her bare ass. He moved and sucked on her neck just below her ear. Dawn's knees buckled, and Robert held her upright.

"God, I love that," she moaned.

"I remember," he whispered.

"You taught him that?" Alyssa whispered from behind Dawn.

"She did," Robert replied.

"God, I owe you. I love when he does that." Alyssa pulled Dawn's hair back and sucked Dawn's neck on the opposite side as Robert.

Dawn moaned, and her legs buckled again. Robert and Alyssa sandwiched her body between them to support her, reaching their hands to each other's sides and holding tight.

Alyssa moved Robert's hands to Dawn's bra, then kissed her way down Dawn's back, snagging the waistband of her panties and pulling them to the floor as she planted kisses on her pale cheeks. Robert unfastened the clasp on Dawn's back, then slid the straps off her shoulders. He stepped back and bent his head to kiss the tops of her breasts, giving the bra a light tug and letting it fall to the floor. He kissed around her breasts, working across the sides and bottoms before sucking Dawn's nipple. Dawn gasped and leaned forward when he sucked hard and pulled back, distending her breast before it popped out of his mouth.

Alyssa moved when Dawn leaned forward, pressing her face between Dawn's cheeks. Dawn jerked upright, then stepped her left foot out a little and bent forward again, pulling Robert's head to her breast. Dawn writhed against Robert as he sucked and nibbled her breasts and nipples, switching from right to left and from soft kisses to hard nips with his teeth. The silences between her grunts and moans shortened, and her legs trembled. Robert dropped a hand to her pussy and inserted a finger, curling it forward, searching for that spongy spot every woman liked. Dawn yelped as he pressed home and repeated the action without losing focus on her breasts.

Alyssa licked Robert's fingers as she ate Dawn from behind. Dawn's breathing quickened, her stomach fluttering against Robert's forearm with each breath. A rosy color spread down her breasts, turning her tan lines pink. Her left leg buckled and caught. Robert moved his free hand behind her back, anticipating her release.

Dawn wailed and clamped her thighs around Robert's hand. Robert felt a small gush of fluid flow over his hand. A moment later, Dawn's legs gave out. Alyssa and Robert held her up, then laid her on the nearby bed.

"Oh, you are a good husband." Alyssa kissed Robert. "Now that she's warmed up, we'll show her how good sex can be."

"Mm. I'm more than warmed up," Dawn murmured.

"Maybe. Billy might have been just fine in bed," Robert deadpanned.

"True, he might know some tricks, but he doesn't have your cock," Alyssa said with a smile that disappeared when she made eye contact with him. Her hand clamped over her mouth. "Sorry, Babe. I shouldn't have said it that way. He ground it into me all night. I'll take yours."

"He never made me feel the way you two just did. That was the best orgasm of my life." Dawn raised her head from the pillow.

"We're just getting started." Alyssa smiled, untied the sash on the hotel robe, and dropped it to the floor beside Robert's pants. "Lie down, Robert." She pushed his chest so he sat on the bed. He moved up and rested his head on a pillow. "Come here, Dawn, let me share my husband with you."

"Are you sure?"

"Um, Dawn, I appreciate your asking, but we are all here, naked, in a room that smells like your cum. Everything is approved until someone says otherwise."

Dawn nodded. "Thank you."

"To be fair," Alyssa continued, "tomorrow morning, I'll make Robert mine again, and he'll be only mine at that point. You might be allowed to play again in the future, or you might not. He and I will decide at that time. For now, though, enjoy!"

"And you, Robert? Are you sure?"

"Dawn, you wouldn't be here if we weren't sure. We want to have you with us."

Dawn took a deep breath and let it out. "So how do we start?"

Alyssa took Dawn's hand and pulled her down to Robert's waist. Taking Robert's hard cock in her hand, she pulled Dawn's head toward it. "Suck this a little, then let me have a turn."

"I don't know if I can get that all in my mouth. Billy isn't that long or wide."

"Start with licking the tip, and go from there."

Dawn licked the underside of Robert's cock, moving to licking the entire head and taking it in her mouth, before licking the underside and repeating the sequence. This time, when she took the head, she went deeper, sucking and fluttering her tongue against the shaft until the tip bumped the back of her throat. She gagged, pulled back, then plunged down again and again.

"Oh, that's good, Dawn," Robert moaned.

"My turn." Alyssa raised Dawn's chin, pulling her off Robert, and plunged her mouth over the hard cock, taking all of it into her throat, not stopping until her nose pressed his stomach. She pulled back and plunged down again, this time remaining in place and extending her tongue to tickle Robert's balls. Robert moaned again and entwined both hands in her hair, showing his appreciation. After another moment, Alyssa pulled off and smiled at Dawn's shocked expression. "Don't be alarmed. You can learn to do that too, with some practice." She kissed Dawn on the mouth, twisting her tongue with the more naive woman's. "Now let's fuck him."

"Slide down a little, Babe. I'm going to ride your face while she rides your cock." Alyssa lifted Dawn's knee so she could straddle Robert's hips. She raised Dawn by cupping her breasts and lifting, then reached down with one hand and guided Robert's cock to Dawn's wet, spread lips. She gripped her breast and pulled downward, lowering Dawn's body the same way she raised it. As his wide head split her lips and entered her, Alyssa released her holds. "You're in control. Take as much as you want as you stretch. I'll show you what's next after you take it all."

Alyssa leaned against the headboard and idly stroked her pussy with one hand and her breasts with the other. "That's it, Babe. Stretch out that tight pussy." She looked at Dawn. "Feel that cock. It really hits all the right spots, doesn't it? You love how full you feel."

Robert watched more of his cock disappear inside Dawn as she rode him. She was tight, and he felt the spongy G-spot with his head. She took more, and her hard cervix pressed against his tip before he slid to the side. Her eyes widened, and she moaned, "Oh god, yes."

Dawn's tan lines started to flush pink. She stayed longer on the downstroke, grinding her hips while she flicked her fingers across her nipples. Her breath grew ragged, and her stomach rippled. She dropped her body down hard to Robert's abs, taking all of his cock. "Oh yes. Oh, fuck me." Dawn put both hands on Robert's chest to steady herself as she began to bounce and roll her hips.

⌀

"Now you're ready," Alyssa smiled as she straddled Robert's head, facing Dawn and lowering her pussy to his searching tongue. She arched her back, pushing her opening onto his mouth. She cupped her own tits, hefting them upward and pinching the nipples between her thumbs and forefingers. She opened her eyes to watch Dawn. Her perfect hair had become tousled, and her hairline was wet with sweat. Her eyes focused where Alyssa's clit rested on Robert's chin as she ground her body on his cock. *She's into it. Into us.*

Alyssa released her own breasts and reached forward to cup Dawn's. Dawn squeaked and looked at Alyssa with wide eyes before raising her hands to Alyssa's tits, mirroring her movements. Alyssa pressed on Dawn's breasts, forcing her to lean back. The shift pressed the large cock inside her against the soft area around her cervix with all her weight, shocking Dawn. She adjusted her movements to drive his cockhead into that spot every time she bottomed out on him.

After another few strokes, Dawn's eyelids fluttered and her mouth formed an *O* shape. *She's coming again.* Alyssa pinched her nipples and pulled them out, driving Dawn to yell. Her body shuddered and stiffened before collapsing forward into Alyssa's arms. Alyssa climbed off Robert, laid Dawn beside him, then turned and straddled him, lining his cock up at her drenched opening and taking him to the root in one movement. She moaned as she chased the orgasm already building within her.

She rode him upright for a few strokes while he played with her tits, then leaned down to kiss him. "That's it, Babe. You thought I wanted someone else tonight, but I love your cock best. Show me why I love it best. Fuck me and make me come."

Robert grabbed her hips with both hands and rolled on top of her, never pulling out. "You were a naughty tease tonight. You need me to remind you what's at home? Here's what's at home!" Robert grabbed behind both her knees and pushed her legs upward, bending her in half and tilting her pelvis. Alyssa's breathing became more difficult, but the top of her pussy tingled in anticipation of what was to come.

From this angle, Robert's cockhead drove into her G-spot and cervix with every delicious insertion. He pounded into her as if his fury could drive her to orgasm. *It can.*

"Play with your tits," Robert commanded, and Alyssa complied. *Yes. Command me like you own me.* She moved her hands to her breasts, squeezing them and rolling the nipples, unable to tell if the intense pleasure sparking between them came from her hard pinches or because he commanded it, and unwilling to care.

Alyssa felt a hand on her belly and looked over at Dawn. She had moved closer and was staring at Alyssa's face as her hand crept down Alyssa's moist stomach to flick her clit as Robert stabbed inside her. Dawn smiled as Alyssa moaned.

Alyssa's vaginal walls rippled against Robert's hard cock, her orgasm coaxing his to begin. She wanted him to come with her. He thrust all the way inside her, spreading her from opening to end, and hot cum splashed on her cervix. She could feel the hot fluid coating her cervix, spreading from the force of his delivery.

He delivered every drop at point blank range, warming her cervix and making her belly spasm as she continued to climax.

Alyssa stilled and breathed two deep breaths before Robert released her legs and rested on her, kissing her gently. "I love you, Alyssa."

"I love you, too, Robert." Alyssa pulled him down for another kiss. He rolled beside her and rested his hand lovingly on her belly.

They both looked at Dawn. She had risen on her elbow, her head resting in her hand. She looked sweaty and content, with the hint of a smile on her face. She had pushed her hair behind her head in one sweaty, tangled mass. Her flushed breasts rose and fell with her deep breathing. Her free hand lazily traced circles around her puffy red pussy.

"You look like you enjoyed it," Alyssa said to her. "How do you feel?"

"God, I feel good. You get that every night? I'd never get out of bed."

They all chuckled. "Ah, to be independently wealthy," Robert mused. "Like everyone else, we do have to get out of bed sometimes."

"Our sex isn't always that good," Alyssa added. "Tonight was better because we were all excited with tonight's events, and the company." She reached out her arm, inviting Dawn to snuggle in.

"No, our sex is always this good. Every single time, no matter what," Robert smiled. "Seriously, though, we had let it get stale for a while. A long while. We rediscovered the excitement and energy we used to have." He stroked Dawn's face, which now rested on Alyssa's shoulder.

"What made it better?"

"I cheated. No, that doesn't tell the story. I had a weeklong sex fest on a trip. I went out of control with multiple partners, both men and women. Nearly ruined our marriage.”

“How did that make everything better?”

“When I got home, I fucked Robert’s brains out. I rode his body to remind myself what I had at home, and to remind him what we used to have. Then I confessed, and he left.”

“That was a bad night.” Robert took a long blink before continuing. “I was hurt and wanted to hurt Alyssa. I was ready to divorce her. I ended up giving her a test. I wanted to see if she was actually committed to our marriage, and I wanted to make her feel the hurt I had felt. I didn’t think she would pass, but as you can see, she is an amazing lady.”

“What kind of test?”

“I had to arrange a woman for Robert to have unbridled sex with for one night, and I had to watch all of it.”

“Oh my god. That’s brutal.”

“It was less than what I did behind his back. The watching was hard, especially when he invited her to fuck and sleep in my spot in our bed. I gritted my teeth and watched. I’m so glad I did. Do you think you would want to try something like that with Billy?”

“No. Well, I don’t think so. Tonight has shown me so much. I have hated Billy for a long time but stayed because I didn’t think I deserved better. Right now, I feel more confident, more worthy. I’ll think about it again in the morning. I’ll have to go home and face him, and he’s never pleasant when he is hungover.”

“You can stay here in the hotel if you want. I booked a room for you through the end of the month, in case you needed to stay. It’s one floor down. The keys are by the TV.”

“Really?”

“Had you told me that,” Robert interjected, “you would have saved some hurt feelings.”

"You walked away from the check-in before I could, and you also declined to walk me to the restroom. I didn't have a chance to tell you my secret elsewhere." Alyssa smiled and reached for his cock, feeling it begin to harden.

"Blaming me hurts, Baby," Robert said with a smile. He looked at Dawn. "You see we don't have this communication thing fully worked out yet."

"Enough talk," Alyssa said, looking at Dawn. "Are you ready to learn more?"

Dawn raised her head. "We aren't done?"

"Not unless you want to be. But if you want to sleep, Alyssa and I will probably bounce the bed a bit first."

"I'm not used to more than once per night. Show me more."

"All right." Alyssa pushed the other two off her and sat against the headboard. "Why don't you use that beautiful mouth of yours to suck Robert's cum out of me? Maybe you make me come before Robert makes you come."

"I have never done this before."

"You'll do fine. Robert will eat you before he fucks you. Do what he does. Then do to me what you like having done to you."

"I'm not sure what I like, so tell me if I do this wrong?"

"Sweetie, dive in with some enthusiasm. There's no way to do it wrong." Alyssa used both hands to guide Dawn between her splayed legs. She tilted her hips upward to give Dawn better access and pulled her head forward. Robert got onto his back behind Dawn and slid his head forward under her hips. He pulled her hips down to his face.

Dawn pulled back from Alyssa. "There is no way you come first if he keeps doing that." She lowered her head and imitated Robert's technique, licking from the base of Alyssa's slit to her clit, flicking it before starting again at the bottom. Dawn swallowed the cum that flowed onto her tongue as she licked.

Alyssa arched her back when Dawn flicked her clit. "Don't be so sure," she gasped.

Dawn licked and swallowed, using her hands to part Alyssa's lips so she could dig deeper. She pulled Alyssa's inner lips with her mouth, just as Robert did to her. She thrust her tongue into Alyssa, pulling cum out to taste. Dawn moaned into Alyssa's pussy, then Robert slid from beneath her.

Dawn looked over her shoulder, but Alyssa grabbed her head and shoved it right back between her legs. "Don't stop. You ready for him to fuck you?"

Dawn nodded, dragging her tongue across Alyssa's clit, making her moan, "So close. Keep going. Use your fingers."

Dawn groaned into Alyssa's pussy when Robert slid into her. The vibration shocked Alyssa's clit, sending sparks deep into her body. Dawn slipped a finger into Alyssa and rotated it until it pressed hard on the back wall before pulling out. Her hand rotated as she slid back in, pressing hard on the front wall. As Dawn's finger pulled out, her tongue kept licking Alyssa's clit. Dawn added a second finger, and the two separated inside her, stretching Alyssa's opening by running the fingers along separate sides from bottom to top. Alyssa squeezed her thighs around Dawn's ears and came. Dawn lapped up the surge of juice that flowed out, bringing the last of Robert's cum with it.

Robert must have noticed how Dawn spread and rotated her fingers in Alyssa's pussy, because his movement changed, taking on a circular motion. Dawn moaned again and began to rotate her hips in time with his strokes. Dawn pulled her hand off Alyssa and reached between her own legs.

Alyssa relaxed her thighs. Robert thrust into Dawn and forced her face tight against Alyssa's mound until her legs stopped quivering.

"Show her some love, Robert, before you finish," Alyssa whispered.

He nodded and rolled Dawn onto her back. He leaned forward and kissed her as he slid his cock inside. After a few strokes, he leaned back. Alyssa smiled, knowing what his curved cock would do to her G-spot in that position. He held her breasts as he slowly stroked in and out of her. Dawn raised her knees and moved to meet his thrusts. "I'm coming again," she panted.

"I'm close too," Robert said.

"Fill me, Robert. Come inside me. Let me feel you." Then Dawn's eyes rolled up, and her back arched. She hooked her ankles behind his ass and held him deep inside her as he moaned. "Oh god, yes," Dawn whispered before relaxing her legs and sagging into the mattress.

Alyssa kissed the back of her husband's head as he lay on top of Dawn, snuggling her while she recovered. She dropped her head and kissed Dawn's cheek. "That is how you deserve to feel every time, honey. You should be this drained every time."

Dawn looked at Robert. "Is that how you make love?"

"No. I only make love with Alyssa. But I made our sex feel like making love. I hope you felt that."

Through blurred vision, Dawn looked at Robert and smiled. "I felt it. Thank you." She sniffed and wiped her eyes. "No offense, but that was so much better than that time after the prom."

Robert laughed. "That was our first time. We loved each other, but we didn't know what we were doing back then."

Dawn's face fell. "That was my best time until tonight."

"Wow." Alyssa stroked Dawn's cheek. "Now you know what you are missing. You can find better, if you decide to."

"I'll need to get divorced first, and I don't want to think about that now. I'm exhausted. Where is that room?"

"Oh no," Alyssa replied. "You're sleeping right here with us."

"That's right. You stay right here tonight. Besides, do you really want to get dressed and wander around the hotel at four in the morning?"

"That sounds so good. Thank you for this. For everything."

25

SUNDAY, MARCH 28, REUNION HOTEL

ROBERT WOKE WHEN he felt the bed move on his left. He watched Dawn pick up her clothes and walk nude into the bathroom.

"She is beautiful, isn't she?" Alyssa whispered in his ear.

"She is. Too bad she stayed with Billy. I hope she can get past it. How did you know?"

"My aunt Phyllis. She was beautiful but downtrodden. Mom always felt sorry for her, but Dad insisted she knew what kind of man she married, and if she wanted to be rid of him, all she had to do was leave. She was protective of her place with him, even though everyone could see how bad it was. Dawn acted just the same way. She had that same look in her eyes." Alyssa moved so her leg and arm draped over Robert, then gave him a full-body hug.

"We haven't seen her in years. Is she still alive?"

Alyssa shook her head. "I remember meeting Phyllis's

husband, David, at a family reunion when I was about sixteen. He was talking to my dad, bragging about how well connected he was. He said, 'I know everything about you, from how much money you make to your wife's bra size, and that makes me the winner.' He made my skin crawl, and that was before he tried to fondle me when we were carrying stuff from the kitchen. Billy acted just the same way. It wasn't hard to put two and two together."

"I'm glad you were right. It would have been a bad night if you had been wrong about her."

"Probably not. I wasn't wrong about him, for sure, and I wanted to show your classmates who the best man is and make him pay for the way he treated you. Helping her was an impulse. If she had been bitchy, she would have been embarrassed by Billy's behavior, and that would have been that."

"Glad I was nice," Dawn said from the bathroom door.

"We are too," Robert responded.

"I thought I'd go to that room now, if the offer still stands. It's still early, so fewer people will see me looking like I just got fucked senseless." She waved her hands from her head down to the hem of her dress like a model showing her wares.

Alyssa cocked her head. "You're a little disheveled, but it's nothing a shower and some fresh clothes won't fix."

"Yeah. I have to figure out how to get my stuff from the house. I can't wear this dress all week."

"You should be good. Tanya has been busy this morning. Robert's phone has been lighting up with texts."

"It has? I didn't notice."

"You never do, Babe. You sleep too soundly. I saw your screen light up every few minutes and looked at the notifications when I went to the bathroom in the night." Alyssa smiled at him. "I hope I never get stuck on the side of the road after you have gone to bed. I'll have to wait until you wake up the next morning."

"I know, I know. Tell Dawn what Tanya has arranged and stop picking on me."

"You're lucky, Dawn. Several classmates have lined up to help you. Tanya, Burt, and a couple of other couples will go with you this morning to your house to help you get what you need. There is another guy who went to school with you, Clint Lawton, who is a divorce attorney. He's ready to talk with you, if that is what you want. Another of your classmates, Jodi Coats, wasn't here last night. She is a therapist who specializes in abusive relationships, and she's available too. That's what I saw. There is probably more. Tanya is quite persuasive."

Dawn sat on the edge of the bed and wrung her hands in her lap. "I never knew people would want to help me. If I had known sooner…" She sighed and looked at Robert. "Can you send me the texts about all this, please?" She handed him her phone. "Text yourself so you will have my number, and forward those." Her eyes went wide, and she snatched at the phone. "Wait. If I am going to get divorced, texts might look like I cheated on him. Shit, and I left the reunion with you two instead of him. Shit. He's going to kick my ass one last time in court."

"Billy works as a home inspector, right?" Robert asked.

Dawn cocked her head. "That's right, but why does that matter?"

"A lot of people have seen how he acted at these reunions. Groping women, propositioning them, maybe getting a few to cheat on their husbands, all in a public place." Robert paused. "That type of information becomes public in court. His employer might not want him to go into other people's homes, particularly homes where a woman is there alone, if he learned of that testimony. You will want to work with Clint, but Billy might be more agreeable once he knows what will be said."

Dawn nodded, then shook her head. "All those people saw us leave together last night too. There was even that discussion of sharing Robert with me."

"And none of those people saw you come in here. They know we walked you to the room we reserved for you and left. You stayed there, alone with your thoughts, all night." Alyssa lifted Dawn's chin and winked at her. "And there is no way I would ever share my husband with another woman. What kind of deviant does that?"

&

"Okay, mister. It's time to take back what's mine." The door had barely closed when Alyssa leaped into Robert's arms and wrapped her legs around him. She kissed him, lowered her feet to the floor, and pushed his chest so he fell onto the bed. "Slide up and get your head on a pillow. This is going to take a while," she purred.

Robert propped his head on two pillows while Alyssa crawled between his legs and dipped her mouth to his hardening cock. She looked at his face and smiled, then raised her ass in the air so he could see it frame her bobbing head. She pressed her tongue against the underside of his shaft, and his head reached the entrance of her throat. "Your cock tastes like pussy, but not mine. I'll have to clean the whole thing, won't I?"

"Yes, you will."

She grinned and took his cock into her mouth again, this time swallowing and pressing her nose against his abdomen as he filled her throat. She cupped his balls as she drooled down his cock with every stroke. She pulled off. "That tastes clean."

She moved up his body until her hips straddled his. She

kissed him, then rose and placed the tip of his cock between her wet lips. As she pushed down, she groaned from deep in her chest and threw back her head. Robert cupped her breasts. Alyssa snapped her head forward, glaring into his eyes and pulling his hands over his head, leaning into his face. "No. I'm doing the work here. You fucked someone else last night, and I will remind you whose pussy fits your cock best. I'm going to reclaim you as mine, and you don't get to pleasure me until I've done that." She kissed him, hard, shoving her tongue deep into his mouth. "You lie back and let me make you feel loved."

Alyssa began pounding her hips up and down on his shaft, the long strokes pulling back until he almost slipped out, then bottoming out when his head hit the end of her tunnel. Over and over, Alyssa pounded him into her. On her last downstroke, she stopped and moved her hips in small circles, rubbing the head of his cock around her cervix. She squeezed her walls together around him, tugging and urging him to come. She pressed her hands against his chest and ran them along his ribs, keeping her balance for the energetic ride. She dripped sweat onto his chest and vaginal fluid down his balls. Her hair stuck to her face as her head lolled back and forth, and she lost herself in pleasure.

She leaned forward to kiss and nibble Robert's neck and shifted her ride to a forward-and-back grind. His breath quickened, and his hands found her ass, guiding her back and forth. "Here I come, Baby," he growled as he shoved his cock into her as deep as it would go and held her in place. Jets of cum soaked Alyssa's overworked pussy and detonated her orgasm.

"Uhn, that's good," she moaned in his ear as her orgasm peaked. She ground her clit against his pubic bone, not letting a drop of his cum escape her clenching pussy. She sagged onto him and snugged her arms and legs against the sides of his body and legs. He wrapped his arms around her, gently caressing her back.

After a moment, he pulled her head up for a kiss. "I love you, Baby. I'll always be yours, and you'll always be mine."

Alyssa kissed him back. "I love you too. I'll always come back to you, my love." She squeezed tighter against him, then raised her head. "As for getting home, if we hurry, we can shower before checkout time. Want me to wash your back?"

26

WEDNESDAY, MARCH 31, HOME

Alyssa kissed Robert as he headed toward the door for work. "Babe, this is the last day of our trial period. Let's not play today. Let's go to dinner early and talk about it tonight. Then, and this is the best part, celebrate between the sheets. Can I talk you into that?"

"That sounds great." He grinned at her. "I'll have to give up nailing the CEO's secretary on his desk before lunch, but if it's what you want, I'm in." He wrapped his arms around her waist and kissed her again. "Where do you want to eat?"

"Surprise me."

"Ruth's Chris it is. I'll meet you here at five thirty?"

"Mm-hmm. See you then, Babe."

Robert sighed when his phone rang at 6:15. "You aren't home yet, Baby. Tough day?"

"Yes. The class this afternoon went terribly. One guy cut his hand so deep we had to call an ambulance, which put us behind. Then another student triggered the fire suppression system. We are just now finishing the cleanup. I'm sorry I'm late."

"It's all right. We can still go out. It won't be Ruth's Chris. They are booked for the rest of the night."

"Shoot. I was looking forward to the stuffed chicken." She was quiet a minute. "I have an idea. Why don't you bring me some clothes, and we can just go across the street to the Embassy."

Robert couldn't believe what he heard. "The Embassy? After what happened the last time you were there? What makes you think I want to go there? What makes *you* want to go there?"

Robert listened to Alyssa breathe through the phone. After her initial gasp, she had calmed, but she had not spoken for nineteen seconds.

"I hadn't thought about it. It's convenient to the office, so it's our default option when schedules are tight. I see what you mean though."

Robert envisioned her spinning her wedding rings as she thought. She needed to resolve this, so he waited.

"Here's what I think, Babe. First, what happened there was a statistically improbable confluence of circumstances."

"Nice way to make it sound scientific."

"I mean it. I was there for a last-minute function. The men I encountered had a room, so they clearly aren't local. I was exhausted, drunk, horny, and leaving alone. All those things played into my behavior, and none of them apply tonight, and you will be there to fend off any unruly hotel guests."

Robert sighed. "Okay, I'll grant you the statistically improbable confluence of circumstances. Don't you have bad memories? Do you think I might?"

"Babe, I have few memories of that night, more of just a general impression. My painful memories are more of the aftermath: seeing the pain on your face when I came home, knowing how I hurt you and Clay when I missed the meeting and our planned rendezvous, the physical pain I know I deserved. Those memories are clear but taint other places, places I love and will not relinquish because of one stupid mistake."

"My memories don't count?"

"Babe, of course they do. Do you remember the first New Year's Eve party we attended when we moved to town?"

"I'll never forget it. We went by ourselves because we didn't know anyone, and ended up meeting friends we still have today. We stayed up all night with them and had to check out before we even slept."

"And the time we had to have the house fumigated because of brown recluse spiders?"

"Yes. We were pissed, but the kids loved the adventure of being in a hotel. They still talk about it."

"And where did those events occur?"

Robert sighed. "The Embassy."

Alyssa's voice softened. "Babe, are you willing to sacrifice those good memories and dozens of others because of one bad one? Don't answer, just think about it. Think about one more thing. Again, practically, how many truly good restaurants are in this town? Five, maybe six? The Embassy is one of them. Are you willing to strike it off the list because of what happened? Something that could statistically never happen again in a million years?"

"You have thought through this, Alyssa."

"Not before this conversation, but I would have had to. We

use it all the time at work, and eventually I would have had to go. I'd prefer it if you were there to protect me the first time I go back."

"Okay, you have convinced me. We can't abandon the Embassy Suites."

"Good. We have made so many memories there. Just like I plan to do tonight. We are going to have a wonderful celebratory dinner, just the two of us. It won't be steak, but the chef there is really good, and it is convenient and casual. We can finish early and get home for some nookie."

Robert laughed. "That's a deal. Do you want clothes in particular?"

"Just jeans and that blue button-down. You'd better throw in a fresh bra and panties, too, if you don't want me to smell too bad."

"Will do. I'll Uber over so we can ride home together."

"Ooh. That sounds great, Babe. I can reward you on the ride home for coming to my rescue yet again."

27

WEDNESDAY, MARCH 31, EMBASSY SUITES

AN HOUR LATER, Alyssa and Robert were sipping wine in a secluded corner booth in the restaurant. "Thank goodness. I didn't think today would ever end. Thanks for grabbing the deodorant when you packed."

"I want to enjoy tonight, so…"

"Funny." She took his hand across the table. "Really, thanks. I wanted tonight to be special for us, and because of you, I don't smell like fire extinguisher."

"Tonight is special because we are together."

"I know. I'm glad." She looked at him a long minute. She had intended to think through this conversation during the day, but life happened. Alyssa's stomach roiled that much more. Not having a good idea of Robert's views made it worse. She had known his mind on almost everything for twenty-two years, but tonight's topic escaped her. *It was your idea, so it's your conversation*

271

to start. Just jump in. "With our trial month of open marriage over, what do you think?"

"It's been difficult. Sleeping with other women has been enjoyable, but knowing you were with other men was hard, especially when it seemed like you wanted something in lieu of me."

Alyssa shook her head but held her tongue. *Maybe in addition to you.* Never *in lieu.*

"That said, our sex together has been great, and I feel like we are a little closer. What about you?"

Alyssa smiled as hope warmed her chest. Robert felt good about their arrangement to the point he thought it had brought them closer. The way he had reacted over the last month, she'd thought he would be done with it. *He won't believe this, but it's the truth.* "I was worried I would be jealous when you slept with other women, but watching you with Summer and Dawn—oh, and Carol too—was so hot. You are like my very own porn star, and you made me so horny." Alyssa paused. She didn't want to tell Robert the rest. It might change his mind on the whole thing. Her feelings embarrassed her, even with him. She clenched her abs and spoke. "The hard part for me was when I was with other men."

Robert's eyes narrowed. He cocked his head to the side like when he didn't understand. "How so? Isn't that the part you wanted?"

The same question I asked myself. I didn't like my answer. Alyssa looked up from the table. Robert was watching her, his face neutral with just enough smile around his eyes to let her know she could tell him anything without repercussion. She made eye contact for what may have been an instant or several seconds, and her stomach calmed. *I can tell him what I think of myself.* "I did want to sleep with other people, men and women. I still do. It's exciting and a little dirty. What I've thought about is that I never sought out these men. I just reacted and fell on my back when the opportunity presented itself. Honestly, that makes me feel cheap. I feel like any horny woman out to get laid."

"Wasn't that the point, to get laid?"

I don't want to be a slut. He doesn't want me to be either. Promoting a plan to have sex with other people as a noble pursuit was a difficult task, particularly advocating it to your husband. Alyssa swallowed the lump in her throat before answering. "Yes. I wanted to add some spice to our love life. I think we did that, and I don't want to give it up, but I want to do it better."

"What do you mean, better?"

Robert's question gave Alyssa hope that he would agree, though she knew he sometimes used questions as barriers. She had to continue to explain. "It started when I dropped Cole for not being a considerate lover. I was a good friend with Jessica, and I got better with Dawn and Billy last weekend. I want to experience sex outside our marriage, but I want it to be intentional, and I want to feel something beyond just pleasure. I want it to be good and for good reasons."

Robert frowned. "Wait a second. This experiment was about just spicing up our sex lives, not falling in love with anyone else. I'm not on board with trying to find people to fall in love with."

He took that the wrong way. A twinge of panic took hold in Alyssa's belly. Her hands quivered on the table as she sought a different way to explain. She shook her head. "Neither am I. I just think, well, I don't want to fall in love with other people, but I want to feel like I helped them in some way, or did some good somehow. Oh, I don't know what I'm trying to say."

"I don't know what you are saying either. It sounds like you are trying to bring people into our marriage. I don't want that." His frown set firmer in his brow, and his lips tightened.

Alyssa felt a clamminess settle onto her face, the way it did when you felt nauseous. *I have to make him understand.* "It sounded better in my head, Babe. I think what I mean is that helping Summer felt right, even though sex with Bryce wasn't very good. Helping Dawn felt right, even though I let Billy grope me like a teenager. Dropping Cole felt right, even though the sex was good." She looked down at the table. *No. Don't hide from this part.* She looked him in the eye. "Being with the three men a couple of weeks ago didn't feel right, even though the sex was—sorry, Babe—mind-blowing. In fact, I almost called off our trial period then." Robert's eyes widened just enough for Alyssa to notice, and her hands stopped shaking. "I still want variety, but I want to be more proactive about who I take those chances with. Does that make more sense?" Alyssa smiled. She knew that look on her husband's face. It was the one she wanted.

Robert nodded. "It sounds like you have worked through the infatuation phase with this relationship. You have eaten your fill of the free candy at the candy store, and you're ready to be a little more selective. Is that it?"

She gripped both his hands with hers across the table and beamed her best smile. "God, I love you. Yes, that is exactly what I was trying to say." She looked at him, lowering her smile, letting him see her sincerity. "I want sex outside our marriage to be good and thoughtful. Sometimes that will be just fun, but occasionally, maybe we can help someone."

"So you want to continue to be open."

His tone made Alyssa look at the table. *He's still deciding. I thought he wanted this too.* "Yes." She looked to his face. Panic exploded from her belly and untethered her mouth from her brain. Her speech accelerated. "Do you? If you don't, I won't pressure you, and the experiment is over. I know this has been hard for you. I'm sorry if it hasn't been good. So do you?" She watched him for any response, nervous like a child asking for a new toy.

Robert looked up, then back to Alyssa. "Yes, Alyssa. I want to stay open also. I like that you want to be a little more deliberate about your partners. I hope that means you will be more deliberate about your communication too."

Her body relaxed in a wave, releasing from her head downward until her toes uncurled with a cramp. *I didn't realize I had been flexing those.* She nodded. "Always. I've learned my lesson."

"You think so? This time?"

Alyssa laughed but understood his seriousness. She waited until her giggle ended, then made eye contact. "Yes, after all these tries, I finally learned. I'll keep you informed of what I'm planning. If I don't, how will you come rescue me?"

Robert shook his head. "We'll see."

⁓

The food was excellent, and the waitress left them alone to enjoy their intimate dinner. They ordered a dessert, and Alyssa stood. "I need to run to the restroom. I'll be right back, Babe."

"The last time you went to the restroom here, you didn't come home. Are you all right, or should I accompany you?"

"Well, I am horny enough to be led to a room but only by you. I'll be right back."

Alyssa checked her makeup before returning to the table. She saw the door open in her peripheral vision. She put the lipstick in her purse and turned to go, then froze when confronted with the person by the door.

"I remember you. The last time you were in here, you wanted a giant cock."

Alyssa crouched to peek under the stalls. *Nobody.* She stood to face the towering redhead. *She's a lot taller when she is off her knees.* "And you had that cock's giant load all over your face and tits."

"I wanted that cock that night. You stole it."

"Believe me, I regret it."

"Did you really take all three of them at once?"

Alyssa's hand went to her chest. "Who told you that?"

"They did."

Oh shit. Shit. Shit. It had been indiscreet enough that she knew about Alyssa's tryst and appeared upset about it, but a bathroom confrontation could make this public and unmanageable. "When?"

"That night. My shift ended at two, and I was going to join all of you in the room. They were leaving for the airport, and we met at the elevator. I rode down with them. The loudmouth one gave me the key and told me I could have you if I wanted to take you."

"They offered me to you?"

She nodded. "Yes. I admit, I came to see you. You were snoring and a mess, so I went home."

She wanted me. Alyssa's nipples hardened. "I'm sorry I took your place that night."

"Don't be. They will be back. They stay here when they come to town every month. I just wanted the one. I didn't know they teamed up." She looked down, then back up at Alyssa. "I wish I had been earlier that night."

"Why? You saw what they did to me."

"Yes, that looked rough. But I wanted to try that big cock. And maybe if I had been there, it wouldn't have been as rough on you. They could have had me too." She blushed. "And maybe we could have given them a show to take a rest from the pounding."

Alyssa smiled at the twinge of heat in her pussy. "That would have been nice. You are beautiful. I wish you had joined us earlier too."

"Thank you for saying that, but you are the beautiful one. Look at you. You are perfect."

"No, sweetie. I'm far from perfect. Thank you for saying so, nonetheless."

The redhead stepped forward just enough to cross one ankle over the other. Her hands met just below her crotch. She tilted her head and looked at Alyssa's chest. "Are you here looking for company?"

"Ah, um, no. I'm with my husband."

"Oh. I hoped you might be in the hotel looking for someone."

"We are having dinner." Alyssa stepped forward. "Are you looking for someone?"

She huffed. "I'm a waitress in a hotel, I don't have to look for anyone. They come on to me." She stepped toward Alyssa. "But I saw you come in here, and I came looking for you."

Alyssa smiled. *I'm getting wet.* "I'm flattered. Like I said, I'm with my husband."

"I'm sorry. I didn't mean to offend you. I wasn't sure if that was husband or 'husband,' but you are too beautiful not to ask."

"What's your name, sweetie?"

"Keegan. Keegan Meyler."

"I'm Alyssa Davis. The man I'm with is my husband, and we're celebrating tonight. We have to work tomorrow, so if you work until two, you won't be able to join us. Maybe another time."

Keegan held up her hands. "I'm working the restaurant tonight, and I'm off at nine. I go both ways. Maybe I can help you celebrate?"

Maybe Robert would want to celebrate one month of an open marriage by using their open marriage. *I think I would.* "Let me make a call." Alyssa dialed Robert.

"Is everything okay, Baby?"

On impulse, Alyssa decided to play a little and surprise him with the beautiful waitress. "It's better than okay. I'll be at the table in a minute."

"So why are you calling, my dear?"

"No need to be sarcastic, Babe. I'm calling because I decided I want to be open tonight, and I wanted to know if you want to be too."

Robert sighed, then said in a low voice, "I thought tonight was just for us, that we are celebrating."

She can bring his dessert, then be his dessert. "We are celebrating. It will be a fantastic celebration. Keegan is just what the doctor ordered."

"Keegan? Jesus Christ, Alyssa. What was all that about being deliberate and selective?"

"Babe, trust me, I'm being very deliberate and highly selective. Will you think about it, and we can decide over dessert?"

"I don't think I want you celebrating with this Keegan guy instead of me tonight, but we can discuss it when you get back. Bye."

Keegan looked at Alyssa. "That didn't sound good. Maybe I'd better leave."

"Nonsense." Alyssa stepped to Keegan and unbuttoned her blouse to show her bra. "We are in the back corner booth. Find a way to take over our table, and everything will be fine. But hurry. He needs to see you before he gets upset with me."

Alyssa sat down, and Robert leaned across the table to speak in hushed tones.

"What the fuck, Alyssa? You can't stop picking people up in the bathroom here? Not even when you're with me? You do remember the part of our agreement about respecting each other, right?"

Alyssa smiled at Robert and reached to take his hand. "I have nothing but respect for you. Well, respect and love. And admiration. And lust. And an almost fanatical devotion—"

"Using old jokes? After what you asked? Not funny."

Alyssa leaned forward, making eye contact with him. His eyes blazed. *Maybe teasing him about this was a bad idea. Be serious.* "I'm not joking, Babe. I think bringing Keegan to bed with us tonight would be a wonderful way to celebrate. But we won't if you don't want to. I won't even make you say 'confessional.' Just say no. But will you at least see what you are rejecting before you do?"

"To bed with us? You want to bring this Keegan home to our bed and let him fuck you while I'm there? What do you want me to do? Watch? Have you lost your mind?"

"You and I both know our home is off-limits. We could get a room here instead, and I expect you to participate. I expect you will want to participate, but if you don't want to, we won't do anything. Would that be acceptable?"

"Here is better than home, but I'm not ready to participate with another man, and I sure as hell don't want to watch. Are you trying to upset me, especially here?"

"Oh, look, Babe. Dessert's here."

They leaned back from the table as the slice of chocolate cake was set between them. Robert's scowl never left Alyssa's face.

Alyssa looked at the server. "Thank you." She looked back at Robert. "Robert, don't be rude because you are mad at me. Look this person in the eye and thank her."

Robert's mouth dropped open, and his head flushed red. He turned to the side and started to speak, then adjusted his face as his eyes roamed up the long, slim body, pausing at the open shirt barely hiding the large breasts beneath. When his eyes reached hers, his face softened. "I apologize. I was rude. Thank you for bringing this, young lady."

"You are welcome, sir. You were only a little bit rude." She smiled. "The look you gave me made up for it."

Robert blushed as the waitress walked away.

Alyssa joined Robert in watching her walk. "She has a great ass too. She's the hottest thing in here tonight, don't you think, Babe?"

Robert turned to his wife and smiled. "No, Baby. Not even close. You are the hottest thing in here tonight."

"Maybe, but I think you are biased."

"Yep. I'm biased. It doesn't mean I'm wrong."

"I think she wants you. Did you see her shirt?"

"It was open before she came over here. She works for tips, you know."

"I think you could have her if you asked."

"Trying to get me to let you celebrate with that guy Keegan again?"

Alyssa laughed. "Babe, she *is* Keegan. I thought you and I could share her as part of our celebration. Are you interested?"

Robert rolled his eyes and blew out a breath. He leaned forward and pointed his finger at her. "Dammit, Alyssa. That was not a nice game you played." He shook his head and smirked at her. "I'm tempted to turn her down and make you only have me tonight, as a punishment."

Alyssa bounced in her seat, clapping her hands. "Excellent! Punish me like that again and again." She took his hand. "I do love and respect you, more than I thought possible, and yet I love and respect you even more each day. We decided to stay open, and I thought a beautiful, towering redhead might be a fun way to celebrate together." Alyssa sat still so he would know she was serious. "If you would rather it just be us, I'm thrilled to have your undivided attention. Either way, I'm happy.

Robert's mouth twisted into a smirk. "You already offered it to her, didn't you?"

"Kind of. She gets off in just a few minutes. We could be in a room naked in…" She turned his wrist to see his watch. "Eleven minutes. What do you think?"

Robert smiled. "You are a devious planner, Alyssa. I'll think about it."

Alyssa groaned. "Making me wait? Is this payback?"

"Payback hasn't started yet."

Keegan brought the check, and Robert handed her his card with a smile and a thank-you. When she returned with the receipt, he looked at her. "I hear my wife gave you an invitation."

"Yes, sir. Well, I kind of asked first."

"You asked to join us?"

"I asked to be with her. She offered for me to join the two of you."

"Are you still interested?"

She smiled and jumped a little, making her breasts jiggle. "Yes. I would love that."

"Are you sure? You really don't know us."

"I heard you on the phone when she asked you. What you said told me how much you love her. I want to feel some of that, if I can. It makes me feel safe even though I don't know you."

"My love is only for her, but I think we, together, will make you feel quite pleasured. And you will be completely safe, of course." He looked at his wife. "We have only one condition. Stay for as long as you would like, but you must leave by six a.m. Alyssa and I will need that time before we go to work to reclaim each other after being with you. Outside of that, we very much want to share ourselves with you. Please join us."

"Wow, you guys even plan how to reconnect? You do love

each other." Keegan grinned. "I'll be gone by six, but not a minute earlier."

Alyssa smiled. "Great! We'll get a room. You clock out, and we'll meet you by the elevator."

Keegan almost ran across the dining room into the back. Alyssa and Robert strolled arm in arm to the desk and got a room, then stood quietly at the elevator bank. Alyssa snuggled her body against him, feeling his hard muscles with her entire length and daydreaming. She opened her eyes when something touched her shoulder.

"Looks like you two are ready for me," laughed Keegan. "I'm so excited!" She hopped again, bouncing her breasts beneath the T-shirt she had changed into.

Alyssa turned and wrapped her hand around the tall woman's waist. "We are too. Let's go." She hit the up button.

⁓

Robert opened the door to allow Alyssa and Keegan to breeze through the living area into the bedroom portion of the suite, slowing only to flip on a light. Robert locked the suite door and followed right behind.

The women were entangled in each other, kissing and fondling. Robert smiled, removed his shoes and socks, and joined the embrace from behind Keegan, dipping his head to nibble her neck and shoulder. Alyssa turned one hand from Keegan's ass to hold his hardening cock, while Robert worked his hands between their chests, using one hand to cup Alyssa's breast and the other to cup Keegan's. Keegan's nipple jumped between his fingers through the thin T-shirt, and he thumbed his wife's through the button-down and thin bra he had brought her.

Alyssa moved her hands to the hem of the taller woman's shirt and raised it over her head, breaking their kiss. Her lips were on one of the rosy nipples before the shirt hit the floor, and Keegan threw her head back to moan, then turned to kiss Robert's mouth over her shoulder.

Robert traced his hands down Keegan's arms and sides, then ran them along her body above the waistband of her jeans, dipping his pinky finger inside the top. After a couple of passes, he stopped in front to unbutton and unzip them, then slid his hand inside on her smooth skin.

Alyssa knelt to pull the tight jeans to the floor and untied the white tennis shoes that prevented her from removing them entirely. Keegan stepped out of the shoes and jeans, supported by Robert's hands on her breast and pussy. Alyssa pressed the freckled thighs apart and began to kiss up the sensitive insides while brushing her fingertips up the backs until she kissed her husband's finger and pulled Keegan's ass cheeks apart to rub between them. She stood and claimed the redhead's mouth from her husband, kissing it hard and caressing Keegan's other breast from the underside. She slid her hand along Keegan's flat stomach and touched her husband's hand.

Robert moved both his hands to the full tits and pulled the hard nipples before kissing down Keegan's back to her ass. He kissed up and down both cheeks several times, nibbling his way to the center. He licked along her crack, sliding to the bottom and her pussy opening. Keegan leaned forward while spreading her legs and jutting her ass, letting Robert tongue her pussy.

Alyssa moved her hands back to Keegan's breasts, cupping them as they hung and pinching the nipples between her middle and ring fingers. Robert curled his hand around and used his fingers to frame the top of Keegan's pussy, then squeezed the lips together to put pressure on her clit. He moved his hand up and down, jacking her clit in time with lapping her opening. Keegan moaned into Alyssa's mouth and stiffened her legs. Robert felt her pelvic muscles clench and release, so he tightened his grip on her lips and lapped harder at her wet opening.

Keegan pressed forward into Alyssa as her ass cheeks clenched. Her pussy released a flood of juices over Robert's tongue, and her legs trembled. She let out a low purr. Robert kept licking her until her hand pushed the top of his head. "Stop, please. I can't take any more."

Robert stood and pulled Keegan upright, allowing Alyssa to stand. He walked her to the bed and helped her lie down. He turned to his wife and kissed her as his hands worked to unbutton her shirt one button at a time. He opened the shirt and let it fall from her arms, then reached behind her to unclasp her bra, letting it fall with the shirt. He kissed her collarbones and up her neck, to her ear as he unfastened her jeans and pulled them and the panties beneath down to her knees. He kissed his way to her breasts, taking time to kiss the full orbs before making his way to the bumpy areolae and hard nipples.

He kissed his way down her ribs and side, his tongue flicking her between the abs and obliques on the way to her pussy. As he knelt, he pushed the jeans and panties to her ankles, and Alyssa stepped out of the sandals, jeans, and panties all in one move. Robert nibbled the top of Alyssa's pussy and pulled his fingers up the backs of her legs and over her ass cheeks. He dipped his tongue again and flicked the end of her hard clit a few times before standing and kissing his wife on the mouth.

"It's your turn, Baby." He motioned for her to lie beside Keegan in the king-size bed. She did, and the women fell right into kissing and groping each other. Alyssa rolled onto her back, and Keegan moved over her, kissing her neck and moving to then suck and nibble her breasts. Robert took his time undressing as Keegan left Alyssa's breasts glistening and heaving to kiss farther down her body, getting on all fours between her legs to dive into her pussy.

Alyssa arched her back as Keegan licked between her legs. The young beauty followed her tongue with her hand, the motion of her elbow indicating she was feeling for Alyssa's G-spot. Keegan's mouth latched onto Alyssa's clit as her fingers worked. Alyssa began to flush red.

Robert watched the tall redhead pleasure his wife while he disrobed. He moved to the side of the bed so he could see while he stroked his cock to full hardness. His wife's eyes were closed in pleasure as she writhed her hips against Keegan's face, and he moved to the end of the bed behind Keegan. He lined his cock up with her wet opening and drove inside.

Keegan tensed when Robert's cock hit bottom inside her. She raised her head off the sopping pussy in her mouth to yelp. His head bumped the end of her tunnel, and her cervix bounced across his head as she rocked her hips. Robert gave her a few hard strokes as she writhed, then he placed his hand on the middle of her back and nudged her back onto his wife's pussy. When the red curls rested on his wife's hips, he drove into Keegan, bouncing her mouth against his wife's pussy and making both women grunt with each stroke.

When Keegan returned her face to Alyssa's pussy, her belly tensed, and she entwined both hands in Keegan's hair. Her chest flushed red, and the veins in her neck strained against her skin. Her legs crushed into the sides of Keegan's head, and although Keegan's arm stopped moving, Robert's thrusts pounded the pretty face into Alyssa's pussy, making her groan.

Alyssa's legs and arms fell to the side, and Keegan rested her head on Alyssa's belly as Robert fucked her from behind. He slowed a bit, rotating his hips to press on all sides of her opening as he slid in and out. She let out a continuous whine between breaths. The fluttering of her cervix across his cockhead typical of an orgasm continued with each stroke, teasing him when he bottomed out.

The pale skin of her ass and thighs flushed pink between the freckles, and her eyes rolled back in her head. Robert's cock swelled. He took one more hard thrust and shot his cum inside her. His weight pushed her limp body forward, moving her head between Alyssa's breasts, and Robert followed her down, keeping his cock in her cunt and lying on her back.

Robert rolled off Keegan, then pulled the limp girl off Alyssa, brushing her hair off her face as she lay on her back, panting. Alyssa rose onto her elbow. "I want more. Are you ready to give it to me?"

Robert laughed. "I'll need a minute, but not too long given the naked women in this room. That was hot. You came really hard."

"I could feel every thrust. It felt like she was fucking me with her face when you moved behind her." She nodded at Keegan. "I think she enjoyed it."

"I did. God, that was hot," Keegan murmured without opening her eyes.

Robert winked at Alyssa, then began to stroke one of Keegan's breasts.

Alyssa smiled at him and mirrored his movements on the other breast. "We thought you had passed out."

"Just enjoying the feeling. You two are amazing. I've never come like that in my life. And if you keep caressing my tits, I'm going to come again, and I have never come from just gentle hands."

Robert smiled and continued his ministrations. "Well, then let's give you a first." He bent his head to kiss her cheek and nodded for Alyssa to do the same. After she did, he stretched his neck to kiss her above Keegan's face, rubbing Keegan's breasts and nipples all the while.

"I love this feeling," Keegan whispered. "I feel loved."

Robert and Alyssa continued to kiss Keegan's face and rub her body. She began to mewl every minute or so when her body twitched. Her chest flushed pink. Keegan's flat belly rolled as her breathing hastened. Alyssa spoke up. "I can't wait any longer. Sorry, Keegan, now you will have to come on my tongue."

Alyssa moved her head between Keegan's lithe legs. Keegan's eyes shot open, and she pulled Alyssa's head into her sex, rolling her hips and tightening her legs against Alyssa's head. Alyssa pulled her head back only far enough to breathe through her nose before diving in again.

Robert stood, taking his hard cock behind his wife. He looked up at Keegan. "Let's flip her over. She really likes this. Roll to your right." Keegan kept Alyssa's head between her thighs and rolled to her right. Robert lifted his wife's hips and turned her body. Alyssa now lay on her back with Keegan astride her face and Robert moving between her legs at the end of the bed. He lined up to plunge into her and stopped, struck by the beauty in front of him. His eyes drifted from the curly red hair down the pale, muscular back to a narrow ass sitting on his wife's chin, with her amazing body lying in front of him, waiting for his cock. He watched Keegan's ass grind and his wife's chin nibble, then stuffed his cock inside. Alyssa moaned into Keegan's pussy, and the redhead smiled at him over her shoulder. He could only see her arms down to her elbows and knew she was playing with her own tits while she rode Alyssa's face. Alyssa was doing the same, pulling and rubbing her breasts while grinding her hips onto Robert.

Robert leaned back and touched his cockhead along Alyssa's front wall. She moaned again into Keegan, and Keegan's hips bucked. He stroked over and over, making Alyssa writhe more and more. Her skin had turned pink from her chin to her waist. She was covered in sweat. She pulled her nipples out far from her chest. She moaned into Keegan, who ground her pussy onto Alyssa's face and let her head flop as she moved.

Keegan climbed off Alyssa. She lay beside her and stroked her breast. "I can't take any more. I need a break."

Alyssa's moans filled the room now that they weren't muffled by Keegan's body. Keegan played with one breast while Alyssa moved her hand to her clit as Robert continued to fuck her. Alyssa balled up and squeezed her body together as she came, wailing. Robert kept fucking into her as best he could with her feet pressed on his belly. She whimpered and went limp. Robert let her legs fall beside him and hang off the end of the bed. Her eyes were closed, and her belly rose and fell with each gasping breath. Her hands still pulled at her nipple and stroked her clit, though much slower than a moment ago. Robert pulled his cock from her. A string of juice hung suspended between her lips and his cockhead for a moment before falling to her ass.

"More."

Robert looked at his wife. She looked asleep but had clearly just spoken. "What, Baby?"

She didn't open her eyes. She answered in a sleepy tone. "More. That was so good. You didn't come in me though."

"No. You look like you need a rest."

"Mm-hmm. You need to come. Give it to her like you did me."

Robert looked at Keegan, who grinned. "If you can make me feel like that, please, fuck me again." She lay beside Alyssa and opened her legs, resting her feet on the edge of the mattress. She reached a hand down to spread her swollen red pussy open for him.

Robert stepped between her legs and slid in slowly. He

rubbed her clit with his thumb, then leaned back to saw in and out of her soaking pussy. She clamped her ankles behind his hips. "Fuck! Right there. What are you doing?"

Robert smiled. "You like that?"

"God, yes. Keep going just like that. I'm going to come a lot."

Robert kept sliding in and out of her, pressing his cock into her G-spot during the stroke and beside her cervix at the end of each one. She pulled her nipples but then dropped her hands to lever her hips upward, letting her breasts bounce on her chest as Robert pounded into her. Her face beaded sweat, and her neck began to flush. The pale skin down her breasts turned pink, and her nipples stood taller. She grunted with each stroke. Her head pressed backward into the pillow, and her firm belly pressed upward above her arched back. Her pussy clamped onto Robert's cock, slowing him only a moment before a gush of fluid flowed out of her pussy and down her ass, to the bed.

Her tightening pussy was more than Robert could bear. He thrust all the way into the nubile redhead and pumped spurt after spurt of cum onto her cervix. Her hips ground onto his, tripping her cervix across his cockhead. He howled in release, then collapsed onto the sweaty girl.

Alyssa's fingertips traced down Robert's back as he lay on Keegan. Her hand trailed down his triceps, then left his body. A moment later, Keegan shivered beneath him. Robert moved off to Keegan's right, leaving the gasping woman between the married couple. Alyssa rose on her elbow and continued to caress Keegan's breasts. "You two should do porn. That was incredible."

"I'll say," Keegan agreed. "You made me come so hard, but god, I could go again right now. You just have to do all the work. I'm beat."

"Thank you, ladies, for the compliments, but I will need a rest first." Robert flopped his soft cock onto Keegan's hip.

Alyssa laughed, then bent her head to lick the cum off Keegan's belly and the tip of Robert's cock.

Robert raised his eyebrow at her. "I thought you were out of it."

Alyssa leaned back to her spot on the bed. "I was, but you bounced me awake. You made me want more. I was out of my mind for sex." She looked away, then back to her husband. "You took care of me. Thank you."

Robert reached to his wife's cheek. "Was that how you were that night? That out of it?"

"Yes. No, I was worse. I had the fatigue and alcohol to make me even less aware of what I was doing. Or, maybe, what I should have been doing." She closed her eyes. "They kept giving me what I asked for, even though I was out of it." She wiped a tear from her cheek. "I'm sorry. This is supposed to be a celebration. I didn't mean to bring everyone down."

Keegan reached to pull Alyssa's head to her chest. She stroked her hair. "You aren't bringing us down. You let it out."

Robert kissed his wife's head and stroked her back. "It will be okay, Baby. I'm going to help you avoid that kind of mess from here on out."

Alyssa raised her head to look at Robert. "It isn't what they did to me. It's what they did to you that I can't forget."

"Baby, don't you worry about that."

Keegan turned to Robert. "What they did to you? The three businessmen a couple of weeks ago? I didn't see you there."

"I wasn't. Somehow they opened Alyssa's phone and texted me some pictures and taunts. It was a hard night."

Alyssa rose from the bed and went to her purse. "It wasn't just pictures and taunts. They were cruel, and they kept us from talking to each other. He didn't even know if I was safe. Look."

She handed her phone to Keegan, the text strand from that night on the screen.

Keegan's mouth fell open. "I can't believe they did this. They offered you to me like a play toy that night, but to do this? With your husband on your own phone? Who does that?"

Robert pursed his lips. "Those fuckers did. They will be lucky if I am never in a position to get even."

"Do you want to get even?" Keegan looked from one to the other beside her on the bed. "They come here regularly. I could let you know when they are coming. You know they are all married, right?"

Alyssa walked to the window. She opened it and stared at the dark city below. Traffic noise filtered through the opening, breaking the silence. Alyssa had one fingernail between her teeth and her other arm across her belly. Her eyes were narrowed and her jaw clenched. She stood still for several minutes while Robert and Keegan lay in bed, watching her. Without turning, she said, "Robert, I am going to be very deliberate."

Alyssa's adventures continue at
www.SageMallory.com/books.
Go there now.

Acknowledgments

I must thank my Proper Lady Business Manager, whose wizardry with the calendar, clock, records, travel, and details of all sorts allows me to do what I love. I must again thank Lyss, who makes me a better writer and who may even help me overcome my debilitating comma habit. If there are errors or shortcomings, they are mine, not hers.

About The Author

Sage Mallory lives near the water, working by day and creating adventures for sexy, determined, evolving women by night. Sage enjoys cooking, hiking the mountains, discussing the meaning of life, and escaping the hectic pace of life inside a great story.